Jack LaCroix was the most unsettling human being she'd ever met.

"What do you want?" She looked into the disturbing depths of his eyes.

"I know you don't trust me." He stepped toward her. "But I need your help."

She'd forgotten how tall he was. A year ago, she'd been taken in by his muscular physique and that reckless glint in his eye. Tonight, the cold reality of what he'd done blurred the sweet memory of how good things had once been between them. Landis raised her chin and met his gaze. "You should have considered the consequences before you committed murder."

"I'm sure this is going to throw a wrench into your undying faith in the criminal justice system, but I didn't kill Evan. Someone set me up."

"I've heard this before. I didn't believe it then. I don't believe it now. Nothing has changed."

"Everything has changed," he said quietly. "I can prove it now."

Dear Reader,

This year may be winding down, but the excitement's as high as ever here at Silhouette Intimate Moments. National bestselling author Merline Lovelace starts the month off with a bang with *A Question of Intent,* the first of a wonderful new miniseries called TO PROTECT AND DEFEND. Look for the next book, *Full Throttle,* in Silhouette Desire in January 2004.

Because you've told us you like miniseries, we've got three more for you this month. Marie Ferrarella continues her family-based CAVANAUGH JUSTICE miniseries with *Crime and Passion.* Then we have two military options: *Strategic Engagement* features another of Catherine Mann's WINGMEN WARRIORS, while Ingrid Weaver shows she can *Aim for the Heart* with her newest EAGLE SQUADRON tale. We've got a couple of superb stand-alone novels for you, too: *Midnight Run,* in which a wrongly accused cop has only one option—the heroine!—to save his freedom, by reader favorite Linda Castillo, and Laura Gale's deeply moving debut, *The Tie That Binds,* about a reunited couple's fight to save their daughter's life.

Enjoy them all—and we'll see you again next month, for six more of the best and most exciting romances around.

Yours,

Leslie J. Wainger
Executive Editor

Please address questions and book requests to:
Silhouette Reader Service
U.S.: 3010 Walden Ave., P.O. Box 1325, Buffalo, NY 14269
Canadian: P.O. Box 609, Fort Erie, Ont. L2A 5X3

Midnight Run
LINDA CASTILLO

Silhouette®

INTIMATE MOMENTS™

Published by Silhouette Books

America's Publisher of Contemporary Romance

SILHOUETTE BOOKS

ISBN 0-373-27329-0

MIDNIGHT RUN

Books by Linda Castillo

Silhouette Intimate Moments

Remember the Night #1008
Cops and...Lovers? #1085
*A Hero To Hold #1102
Just a Little Bit Dangerous #1145
*A Cry in the Night #1186
The Phoenix Encounter #1208
Midnight Run #1259

Silhouette Books

Uncharted Waters

*High Country Heroes

LINDA CASTILLO

knew at a very young age that she wanted to be a writer—and penned her first novel at the age of thirteen. She is the winner of numerous writing awards, including a nomination for the prestigious RITA® Award, the Holt Medallion and Golden Heart. She loves writing edgy stories that push the envelope and take her readers on a roller-coaster ride of breathtaking romance and thrilling suspense.

Linda spins her tales of love and intrigue from her home in Texas, where she lives with her husband and four lovable dogs. Check out her Web site at www.lindacastillo.com. Or you can contact her at P.O. Box 670501, Dallas, Texas 75367-0501.

To my editor, Kim Nadelson, for seeing the magic
and helping to make this story a reality.
You have my admiration and heartfelt thanks.

Prologue

Fate had a twisted sense of humor, Jack LaCroix decided when the first shot rang out. Branches slashed at his clothes and face as he sprinted through the dense brush and low-growing trees. His prison-issue boots pounded through the mud in a rhythm that had pushed his body to the limit for what seemed like eternity. Behind him, the hounds were so close he could hear their frustrated baying over the sound of his own labored breathing.

He'd always considered himself a lucky man. At least up until a year ago when Lady Luck turned on him and bared her fangs. Damn, he wished he'd remembered how capricious she could be before trying a crazy stunt like breaking out of prison. If only he could charm her into keeping the dogs off him long enough for him to reach the river.

Desperation hammered through him as he calculated how far he had yet to go. Two hundred miles separated him from freedom. From justice. From the truth. A bitter laugh escaped him as the odds of his getting away struck him. Even if he made it to the river, he still faced his biggest obstacle yet. The only person who could help him believed he was a murderer.

Panic reared inside him at the thought. Everything he'd ever worked for or believed in—his very life in fact—hinged on whether he could convince her to help him. If she refused, or if they caught him before he reached her, he would be sent back to prison. He couldn't let that happen. Not now. Not when he'd already ventured beyond the point of no return.

Plummeting down a steep embankment, he reached the flood plain of the river. Hope curled through him when he heard the sound of rushing water. He picked up speed and ran blindly in the darkness, stumbling over rocks and stumps, no longer feeling the branches cutting his face or the rain that pelted him.

He stopped at the edge of the clearing, listening, his breaths rushing out in great white puffs. Behind him, the dogs howled in an eerie bloodlust symphony. The rain-swollen river loomed beyond the trees, the black, swirling water teasing him with the seductive promise of escape.

Every muscle in his body tensed as he stepped into the clearing. He could barely hear the dogs over the frenzied beating of his heart. He was in plain sight now, an easy mark for any government-paid sharpshooter looking to cut a notch in the butt of his rifle. Crouching, he started for the river, knowing fully if fate decided to dupe him again, she would win for good.

White-hot pain streaked through his left shoulder. An instant later the clap of a rifle shattered the air. He heard himself cry out as the impact of the bullet spun him around. Clutching his shoulder, he lost his footing and tumbled down the muddy bank. Shock tore through him when he realized he'd been shot, then again as the icy water enveloped him.

Damn, he didn't want to bleed to death in this godforsaken river. Not like this. He didn't want to die like a criminal.

An eerie calm descended. Instinctively, he began to swim. The dogs couldn't scent him here, he thought as the current tugged at him. He wouldn't leave any footprints. The trackers would find blood on the bank. Hopefully, they'd think he succumbed to the cold and drowned. With a little help from Lady Luck, he might just live long enough to see daybreak.

Chapter 1

With the thrill of victory still humming through her veins, the last thing Landis McAllister wanted to deal with was the weather. She could handle a few snow flurries. Even an inch or two on the roads didn't bother her. It was when Mother Nature went overboard and dumped two feet of the stuff that she questioned the wisdom of mountain living.

Determined not to let something like a little snowstorm dampen her spirits, Landis flipped on the radio and sang along with an old Christmas tune, her voice carrying over the din of the windshield wipers and the sound of tires crunching through ice. She didn't care that she sang a little off-key as she steered the Jeep up the driveway. She didn't care that it was snowing so hard she could barely see as she parked in her usual spot and shut down the engine.

Landis had just won the first major case of her career. Twelve weeks of dealing with a team of egocentric defense attorneys, a temperamental jury and a judge with a grudge against female prosecutors had finally paid off. Not only had she put the worst kind of criminal behind bars, but she'd ended a child's suffering. That, she knew, was the biggest reward of all.

But despite her efforts to convince herself otherwise, Landis hadn't walked away from the case unscathed. This one had taken something out of her. The child abuse cases always did. She felt spent, as if all the energy she'd thrown into the past twelve weeks had been sucked out of her. She'd tried not to let the ugliness affect her, but the testimony, the witnesses—and most of all the little victim herself—had hit home with the force of a sledgehammer.

Laying the memories of her own childhood aside, Landis focused instead on what the victory meant to her professionally. She'd taken a giant leap toward building the reputation she'd dreamed of her entire life. Her win today had opened doors for her, and she had every intention of breezing through those doors all the way to the district attorney's office.

She poured her heart and soul into the cases she prosecuted, and she was damn good at what she did. Justice was important to her, especially since her older brother had been killed in the line of duty.

Refusing to let the past tarnish her mood, she hefted the bag of groceries and got out of the Jeep. Tonight was reserved for celebration, she told herself. It didn't matter that her guest list consisted of a cat, a mystery novel and a fire—if she could manage to dig some wood out of the snow.

The tang of chimney smoke hung pleasantly in the frigid air as she made her way to the cabin. Snow blanketed the ground, reminding her that Christmas was less than a month away, and she had yet to begin her shopping. Struggling with the groceries and her perpetually overstuffed briefcase, she unlocked the door and stepped inside.

Pleasure fluttered through her as the familiar smells of

home engulfed her. Vanilla. Old pine. The lingering aroma of this morning's coffee. Out of the corner of her eye she spotted BJ, her three-legged alley cat, as he darted from behind the Indian-print sofa. Knowing the crafty tom was angling for a field mouse before dinner, she used her foot to close the door and lugged the grocery bag into the kitchen.

The cabin had been a gift to herself on her thirtieth birthday last year. It was the first home she'd owned, and she loved every square inch of it right down to the squeaky floors and drafty upstairs bedrooms. The isolated location satisfied her need for privacy while the view of the mountains to the west never ceased to take her breath away.

As Landis stacked the last of the cat food in the pantry, thoughts of the cabin gave way to an uncharacteristic bout of uneasiness. The hairs at her nape prickled. If she didn't know better, she might have thought she was being watched. But that was crazy. She was alone.

Closing the pantry door, she turned, expecting to see her cantankerous tom stalking her. ''BJ?'' she called and froze. Her heart slammed against her ribs when the silhouette of a man moved out of the laundry room. Shock riveted her in place. She stared in stunned disbelief as his dark, familiar eyes latched on to hers.

''Jack,'' she gasped, telling herself it was an absolute impossibility for Jack LaCroix to be standing in her kitchen dripping water all over the floor. ''My God, how did you—''

''We need to talk.''

She smelled the desperation on him as clearly as she saw the dangerous light in his eyes. Melting snow clung to his black hair and dripped on to his face. On his temple, a cut stood out stark and red against the prison pallor of his complexion. A heavy five o'clock shadow darkened his jaw.

For a moment, Landis couldn't speak. Her mind grappled

for logical explanations, but she knew there was only one that explained his presence. "You escaped."

"You always were a quick study."

It wasn't really fear that speared through her, but it was close. Something volatile and powerful she couldn't put a name to. Adrenaline danced through her midsection, but she didn't move. She couldn't take her eyes off him. "How did you get in?"

"Through the back door." He regarded her through piercing eyes. "Sorry about the pane."

She choked back a hysterical laugh as the irony of his words struck her. A murderer with a conscience, she thought bitterly. But she knew his gentle voice and polite words didn't mean he wasn't dangerous. After all, tigers were wild and beautiful, but they were killers at heart. Just like Jack LaCroix.

"I don't want you here," she said with a calm she didn't feel.

"I don't care. I need your help."

She didn't think he would harm her, but she'd been wrong about him before. Dead wrong. In the back of her mind, she wondered if she could reach the phone before he stopped her.

Why had he come to her when a sane man would have fled to another country where the police weren't looking for him? When surely he knew she was the last person on earth who would help him?

Her gaze flicked to the telephone on the wall. "I'm calling the police."

"I'd tell you not to waste your time, but I know you won't listen. You never were much good at listening." His lips twisted into a wry smile. "That's one of the things I always liked about you."

With forced calm she strode to the phone, her every sense honed on the man behind her. She felt his gaze on her as she moved, vaguely aware that he didn't follow. Snatching up the receiver, she punched 9-1-1 only to be met with silence.

Her heart thrumming in anger, she turned to him. "You had no right—"

"Don't talk to me about rights," he cut in. "Mine were taken away from me, and I damn well want them back."

She watched him stride to the sofa, pick up her purse and dig out her cell phone. "What are you doing?" she asked.

Without looking at her, he dropped the phone to the floor and crushed it with his boot. "Trying to stay out of jail."

Landis stared at her broken phone. "Destroying my phone isn't going to help."

"Maybe not, but it will buy me some time." His expression was inscrutable, but then she'd never been able to read him. She wasn't even sure she wanted to. To know what was going on behind that enigmatic expression was a frightening notion. Jack LaCroix was the most unsettling human being she'd ever met.

"What do you want?" She looked into the disturbing depths of his eyes. The intensity burning there nearly sent her back a step. But she held her ground, telling herself she was still in control, knowing deep down inside she'd never been in control when it came to Jack.

He looked like he'd been to hell and back. Mud streaked his face and clung to his clothes. The elegant hands she remembered so well were grimy, bruised and scratched. A red stain darkened his shirt from shoulder to waist. Landis stared at it, praying the hole in the fabric wasn't from a bullet. She tried to ignore that he was shivering with cold, telling herself he didn't deserve compassion, least of all hers.

"I know you don't trust me." He stepped toward her. "But I need your help."

She took a reflexive step back, knowing immediately it was a tactical error. Never show weakness. Never give up ground. Not in the courtroom. Not in any situation. They were the rules of her trade, and she followed them unerringly. Too bad she hadn't been as successful in assimilating them into her personal life.

But she'd forgotten how tall he was. Thinner than she remembered, but it wasn't for lack of muscle. He looked hard-as-rock and lean as a marathon runner. A year ago, she might have been taken in by his muscular physique and that reckless glint in his eyes. Tonight, the cold reality of what he'd done blurred the sweet memory of how good things had once been between them.

Forcing back the memories, Landis raised her chin and met his gaze. "You shouldn't have come here. You shouldn't be—"

"I shouldn't be a lot of things." Bitterness laced his voice. He'd never been a bitter man, but she supposed there were worse fates for a convicted murderer. "I shouldn't be in prison for starters."

Her temper stirred. She didn't like mind games. She didn't like being frightened. Or lied to. Especially when it came to the man who murdered her brother. "In my business I hear that so often it makes me sick."

"Still putting them away, are you?"

"I happen to believe people like you belong in prison."

"That's my girl. A lawyer first—a human being second. Your daddy did a real number on you, didn't he?"

Her heart kicked with another jab of anger. She didn't want to discuss her father or what he'd done. Not with a man whose betrayal had cut her even deeper than her old man's.

"Have you lost your mind or merely your sense of decency?"

"I lost any decency I might have had the day they put me in a cage."

"Maybe you should have considered the consequences before you committed murder."

He raked a shaking hand through his hair. "I'm sure this is going to throw a wrench into your undying faith in the criminal justice system, but I didn't kill Evan. Someone set me up. The money. The gun. The bogus witnesses. I tried to tell you—"

"I've heard this before. I didn't believe it then—I don't believe it now. Nothing has changed since your trial."

"Everything has changed," he said quietly. "I can prove it now, but I need some time to do it."

The night of the murder skittered through her mind. She winced with pain, then fury rumbled through her with such force she felt it all the way to her belly. She wasn't a violent person, but she wanted to hurt him. He'd caused her so much pain. He'd taken so much away from her. First her heart. Then her brother.

"You were his partner, for God's sake. He trusted you. I trusted you." The need to strike out nearly overpowered her, but she maintained control if only by a thread. "I'd have to be insane to believe anything you say now."

"I thought you might want to hear the truth," he said. "I never had you pegged as a hypocrite, but Lord knows I've been wrong about you in the past. You claim to love the law so much. Maybe you believe in your beloved laws when it's convenient. When they suit your needs. When it's easy. Or maybe you hide behind justice when you're not brave enough to face the truth."

The words sliced her like a blade. It outraged her that he would take the one thing she truly believed in and use it to manipulate her. "It was your revolver that killed Evan. You took money from a known criminal. Two witnesses placed you at the murder scene. What am I supposed to believe with such overwhelming evidence staring me in the face?''

''You of all people should know the truth isn't always handed over on a platter,'' he said. ''Reality isn't that neat.''

''Don't preach to me about reality. Of the two of us I'd say I'm a hell of a lot more grounded in reality than you. Damn it, Jack, what were you *thinking* breaking out of prison?''

As if the weight of the world suddenly settled on his shoulders, he sagged against the wall. The unpredictable light went out of his eyes, and Landis felt a new kind of tension tighten in her chest. For an instant he looked incredibly vulnerable, as if the odds stacked against him had finally worn him down and crushed him.

An alarm trilled in her head when she saw fresh blood coming through his shirt. He looked pale and shaken, but far too dangerous to touch. Like a snarling, wounded animal.

''You're bleeding,'' she said.

''I've got worse problems than that.''

For a fleeting instant she wanted to reach out and offer comfort. Just as quickly, she shoved the notion away, telling herself that caring for him would not only be self-destructive, but dangerous. He was no longer a detective with the Salt Lake City Police Department. He was no longer a free man. And he was certainly no longer the man who'd stolen her heart.

Jack LaCroix was a cold-blooded murderer.

''Don't shut me out, Landis.'' He reached out with his uninjured arm and traced the line of her jaw with his thumb. ''At least listen to me. Hear me out. That's all I'm asking.''

Angered by the contact, she slapped his hand away. She knew better than to trust him. He'd lied to her, taken her heart and torn it to shreds, then proceeded to turn her life

upside down. She refused to put herself on the line again.
Certainly not for a man who wouldn't hesitate to do it all
over again.

"You could have left the country, Jack. What could you
possibly want from me?" The instant the words were out
she regretted them, realized she didn't want to know.

"You're the only person I know who gives a damn about
the truth," he said. "At least you used to."

He stood so close she could smell the sweat and dirt and
the lingering redolence of panic. His gaze pierced her so
that she couldn't look away. If she hadn't known better,
Landis might have been taken in. His bedroom eyes and
whiskey-smooth voice could be very convincing. But she'd
learned the hard way that he was a capable liar and master
manipulator. She wasn't foolish enough to fall into the
same trap a second time.

"I can't help you," she said. "I won't."

Jack flinched, closed his eyes briefly. He looked miser-
able. Cold. Dirty. She watched, stunned, as a single drop
of blood rolled off his fingertips and splattered on the floor.
That he didn't notice told her a lot about his frame of mind.

"You've got to turn yourself in," she said.

Something dark flickered behind his eyes. "I'm a dead
man if I go back."

"By the looks of you, you're not far from that now. For
God's sake, you were under appeal. How could you be so
stupid—"

"Duke put a contract on me."

The words stopped her cold. Cyrus Duke was Salt Lake
City's most infamous drug kingpin. With roots running
from Miami's seedy underworld to his hierarchy in Los
Angeles, he was powerful, ruthless and completely untouchable.

"Why would Duke put a hit on you?" she asked.

"He knows I'm going to take him down."

"You're not a cop anymore. You weren't a threat to him in prison. You're certainly not a threat now."

"As long as I'm alive, I'm a threat. He knows I'm close to getting the goods to nail him."

Landis didn't buy it. She wouldn't even consider it. The repercussions were too far-reaching. Jack had every reason in the world to lie; she had every reason in the world not to believe him. "I'm not going to let you do this to me," she said.

"I'm going to nail him, Landis. I'm on to something big. I'm so close I can taste it. I just need a few hours to pull myself together. I need some dry clothes. Food. Money."

A hundred questions rushed through her mind, but they were jumbled by emotions and memories and the cold, hard fact that she didn't want to get involved. "As an attorney, the only advice I can give you is to turn yourself in."

One side of his mouth curved. "Not my style, Red."

The endearment affected her, reached into her and touched a part of her heart she'd carelessly left unguarded. A heart that had once belonged to him—no holds barred. She cursed him for having that ability. She cursed herself for responding, wondering what kind of a person that made her. How could she feel anything but disdain for the man who killed her brother?

"You'll only make things worse if you don't go back," she said.

"Things can't get any worse."

"Things can always get worse. I don't want to see you hurt."

"Worried about me?"

She stared at him, aware that her pulse was racing, that she didn't have an answer.

Jack sighed. "Look, I can give you Cyrus Duke, but I need some help."

Landis stomped the quick flare of interest. "I'm not naive enough to risk everything I've ever worked for on the word of a convicted murderer.''

''You don't have to be naive to listen to the facts.''

''You murdered my brother. I won't help you. And I'll never forgive you. My loyalty runs deeper than that.''

''What do you know about loyalty?'' Though his voice remained calm, his hands clenched into fists at his sides. ''If I recall, you were pretty quick to turn tail and run when the going got rough.''

''Loyalty to my family—not you! You don't deserve loyalty. You don't know the meaning of the word.''

''What about loyalty to Evan? Don't you want to know what really happened? Don't you want to know who really murdered him? Or do you prefer sweeping the entire mess under the rug so you don't have to get those pretty hands of yours dirty? So you can get on with playing Lady Justice? Isn't that what they call you these days?''

''I believe in what I do, but that isn't the issue, is it?'' She hated the defensive ring in her voice. She didn't have to defend her choices to anyone, especially Jack.

''What is the issue, Landis?'' He offered a cynical smile. ''Justice?''

''Justice is real—''

''Justice is an illusion!'' He stepped closer. So close she felt the searing heat of his stare, the warmth of his breath, the startling power of his presence. ''I'm living proof of that. So, *Counselor*,'' he snarled, ''if you believe in your precious justice so much, I suggest you come look for it, starting with me.'' He rapped his fist against his chest with the last word. ''Somewhere out there, Evan's murderer is a free man, while I've spent the last year in prison for a crime I didn't commit!''

The words pounded through her. Simultaneously, her emotions clashed with the logical part of her brain. She'd always prided herself on her ability to keep her feelings removed from her judgment. That was one of the things that made her a good prosecutor. But when it came to Jack, her logic and emotions tangled and melded into a big, confusing ball.

Was it possible he was telling the truth? Or was he a desperate man willing to do anything to avoid going back to prison? It took every ounce of courage she could muster to meet his gaze. "I want you to leave. Now."

He choked out a humorless laugh. "I don't have anywhere else to go. To hell perhaps, but I've been there, and I can tell you it's not all it's cracked up to be."

She wasn't sure why the words hurt. But they did, and the pain was so sharp she had to turn away. She couldn't face him with uncertainty etched into her every feature. Jack was a perceptive man, and he'd always been able to read her. She didn't want him to get inside her head. In the year he'd been away, she'd simplified her life, focusing solely on her career and her future with the D.A.'s office. She refused to let him destroy what she'd worked so hard to achieve. She wouldn't jeopardize her professional reputation or risk hurting her mother and younger brother.

With her professional mask in place, she turned to face him. "I'll turn you in," she said. "You know I will."

His eyes flicked over her. He looked into her, through her. She sensed the appraisal, and her knees went weak with the power of it. Her heart banged against her ribs with such ferocity she felt certain it might pound its way right out of her chest.

"Sit down," he said.

"You're not staying."

"I can't force you to help me. But I can make you listen. It's up to you whether or not you care enough about the truth to get involved." Raising his arm, he wiped the blood from his fingers on to his shirt, then stared at the crimson smear as if its presence stunned him. "If you still don't

want to help me after you've heard me out, I'll find another
way to do this.''

Landis watched him walk to the kitchen table. He moved
with the grace of a wild, hunted animal. One that was tired
and injured and anxious for the hunt to end. If it hadn't
been for his eyes, she might have thought he'd given up.
But that would have been as out of character for him as if
he'd thrown in the towel and gone to prison without a fight.

No, she thought, Jack was definitely a fighter. He fought
hard, long and dirty for what he wanted. If she didn't get
him out of her house; if she didn't get to a phone and call
the police, she was in for the battle of her life.

Jack had known she would affect him. What he hadn't
realized was just how profoundly. Seeing Landis McAllister after a year was like taking a sledgehammer to the solar
plexus. The ache was so sharp that he questioned the wisdom of coming here tonight. He'd been foolish to believe
his feelings for her had dulled with time. Funny how much
a man forgot in a year.

He watched her walk to the pantry, trying in vain not to
notice the way those slacks skimmed over her hips or wonder if she still painted her toenails the color of cherry bub-
blegum. Even from a distance he could smell her hair, that
exotic mix of coconut and musk that made him want to
reach out and run his fingers through it one more time. She
looked very much the part of tough prosecuting attorney in
her black suit and leather boots. A year ago he'd known a
part of her that was soft and kind and compassionate. He
wondered if that part of her still existed, or if she'd managed to eradicate it along with the feelings she once had
for him.

Her movements were controlled and deliberate as she
walked to the counter and started a pot of coffee. He knew
the gesture had nothing to do with the fact that he was

shivering with cold, but because her nerves were strung tight and she needed to do something.

Once upon a time she'd loved him. She'd seen him as decent and kind and honorable. Jack had loved her more than his own life. He'd needed her more than his next breath, would have died a thousand deaths for her. What a fool he'd been to believe any of those things would matter now.

It tore him up inside knowing she thought he was a cold-blooded killer. That knowledge had tortured him every second of every day he'd been locked away. He knew if he gave her the chance, she'd go straight to the police. He didn't plan on giving her the chance.

Every muscle in his body protested as he lowered himself into the chair. He'd covered over one hundred cold, rugged miles in the past two days, some on foot, some in a filthy cattle car courtesy of Burlington Northern. He couldn't remember the last time he'd stopped moving. Or eaten. Or slept. He couldn't remember the last time he'd been in a civilized place that spoke of warmth and comfort and home. Most of all, he couldn't remember the last time he'd been in the company of a woman. Especially a woman he'd spent the better part of a year trying to get out of his system.

He watched her scoop coffee and wondered if there was a man in her life, if she was seeing anyone, but quickly thwarted that line of thinking. Her personal life was no longer his concern, he reminded himself darkly. Wanting was a dangerous thing for a convict. A man could drive himself crazy if he wasn't careful.

Jack had promised himself he wouldn't let his feelings for her interfere with his mission of clearing his name. She'd deemed him guilty based on circumstantial evidence, paid witnesses and manufactured proof. How could he still want her when he felt so bitter? How could he be attracted to a woman he hadn't been able to forgive? He couldn't let it matter. Damn it, he couldn't let *her* matter.

Survival had dictated his jailbreak. It had taken months of planning and physical conditioning. Every evening the inmates were herded into either the gymnasium or exercise yard to work off steam. It had been raining the night of his escape. The gymnasium was crowded. While one of the inmates he'd befriended created a diversion for the corrections officers, Jack had shimmied twenty feet up a water pipe mounted to the wall and climbed out the window. Once outside, he'd used the wire cutters he'd gotten from another inmate to traverse the concertina wire. He'd almost made it to the river when the dogs began to bay....

Shaking the memory from his head, he folded his hands in front of him, realizing for the first time how battered they were. The last two days were a blur of pain and cold, and he felt mildly shocked he'd survived at all. The bullet had put a deep graze in his shoulder, sparing the bone and joint, but leaving him weak from blood loss. He'd survived on little more than adrenaline and desperation. When those two things had waned, his memories of Landis sustained him the rest of the way.

She carried a cup of coffee to the table and set it in front of him. "You've never been stupid, Jack. You know the police will find you. You're only making things worse by running."

"There's not a whole hell of a lot they can do to me that they haven't already done. I'm a lifer, Landis."

"They could kill you, for God's sake."

Jack looked down at his coffee, wondering if she realized there were times when he considered death a better alternative than spending his life behind bars.

Shaking her head, she took the chair across from him. "How can you possibly believe you're going to get away?"

He returned her gaze, pulling back just in time to keep

himself from tumbling into its emerald depths. He'd been in the cabin less than an hour and already she was getting to him. He'd thought he was over her. He'd thought the bitterness would keep him from wanting her. It galled him that he was wrong on both counts.

"Maybe getting away isn't my goal," he said.

Landis remained silent, looking at him like a cat that had been kicked by a cruel child.

"On the night Evan died," Jack began, "he left a voice message, asking me to meet him at the warehouse where Duke's people had been operating. Allegedly, there was a shipment of cocaine coming in from L.A. Sixty kilos of Peruvian flake. Uncut. Evan was supposed to keep his mouth shut. But this stuff was pure. White death for anyone who didn't know what they were getting into. He was afraid it was going to hit the street and start killing people. So he told me about it." Jack remembered his partner's voice as if it were yesterday. The memory still wielded the power to make his hands shake.

"I know the story, Jack. All this information came out during your trial. There was no shipment of cocaine." Tucking a shock of flame-colored hair behind her ear, Landis sighed wearily. "I've gone over it in my head a hundred times. I even reviewed the transcripts."

"Things have changed since the trial," Jack said. "You hear things in prison, Landis. Bad things. Things I suspected all along, but couldn't prove."

"Like what?"

"Like Evan wasn't the only cop who knew about the shipment."

"I don't believe you."

"There are cops on the take. Salt Lake City cops. Sheriff's office. DEA. Customs—"

"Even if you *can* prove corruption, that doesn't exonerate you."

"It will if I can prove someone inside the department set me up to take the fall."

"Who, Jack? What proof?"

He sighed in frustration. "I don't have anything solid yet. Just a few pieces of the puzzle. I need some time to work it. I've got to talk to some of my old snitches."

"Nothing you've told me disputes the fact that your revolver was the gun that killed Evan or that over fifty thousand dollars somehow found its way into your bank account. It doesn't dispute the two witnesses who put you at the scene the night Evan was killed."

His temper flared with the accusation. "Two witnesses I've since tied to Duke. That reeks of setup and you know it."

"You haven't given me a single fact I wasn't already aware of," she shot back. "Your story sounds desperate and pathetic, and I don't believe a word of it."

Reining in anger, Jack looked down at his coffee and concentrated on the warmth radiating into his hands. Frustration hammered through him that he didn't have any solid evidence. All he could offer was his own gut instinct and the word of a dead convict who'd talked too many times to the wrong person. Unfortunately, Landis had never been big on gut instinct.

"Evan was dying when I reached him that night," he said. "He'd taken two slugs. He was bleeding. Scared. In shock. He kept trying to talk. I tried to quiet him, but he wouldn't listen. Damn hardheaded cop—"

Shaken, he broke off. The room felt overly warm. Chills wracked his body, but sweat streamed down his back. A curse escaped his lips when he realized he'd reached the end of his physical endurance. His concentration was shot. He wasn't sure why he was talking, dredging up the past. He could barely speak. But there was so much to say. So many emotions tangled inside him.

So much at stake.

Jack raised his eyes to hers. It tore at his heart to see the shimmer of tears. She still mourned her brother. He wondered if there was any grief left over for him. For the part of him that died that night.

"Evan had seen enough shootings to know he was dying," he continued. "I guess the cop in me expected him to use those last minutes to name his killer, but he didn't. Instead he used the last of his strength to make sure I knew about that telephone call he'd made to you."

Across from him, Landis went perfectly still, as if knowing something terrible was about to be flung her way. "Evan and I were close," she said. "He called to tell me he loved me. I testified—"

"Did he often call at midnight to tell you he loved you?"

She blinked at him. "Well, no."

"He knew he was a marked man. He called to tell you something."

"Why didn't he? For God's sake, why didn't he tell me he was in trouble? Why didn't he tell *you* he was in trouble and ask for your help?"

The latter question hit a nerve. It always did. But Jack didn't let himself react. He would spend the rest of his life wondering if Evan might still be alive if the trust between them had been stronger. "I can't speak for Evan. Maybe he didn't trust me enough. Maybe he didn't want to drag me into it. But, Landis, he knew they were going to kill him. That's the only scenario that fits."

"Who?"

"Cyrus Duke." He clenched his jaw against the pain spreading down his arm like hot lava. He ached to get out of his wet clothes and fall into a warm bed for a few hours to recoup. He needed to eat to regain his strength. But he couldn't stop now. She was listening. If only he could make her believe.

"Evan tried to play both sides of the coin," he said. "He wanted the money. But he also wanted out."

"Out of what?"

"Evan was taking money from Duke."

"No!"

"But he wanted out, Landis. He feared for his family's safety. But he knew if he rolled over on Duke, the scumbag would go after Casey and the girls."

Landis lurched to her feet. "I don't want to have this conversation."

Jack rose with her. He didn't give a damn that she didn't want to hear the truth about her brother. Six months ago, when he'd been stuck in a jail cell for a crime he didn't commit, Jack hadn't wanted to hear it, either. But he had. From a reliable source who'd just happened to get himself murdered in the shower room a few days later. "Evan was a dirty cop, Landis."

She looked at him, her eyes large and dark against her pale complexion. "I don't believe you. And I won't stand by and let you defile my brother's name or shame his widow with lies you fabricated to save yourself."

The anger struck him with such ferocity that for a moment he was dizzy. Whoever framed him had taken everything from him. His career had been destroyed. His reputation dragged through the mud. His partner was dead. The passionate and intense love affair he'd once shared with Landis had been reduced to a bitter memory steeped in resentment and lies.

"Evan knew he couldn't talk to Casey, and he couldn't tell me because he knew I'd bust him." Jack nearly laughed at the absurdity. Evan had always been the straight arrow while Jack had always skated that thin, dark line. The irony of how things had worked out in the end burned.

He looked at Landis. "So he chose you. His sister. Someone he could trust. A *prosecutor.* He wanted you to know, but for whatever reason never got the chance to tell you. He wanted you to go after Duke because Evan knew he was a dead man. He knew you'd protect his family and get to the bottom of it.''

Her eyes flashed. ''I don't believe any of it.''

A cold sweat broke out on his forehead, and Jack knew with dead certainty the last two days had finally caught up with him. His shoulder throbbed with every beat of his heart. His head felt like the business end of a jackhammer.

''I knew Evan better than anyone,'' he said. ''I knew how he operated. I knew his weak points, his many strengths. I knew him like a brother, Landis. I knew he was in to something.''

''He wasn't dirty!''

''He fed Duke inside information. Warned him of impending busts. Kept his competition off the street. Damn it, he got in over his head.'' Jack blinked at her when the room tilted abruptly. Heat infused his face. Nausea seesawed in his gut. He cursed, knowing he was going to pass out. Grabbing the back of the chair, he steadied himself, determined to continue.

Landis started to speak, but he cut her off. ''Duke bought and paid for your brother, then he killed him. The bastard knew I'd come after him so he framed me for his murder. He had help from the inside.'' His voice echoed inside his head, and for a moment he wondered if he'd actually spoken at all.

Words flowed out of her, but Jack no longer understood. It was as if he'd stepped out of his body and watched with detachment as Jack LaCroix went through the motions without him. He fought the dizziness but knew the darkness was going to win.

One by one his senses shut down. Desperation clawed at him. He didn't want it to end this way. He knew the moment he went down, she'd leave and call the police. He expected no less, and he hated her for it.

Knowing he had to stop her, he reached out, stumbled and went down on one knee. Pain ripped through his shoulder. He groaned deep in his chest. Around him, the room shifted, darkened. He heard himself utter her name, then the floor rushed up and slammed into him.

Chapter 2

Landis stared in horror as Jack collapsed onto her kitchen floor. It was the last thing she expected to happen, but she'd learned long ago to expect the unexpected when it came to Jack LaCroix. Tonight, it seemed, he was just chock-full of surprises. Dark, unpleasant ones, she thought wildly. Leave it to him to toss her into a compromising position, then bail out.

Heart racing in perfect cadence with her mind, she fell to her knees next to him at a complete loss as to what to do next. She didn't want to touch him, but quickly realized there was no way to avoid it. He'd fallen on his side with his left arm pinned beneath him; she couldn't leave him twisted like that. What if he were seriously injured and stopped breathing? What if he died right there on her floor?

Frustrated and scared, Landis placed her hand gently on his shoulder. "Jack?" His clothes were wet and cold beneath her palm. Good Lord, he was soaked to the skin. Cautiously, she rolled him on to his back.

His body was long and lean and looked as out of place on her kitchen floor as a bearskin rug might have. Even unconscious, his muscles were as hard as steel. But he didn't seem quite as dangerous with his eyes closed. Oddly, Landis felt relieved that she didn't have to look into those eyes. The last thing she needed was to get ensnared in that compelling gaze of his.

"Damn you, LaCroix," she muttered.

His breaths came slow and regular. She pressed a finger to his throat and found his pulse steady and strong. She didn't see much fresh blood, but he was wet and muddy, so it was difficult to tell how badly he was bleeding.

Crossing to the counter, she opened a drawer, yanked out a clean dish towel and wet it beneath the faucet. She didn't possess a shred of medical expertise but knew enough about first aid to know he should be kept warm and comfortable.

At least until the police arrived.

The thought wasn't a pleasant one. Why had he come to *her* for help? Why not one of his cop friends? Surely one of them had kept in touch throughout the pandemonium of the last year, hadn't they? But Landis knew how cops felt about cop killers. Jack might have been one of their own for the better part of twelve years, but they'd branded him a traitor. He was smart enough to know there wasn't a soul on the force he could trust.

So he'd come to her.

Dismayed by the implications, she folded the towel and pressed it against his forehead, trying not to notice how pale he was. "How could you do something so incredibly stupid?" she murmured.

He couldn't have put her in a worse situation. His very presence threatened everything that was important to her, everything she believed in. She refused to compromise her reputation, her career, or her family for the likes of a man who didn't deserve her compassion.

Pulling in a calming breath, she rose. The only thing she could do was drive down to her neighbor's cabin and call the sheriff. Dread swirled through her as she imagined a swarm of cops converging on her tidy cabin. Jack would be taken into custody. She would be asked to come down to the sheriff's office to make a statement. Eventually, the media would catch wind of Jack's capture.

Then all hell would break loose.

Shuddering at the scenario her overactive mind had drawn, Landis considered her options—all of which boiled down to one. She had to call the sheriff. Jack was a murderer. An escaped convict. He belonged in prison. As the saying went, he'd made his bed and now he must lie in it. She refused to accept responsibility for his woes.

A brightly colored afghan lay folded across the back of the sofa. Landis dashed to it and snapped it open. Kneeling beside Jack, she draped it over him, tucking the ends beneath his arms and legs. As she straightened, he thrashed and called out her name with such clarity that for an instant she thought he'd regained consciousness.

She stared at him, the memories pounding through her like fists. Ironically, it had been Evan who'd introduced them. In spite of her self-imposed rule never to date cops, she'd fallen for the strikingly handsome vice detective with the magnetic eyes and captivating smile. He'd swept her off her feet and into a breathtaking relationship. Level-headed Landis had been so caught up in the intensity, she didn't even realize it when she lost her heart. Jack wouldn't have it any other way. He was all or nothing, and she had definitely given him her all.

But even back then she'd known he skirted that dark edge. He'd always unnerved her with his rule breaking and disdain for authority. Jack LaCroix wasn't for the faint of heart. He existed in a world of gray. A world where he could stretch the rules and turn wrong into right if it suited him. Landis's world was black and white. She followed the rules, embraced them. Still, for a year she'd loved him with every fiber of her being...

Shaken by the memories twisting through her, she turned away, aware that her heart was beating too fast. How could she have been so wrong about him?

Knowing there was nothing she could do for him except, perhaps, keep him from self-destructing, she reached for her coat. Just as her fingers closed around it, Jack's voice rang out. She froze at the sound of her name and turned, half-expecting to see him sitting up, hitting her with that devastating smile. But he wasn't sitting up. He wasn't smiling. His eyes were closed. A sheen of sweat coated his forehead. His face was contorted in pain.

Alarmed, she walked over to him, straining to hear as he mumbled something unintelligible. His voice was soft and deep and achingly familiar. Her heart stuttered as she recognized a single, profound word—*innocent.*

In all her years of working in the court system, she'd never heard such despair. It wrenched painfully at her conscience. Was it the voice of a desperate killer? she wondered. Or was she hearing the voice of an innocent man wrongly accused of a horrific crime? The questions haunted her, the implications taunting her with terrible possibilities. Telling herself she could sort out her feelings later, Landis threw on her coat and headed for the door.

Twenty minutes later, Landis sat in the Jeep in her driveway and waited for the sheriff's department deputy to arrive. She told herself it was the cold that had her shaking uncontrollably, but the heater wasn't helping. Relief billowed through her when she saw the flashing lights of the sheriff's Tahoe. By the time the deputy climbed out, she'd already reached his vehicle.

"Evenin'." The man was the size of a grizzly, wore cowboy boots and a Stetson the size of a Volkswagen. "You called about a prowler?"

"He was here when I got home from work about an hour ago. It looks like he broke a pane and came in through the back door. He's either injured or suffering from exposure because he fainted on my kitchen floor."

The deputy cocked his head. "Fainted?"

Realizing she was talking too fast, she took a deep breath and silently counted to three. "I think he's been—" Landis broke off when the deputy withdrew a pistol the size of a cannon.

"Is he still inside?" he asked.

She stared at the gun, not wanting to imagine what a bullet would do to human flesh. "Yes," she answered, steeling herself against the sense of foreboding that welled up inside her. If the deputy knew he was going in to arrest infamous cop killer Jack LaCroix, would he be more apt to use deadly force?

"Is he armed?" he asked.

"I don't think so." She prayed Jack gave himself up easily. She didn't want to see him hurt. She didn't want to see *anyone* hurt.

"Have a seat in your vehicle, Ms. McAllister, while I take a look." Pistol in hand, the deputy jogged toward the cabin.

Landis watched him disappear inside, then walked back to the Jeep and climbed inside. It only took a couple of minutes for her to realize she couldn't just sit there and do nothing. She was too keyed up, and the deputy was taking too long. Oh, dear God, she'd never be able to live with herself if either of them got hurt....

Cursing Jack, she climbed out of the Jeep and began to

pace, keeping her eyes trained on the front door of the cabin. Were they negotiating the terms of Jack's surrender? Or were they in the midst of a standoff?

The path she was wearing in the snow grew as she paced—much like the doubts swirling in her head. Did Jack's story warrant consideration? Was it possible Cyrus Duke was involved in her brother's death? The questions pummeled her, but Landis knew that aside from offering legal advice there was little she could do to help Jack. Not that she felt compelled to do so, she reminded herself. She was an officer of the court and saw clearly the line between right and wrong. If Jack believed he'd been wrongly convicted, the only way he could help himself was to operate through the proper legal channels.

But as she rationalized and reasoned through everything that had been said and done, something nagged at her. Something obscure and uncomfortable that had lodged like a fist in her chest. Landis had never been overly intuitive. She preferred dealing with facts. Tangibles. Gut instinct never entered the picture when it came to drawing conclusions or making decisions. But even as she denied the possibility of Jack's innocence, she knew something wasn't right. He was one of the most intelligent people she'd ever known. If all he'd wanted was his freedom, he would have fled to Mexico or Canada. He wouldn't have come to her knowing she blamed him for Evan's death. It didn't make sense for him to risk his life in a daring prison escape only to jeopardize it by coming to her.

Landis stopped pacing and looked toward the cabin, aware that her heart was beating too fast, that her palms were wet despite the cold. What was taking the deputy so blasted long?

Too impatient to wait any longer, she changed direction and started for the door. Jack might be desperate, but he wasn't crazy enough to get into a physical confrontation with a cop. Surely the deputy had the situation under control, didn't he?

Her pulse kicked when she stepped on to the porch. The front door stood open. Shadows ebbed and flowed within. As familiar as the cabin was to her, it now seemed menacing. Moving closer, she stopped and peered inside.

"He must have run out the back."

Barely suppressing a scream, Landis spun. The deputy stood a few feet behind her. She was about to give him a piece of her mind for scaring the daylights out of her when his words registered.

"Gone?" she cried. "That can't be. He was right there on the kitchen floor." Jack *had* to be there. He'd been unconscious when she left. He was in no condition to get up and walk away.

Not bothering to wait for a response, she whirled and darted through the door. Her boots cracked sharply against the pine floorboards as she ran to the kitchen. The room was just as she'd left it, less one unconscious man. She stared dumbly at the floor where a single drop of blood was the only sign he'd ever been there.

"A set of footprints leads to the road," the deputy said. "Looks like he cut his hand on that pane. I found blood in the snow."

Landis watched the deputy saunter to the French door where the pane had been broken. Shards of glass sparkled like broken diamonds on the floor.

"Did you get a look at him, ma'am?"

She met his gaze, her mind speeding through the ramifications of the question. He was a large man with sandy hair and a handlebar mustache. He appeared capable and professional in his sheriff's department jacket and ostrich boots. But she'd noticed the aggressive glint in his eyes. She'd seen that glint before and knew well the difference

between a lawman who enjoyed his work and a cop with
an ego to sate and an itchy trigger finger to boot.

"No," she answered, thinking she knew how Pandora
must have felt after opening that blasted box.

She answered the rest of his questions truthfully, but
without the kind of details that would have made his job
easy. No, the intruder hadn't stolen anything. She hadn't
seen a gun. No, he hadn't harmed or threatened her in any
way. Even her description of him came out vague.

It wasn't that she didn't want the police to find Jack. She
did. He'd murdered her brother and deserved to spend the
rest of his life in prison. Landis just didn't want this deputy
going after Jack half-cocked. She believed in justice, not
vengeance.

Discomfort washed over her when she realized her other
motives weren't quite as noble. If she identified Jack, his
name would be plastered on the front page of every newspaper in Utah. Their past relationship would be sensation-
alized. The first major victory of her career would be overshadowed by scandal. Regardless of the fact that she was
an innocent party and had acted properly and lawfully, she
knew the gossip and speculation would affect her career.
Perceptions were everything when you were a public ser-
vant. She'd sacrificed enough for Jack LaCroix. She'd be
damned if she sacrificed anything more.

The most important thing was that he was gone, she told
herself as the deputy drove away. She could get on with
her life and try to forget he'd ever shown up. She wouldn't
even have to admit to herself that as she'd listened to his
declarations of innocence, a small, gullible part of her had
been tempted to believe him.

She knew there was a possibility of Jack returning, but
she didn't think he would. She'd made her position clear.
He was a lot of things, but a fool wasn't one of them.
Tomorrow, she would call his lawyer, Aaron Chandler, and

fill him in on the situation. If Jack got in touch with him, perhaps Chandler would be able to persuade him to turn himself in.

Turning away from the door, Landis walked to the living room. She was still shaking, and her hands were ice-cold. Guilt sat like a rock in the pit of her stomach. The knowledge that she'd protected her brother's murderer weighed heavily on her shoulders. As she stared at the drop of blood on the kitchen floor, she realized with dismay that her hard-won victory earlier in the day was overshadowed by what she'd done. She felt like a charlatan.

Shaking off thoughts she didn't want to deal with, she stripped off her coat and tossed it on the sofa. BJ brushed against her leg and mewed. She scooped the cat into her arms and hugged him tightly, wondering why she suddenly needed the comfort of his warmth, why she suddenly felt so alone.

"How about that fire?" she said aloud.

The woodpile was in the backyard. Not bothering with her coat, Landis crossed through the kitchen. The deputy had taped a piece of cardboard over the broken pane to keep out the cold. She'd have to go to the hardware store tomorrow and pick up a new pane. Unlocking the French door, she opened it and started for the cord of wood stacked against the fence a few yards away.

The snow was still coming down, but not as hard. Such a serene picture, she thought as she pulled two logs and some kindling from the stack. If only she felt as serene. Seeing Jack had been a tremendous shock. It galled her that she still felt something for him. Not love or anything so profound. But a connection that ran a lot deeper than she wanted to admit.

Movement off to her right sent her heart hard against her ribs. Gasping, she dropped the wood and spun. Before she'd taken two steps toward the cabin, strong arms closed around her from behind, trapping her against a solid wall of muscle. A hand clamped over her mouth, cutting off her scream.

"Easy, Landis, it's me." Jack's voice sliced through the fog of fear. "Don't scream. You know I won't hurt you."

She berated herself for being foolish enough to believe he'd gone. Cursing him, she tried to break his grip on her and wriggle free, but he held her tightly against him. Angry and afraid, she did the only thing she could think of and bit his palm.

He jerked his hand away. "Ouch! Damn it!"

"Let go of me!"

"Hold still!"

Furious, Landis spun to face him. "How dare you come at me like that!" Bending, she scooped up a piece of kindling and swung it as hard as she could. Air whooshed.

Jack lunged sideways, stumbled and went down on his knees. The kindling missed him by an inch. Scrambling to his feet, he moved toward her. "You could have taken my head off with that!"

"You don't use it anyway." She swung again.

He ducked, then lunged for her. His arms went around her waist. The momentum knocked her off balance, but she didn't fall. She raised the stick, prepared to defend herself. But his hand snaked out and braceleted her wrist. "Don't even think about hitting me with that," he growled.

Jack had forgotten how small she was. How delicately she was built. How good she smelled when he got this close—a subtle mix of coconut and musk and woman flesh. He'd forgotten how soft her body was when she was pressed up against him. How her eyes flashed like cut emeralds when he ticked her off. He'd forgotten a lot of things about her in the past year. Or tried to, anyway. Holding her against him, they all came rushing back....

"Damn you, Jack!" She struggled to free herself from his grasp. "Let go of me!"

She was surprisingly strong for her size. "Let go of the stick," he said between clenched teeth.

She lashed out with her right foot. The heel of her boot connected solidly with his shin. He felt pain on top of pain, but he didn't let go. "Stop fighting me."

"You're hurting me!"

"Yeah, well your heel grinding into my shin didn't exactly feel good."

He squeezed her wrist. Her hand opened; the kindling fell to the snow. Growling in annoyance, he shoved her away. For several long seconds, they faced each other, breathing hard, their breaths mingling between them in a white cloud of vapor.

Despite the fatigue and pain fogging his brain, Jack couldn't help but notice the rise and fall of her breasts. That her cheeks were blushed with cold. Or that she was still the most beautiful woman he'd ever laid eyes on. He steeled himself against those observations, knowing it was crazy to think of her in those terms now.

"I'm sorry if I hurt you," he said.

"In the scope of things, I'm sure a bruised wrist is the least of my worries," she said dryly. "Why sweat the little things when you're determined to ruin my life?"

"I'm not going to ruin your life. Nobody has to know I was here."

"I hate to remind you of something so obvious, but that deputy sheriff was just here looking for you."

"Yeah? So then why the hell did you send him away?"

She blinked. "I…didn't. I mean, he went back to the sheriff's office to put together a search party."

The realization that she hadn't identified him staggered him. Something that felt vaguely like hope fluttered in his chest. "You know, Red, for a lawyer you're not a very good liar."

"He's coming back. I swear he's coming right back."

He contemplated her, feeling more for her than was prudent. But then, he'd never been a prudent man when it came to Landis. "If I understood your motives a little better, I might thank you."

"Don't bother." She met his gaze levelly. "I'm not going to let you drag me down with you. I'm not going to let you ruin my life."

A sudden shiver wracked his body. Another wave of dizziness followed with such force that for an instant he thought he was going down again. Fighting nausea, he leaned against the trunk of a pine tree for support. "Damn it..."

"Jack—"

"I need to call Aaron Chandler," he ground out.

"You're turning yourself in?"

"Don't count on it." He'd hoped she would be able to put her hatred for him aside in the name of justice, but it didn't look like she wasn't going to help him. Chandler probably wouldn't, either. But calling his lawyer might buy him some time. Under the circumstances, Jack figured it was the best he could hope for.

"I'll have to drive down to Mrs. Worthington's to use the phone," she said.

"Like I'm going to let you drive away," he snapped. "Get me a knife. I'll splice the line together."

Landis glowered at him a moment before picking up the fallen firewood. Following her cue, Jack gathered the remaining kindling and trailed her to the cabin.

The heat inside made him feel feverish, but it wasn't enough to warm him. He felt cold all the way to his bones. He prayed he could function long enough to repair the phone line and make the call to his attorney.

Setting the kindling on the hearth, he watched Landis approach him with a small utility knife. Her cheeks were flushed with cold. Her hair was damp and clung to her face in wisps. That she appealed to him even now annoyed the hell out of him. He couldn't count the times he'd thought of her when he'd been locked away, lying on his cot, staring at the ceiling, trying to block out his surroundings. She would never know how many endless nights he'd dreamed of her, of touching her. She would never know that those dreams had sustained him, given him a reason to live.

He'd known she wouldn't welcome him back. In the months he'd spent in prison, he'd tried desperately to convince himself it didn't matter, that he didn't care. But the truth had eaten at him, like an acid gnawing at his heart until there was nothing left but an empty shell.

Shaking off the memories, Jack took the knife and walked back outside to splice the telephone line. A few minutes later, he returned to find Landis at the hearth, building a fire. Without speaking, he went directly to the phone. A sigh of relief slipped between his lips when he got a dial tone. He dialed Aaron Chandler's number from memory.

He looked at Landis. "Come here."

Wariness flashed across her features. "Why?"

Ignoring the question, Jack thrust the phone at her. "Tell him to meet you here. Tell him you've got a mutual friend who needs clothes and money. Don't mention my name in case there's a tap. He'll know it's me. Tell him it's an emergency. Make sure he drives up here *now*."

Protest registered in her eyes, but Chandler must have answered, because she turned her attention to the phone. Jack watched her shift into lawyer mode, listened as the cool, detached professionalism slipped into her voice. Quickly and without emotion she informed Chandler of the situation. If Jack hadn't been watching her, he wouldn't have known her hands were trembling. Or that the pulse point just above the mole on her throat was thrumming.

Hanging up the phone, she turned to him. "He'll be here in a couple of hours."

"That'll give me time to eat and shower."

"You realize Aaron's going to insist you turn yourself in, don't you?" she asked.

"He can insist all he wants. That doesn't mean I'm going to do it."

"As an attorney—"

"Cut the lawyer crap. Nothing personal, but I'm not too keen on lawyers these days."

"Maybe you should have gone somewhere else."

Jack bit back an angry retort. He was cold and hungry and ached all the way to his fingernails. The last thing he wanted to do was argue with Landis. "It's been a rough couple of days." Argument leaped into her eyes, but he raised a hand to silence her. "I've got a bullet wound in my left shoulder."

Her mouth opened slightly and her gaze flicked to the bloodstained shirt. But she didn't speak. She didn't offer help. Maybe she wasn't as compassionate as he'd thought. "You need to go to the hospital," she said.

"That's not going to happen."

"I'm a lawyer, Jack. I don't do bullet wounds."

"Yeah, well, you're going to make an exception tonight." Never taking his eyes from hers, he began unbuttoning his shirt.

Landis stared at him as if he'd slashed her with a machete. Her gaze flicked from his eyes to his hands as he worked the buttons. At least that cool, detached mask was gone he mused, vaguely satisfied.

Easing one side of the shirt off his shoulder, he stole a look at the wound. His stomach flip-flopped as his eyes took in the mass of jagged flesh. The skin was the color of eggplant, swollen and hot to the touch. No wonder it hurt like hell.

Landis gasped and covered her mouth with an unsteady hand. "My God, Jack, I had no idea you were… You need to go to the hospital. A doctor. Stitches…" She stepped back, as if distancing herself would make him go away.

He knew she wasn't necessarily worried about his well-being, but it was good to know she was concerned. He couldn't remember the last time someone had worried about him. Hell, he couldn't remember the last time someone had cared whether he lived or died.

The feeling was bitterly familiar. Orphaned at the age of eight, Jack had grown up in a series of foster homes, some good, some not so good. He'd been moved around so often, the constant shuffling from home to home had become a way of life. He'd dealt with it by convincing himself he didn't care. If that didn't work, he went looking for trouble—something he'd always had a knack for finding.

He thought about the man who'd helped him turn his life around and wondered how Mike Morgan would feel about what was happening now. The prospect of Mike's disappointment left a bitter taste at the back of his throat.

"Why don't you let me drive you over to the clinic in Provo?" Landis said.

Taking in her wide eyes and pale skin, he almost smiled, realizing that even after everything that had happened between them, he was still hungry for her attention. Hungry for a hell of a lot more than her attention if he wanted to be honest about it. God, he was a fool…

"Because by law all bullet wounds are reported to the police," he snapped.

"I'm not equipped to treat a wound like that, Jack."

"It's only a graze. You can handle a bandage." He looked down at his muddy clothes. "Right now I'd like a shower and some dry clothes. I need something to eat.

Some aspirin and a bed. I need to have a clear head when Aaron gets here.''

He gazed through the French door, gauging the snow. Not exactly a snowstorm, but it was coming down again. In another hour the roads would be treacherous. Hopefully, Chandler kept a set of tire chains in the trunk of his Mercedes.

Surprising him, Landis stepped closer, until she was standing a mere foot away. He knew it was a tactic she'd learned at some point in her education. Some nonsense about invading personal space. Too bad she hadn't yet learned the tactic didn't work on him.

"All right, Jack. You can take a shower. I'll fix you something to eat. I'll even do my best to get your shoulder taken care of. But the moment Chandler gets here, you become his property, and he'll damn well take you with him when he leaves."

Jack tried to be amused, but his sense of humor had all but vanished in the last hours. "And if he doesn't?"

Narrowing her eyes the way a cat might an instant before it pounced on an unsuspecting mouse, she moved even closer. "Then you can add another twenty years to your sentence for holding me hostage."

Chapter 3

Landis's every sense was honed on the man standing at the hearth as she made her way toward the linen closet for a towel and an extra bar of soap. She told herself the only reason she was helping him was because she wanted him gone. The sight of him shivering with cold and pain had nothing to do with it. Damn it, it didn't. She was immune to his suffering. She might have cared for Jack once, but those days were over for good—for too many reasons to count.

As long as she kept her interaction with him to a minimum, she would get through this. Of course, maintaining a safe distance was going to be difficult considering the size of her cabin. For the first time since owning the place, she wished she'd gone for square footage instead of privacy.

She looked down at the bar of soap in her hand and willed her hand to stop shaking. The last thing she wanted to think about was Jack taking a shower in her bathroom.

The image of him lathering that large male body with her
perfumed soap disturbed her more than she wanted to admit. Maybe because she remembered every detail of that
body with startling clarity. A wide, muscular chest that tapered to a washboard belly. Narrow hips that connected to
long, powerful legs. She remembered running her fingers
through the dusting of black hair on his chest and thinking
she'd found heaven in his arms. She remembered kisses hot
enough to melt steel. Lovemaking so intense it had left
coolheaded Landis in tears...

With those disturbing memories came the darker memories of their last terrible night together. The night Evan
died, it had been Jack who broke the news. It was a night
of disbelief, of rage, of wrenching grief. But even as her
heart had cried out with the pain of losing her brother, she'd
reached out to Jack. He was Evan's best friend, and it had
seemed so right that he would be the one to share her anguish. A man and a woman, lovers bound by sorrow, seeking comfort in each other's arms. Landis had slept with
him one final, earth-shattering time before the investigation
and trial tore them apart.

But she'd never been able to erase the memory of his
words of solace, the tormenting sight of his tears or the
outrage burning in his eyes. Nor had she been able to forget
his gentle kisses, his steady, elegant hands, or the way his
eyes glittered with passion when he was inside her.

Shaken by the memory, appalled by the thoughts streaking through her traitorous brain, she opened the closet door
and yanked a towel from the shelf, vowing not to let the
past cloud her judgment. Granted, Jack was an attractive
man and they had once been lovers, but she respected herself too much to fall victim to his charms knowing what
she did.

"Where do you want me to put my clothes?"

Landis jumped at the nearness of his voice. Realizing

he'd come up behind her, she spun and thrust the towel into his midsection hard enough to elicit a grunt. "Don't sneak up on me like that."

Jack studied her carefully for a moment. "If I didn't know better, I'd say you were blushing."

"I'm not blushing," she snapped, hating it that he'd noticed. The curse of being a redhead, she supposed. Unable to meet his eyes, she focused on the towel between them— only to notice how large and strong his hands looked wrapped around it. She remembered seeing those same hands on her body, touching her, his palms warm and slightly roughened against her most sensitive flesh....

Disgusted with herself, she stepped back. "Take a shower." She sniffed. "You need it."

"You'll come check on me if I pass out, won't you, Red?"

Her heart did a weird little roll when his hands went to the remaining buttons of his shirt. Jack had never been shy. He was a boldly sexual creature, and Landis had always felt a little overwhelmed by his intensity. She wanted to snap at him to stay dressed until he was locked in the bathroom, but she knew that was silly. She was a grown woman and had seen plenty of male chests. This particular chest shouldn't be any different. Especially since she didn't even like the man it belonged to.

"Unless you want to spend the night in jail, I suggest you refrain from passing out," she said.

"It'd be hell explaining to the police how an escaped con got in your bathtub."

She didn't want to think about that. "Toss me your clothes from inside. I'll throw them in the washing machine."

Abruptly, he reached out. Landis tried to avoid the contact, but he was too quick. He brushed his knuckles along her jaw, but she felt the contact like an arc of electricity that snapped through her body and went all the way to her toes. Her intellect told her to pull away, but her body refused the order. Instead she found herself melting and softening, and she had to resist the impulse to lean closer....

"Thank you," he said.

She swatted his hand away from her face. "Don't read too much into it. You're not in jail right now because you've led me to believe you're going to turn yourself in."

A smile traced the corners of his mouth. "You still have a weakness for strays, don't you, Red?"

"You're not a stray, Jack. You're a wolf, and I only hope you don't turn on me." She raised her chin and looked him in the eye. A year of bottled-up pain and anger burgeoned in her chest and began to flow. It was as if he'd reached into her and wrested the plug from her damaged heart. "Don't assume you're going to flash that smile, hand me a few tidbits on Cyrus Duke and expect me to help you."

"The thought never crossed my mind," he said dryly.

"Don't insult my intelligence by thanking me for something I would never do for you."

"I'm going to enjoy proving you wrong."

"For your sake, I hope you can. Personally, I don't care as long as you stay out of my life."

"A couple of hours," he said. "Until Chandler gets here. That's all I'm asking."

"You have no idea what you're asking."

"Listen to your heart, Landis."

"My heart has been wrong about you every time it got involved."

"Not this time." His voice was like a caress, so soft and gentle that for a moment, she wanted to believe him....

Never taking his eyes from hers, Jack worked off the shirt and handed it to her. It took all of her discipline not to let her eyes drop, to explore what she knew was a magnificent chest. But she didn't; control was too important to her. And Jack had always been a threat to that control. He'd always wreaked havoc on her in one way or another. Mentally. Physically. Emotionally. Landis only hoped she could keep a handle on her emotions long enough to get him out of her life once and for all.

Needing to get out from under his discerning gaze, she turned and started down the hall. She could feel his eyes on her as she walked, but she didn't stop, didn't even look back. And for the first time since his arrival, she knew she was much more vulnerable to him than she'd thought.

Leaning forward with his hands against the tile, Jack let the hot spray pound away the dirt, the aches and the bone-deep chill. The water felt like a hot branding iron against his shoulder wound, but there was no getting around a shower so he simply endured. He gladly put up with the pain to get clean. The water ran brown with grime and dirt and blood. He'd never wanted a shower so badly in his entire life. Prison had a way of making a man feel dirty right down to his soul.

He closed his eyes against a bout of dizziness, and for a moment the darkness transported him back to the peniteniary. He heard the steel doors banging shut, the locks turning with the kind of finality that could drive a man insane. He heard the crude shouts, listened to the words of hatred and bitterness and felt his humanity slip a little bit more.

Jack had always considered himself a strong, resilient man. But the year he'd spent in prison had come very close to destroying him. He'd tried to adjust to the routine of prison life; he'd tried to accept the reality that he would be pending the rest of his life behind bars. But something inside him refused to acquiesce no matter how impossible the situation.

Back when he'd been a troubled teen, he'd been unable o fight the injustices inflicted upon him by a system that wasn't perfect. But Jack was a man now. Deep down inside he was still a cop. And even if that title had been stripped from him, he would draw his last breath fighting for what was right.

Or die trying.

Using a heart-shaped soap, he lathered his body twice, marveling at the feel of being warm and clean. He washed his hair with shampoo that smelled startlingly like Landis. For a moment, he lost himself in her scent and wished for the hundredth time he could turn back the hands of time.

But Jack was through lamenting the past. For the first time in over a year, his fate was in his own hands. He didn't intend to squander it. He wouldn't waste one second of that time wishing for things he couldn't have. The relationship he'd once shared with Landis was over. She'd turned her back on him when he'd needed her desperately. She would do it again if he gave her the chance. The sooner he accepted that, the better off he'd be.

He didn't have much time. Twenty-four hours. Thirty-six hours tops. He had no idea when the police or the department of corrections would catch up with him. The way his luck was running, capture seemed imminent. He hated to waste time on sleep, but he hadn't slept for two days. His brain was barely functioning. His body was operating on sheer will alone. He needed food and a few hours in a bed. He needed a clear head for his meeting with Chandler because it wasn't going to be easy convincing his attorney to look the other way while his client became a fugitive from justice.

He switched off the water and opened the glass door. A fluffy pink towel hung neatly on the rack. Jack stared at it, realizing with mild amusement that he had nothing to wear while his clothes were being laundered. Cursing mildly, he stepped out of the tub and reached for the towel. The fabric elt soft against his fingers. Even before bringing it to his nose, he knew it smelled like Landis.

Pleasure jumped through him as her scent wrapped round his brain. Despite the fatigue, and the pain of his injury, his body responded. Closing his eyes against the ard tug of longing, he whispered her name. ''Landis...''

Landis's hands shook as she tossed sliced mushrooms into the omelet. Cooking usually calmed her, but tonight er battered nerves refused to cooperate. She couldn't stop thinking about Jack. The way he'd looked at her when he'd proclaimed his innocence. The sound of his voice when e'd whispered her name. The way he'd touched her. Oh ear God, why had she allowed herself to get sucked into his maelstrom?

''Don't tell me you finally learned to cook.''

She jolted at the sound of his voice. The slice of toast he'd been buttering slipped from her hand and landed butter-side down on the floor. She was about to utter a very nlady-like curse when the sight of him wearing nothing ut a towel froze her in place.

Her eyes swept over him. Shock and a jolt of something at felt vaguely electrical ran the length of her body. Water om his shower glistened on broad shoulders. She saw a nest that was rounded with muscle and covered with thick ack hair. The towel was wrapped snugly around an abomen that was flat and rippled with muscle. Even as she ld herself she wasn't going to let the sight of all that hard ale flesh get to her, she felt the burn of a blush on her eeks.

Appalled by her reaction, she quickly turned away, telling herself it was stress that had her blushing and speechss when she should have been doling out ultimatums.

Plucking a paper towel from the roll, he stooped to re-

trieve the fallen toast. "The omelet's singeing," he sai
easily.

Landis reached for the spatula and proceeded to mangl
the omelet.

With the self-assurance of a man who knew his wa
around the kitchen, Jack moved in beside her and usurpe
the spatula. "Let me do that."

She watched him expertly fold the eggs and shovel ther
on to waiting plates. "Where did you learn to do that?
she asked, determined to get a grip before he got the wron
idea. Just because he'd flustered her didn't mean she wa
going to change her mind and help him.

"I cooked for cellblock C six days a week," he sai
"Breakfast shift, mostly."

When he looked at her she knew instinctively the smil
was there only to hide something he didn't want her to se
Sadness. Humiliation, perhaps. The thought put an uncon
fortable twinge in her chest.

"I make a pretty mean beef stew, too," he said. "Bat
carrots. Turnips. You ever had turnips with beef stew?"

He was the only person she'd ever known who coul
make her smile when she didn't want to. None of what ha
happened in the past year was even remotely funny. It wa
sad more than anything, she realized. So many lives ruine
Others irrevocably changed.

"Ian left a flannel shirt behind the last time he wa
here." Unable to look at him, she dropped her gaze to th
skillet in front of her. "I'll get it for you."

"Why won't you look at me?"

"Because I'm trying to fix you something to eat," sl
said, her voice filled with exasperation.

"It doesn't bother you to see me in a towel, does it?"

"Don't be an idiot." She glared at him, refusing to a
knowledge that her heart was pinging hard against her rit

One side of his mouth curved. "Red, you're refreshing as hell."

"I'm glad at least one of us is finding the situation amusing." Turning away from him, she stalked into the living room, swung open the closet door and jerked the blue flannel shirt off a hanger. Back in the kitchen she thrust it at him. Because she couldn't quite meet his gaze, she found herself staring at the sterile gauze he'd taped haphazardly to his shoulder. She could see that the surrounding flesh was swollen and discolored, and hoped to God it wasn't as serious as it looked. "That's a pathetic excuse for a bandage."

"Yeah, well, I couldn't do a very good job with one hand." He gazed steadily at her. "I'm going to need you to butterfly me."

She didn't want to get anywhere near him, let alone administer first aid. "Look, Jack, the only stuff I know about first aid comes from the occasional episode of *E.R.*"

"That's good enough for me." Wincing a little, he eased into the shirt, then looked down at the pink towel wrapped around his hips. "How long until my pants are dry? I want to be out of all this pink by the time Chandler arrives. It doesn't do much for my credibility."

"I hate to tell you this, Jack, but you don't have any credibility."

His smile was cold. "I'd almost forgotten how cutting you can be."

"I don't want you here. What do you expect?"

"The benefit of a doubt."

"Maybe we should just concentrate on getting through the next couple of hours without coming to blows." She carried their plates to the dining room table. Though she didn't look at him, she felt his gaze on her as she pulled out a chair and sat.

Momentarily, he followed and sat next to her. Without

looking up or speaking, he ate like a man possessed, making her wonder how long it had been since he'd had any food.

As she watched him, a sudden jolt of despair wrenched at her. She told herself it was the feelings she'd once had for him fueling the doubts inside her. Damn it, she trusted the criminal justice system. He'd had a fair trial. Justice had been served. She'd seen the evidence. She'd heard the witnesses testify against him. Yet buried in the recesses of her mind, a shadow of doubt had taken root. Was it possible Evan had gotten himself into trouble and been killed for it? Was Cyrus Duke involved? Could Jack be innocent?

She tried not to imagine what he'd been through. As an assistant prosecutor, she'd been inside prisons before. She knew how the inmates were treated. She knew the humiliations, the violence and the lack of humanity that was an integral part of prison life. She knew what being locked in a cage did to a man. She knew what it had done to her own father. The parallels between the two men made her shiver.

Jack had lost everything in the past year. His best friend. His career. His freedom. Yet he'd endured, never sacrificing his dignity. What kind of a man did that make him? A murderer who wanted freedom at any cost? Or a survivor who was willing to risk it all to prove his innocence?

"Do you have a first aid kit?"

The sound of his voice startled her, and Landis realized with some embarrassment that she'd been staring. "Everything I have is in the medicine cabinet. Gauze and tape."

"Antibiotic cream?"

"Yes." His politeness was beginning to annoy her. It would be easier to hate him if he were rude.

"What you need is a doctor," she said, praying that for once in his life he would agree with her. "Not me to play nursemaid."

Rising, she gathered his dishes, her own untouched food

and took them to the sink. Even without looking at him, she knew he was assessing her, trying to read her body language. Mercy, she knew him too well. It was disconcerting to know he knew her just as well.

"It might be a few days before I get to the doc," he said.

Landis closed her eyes, dread gathering in her chest. It was crazy, but a small part of her wanted to help him. She wanted to ease his pain. She wanted to do this one, compassionate thing for him because she knew it would be the last kindness she would ever show him. After tonight he would be gone, and she would never see him again. Oddly, the notion wasn't as comforting as she wanted it to be.

Taking a calming breath, she faced him. "The cut above your eye looks bad, too."

"Pretty careless of the prison system to string barbed wire where the inmates could get hurt. Think my lawyer could get a settlement out of them?"

"That's not funny."

Irked by his flippant tone, Landis left the kitchen. In the bathroom, she found the gauze, tape, peroxide, aspirin and a crinkled tube of antibiotic cream. Dreading the job ahead, she entered the living room to find Jack slumped on the sofa, watching her through heavy-lidded eyes.

"You got anything stronger than aspirin?" he asked.

Despite the intrepid facade, she could tell he was tense about the wound. He should be, considering what he expected her to do. "I guess you're not going to let me talk you out of this," she said.

"Think revenge, Counselor. That should get you through it."

Frowning, she went to the bar and found the old bottle of brandy she'd gotten for Christmas last year. Working off the cork, she snagged a good-size tumbler from the cabinet, and walked back to the living room.

"Ah, a little brandy for the soul," he said. "That ought to do nicely."

She set the bottle and glass on the coffee table and looked down at him. "That wound is serious, Jack. If it gets infected you could find yourself seriously ill."

"Careful Landis, or I might think you still care about me."

"Like you said, Jack, I've always had a weakness for strays—even when I know they're likely to bite." She poured two fingers of the amber liquid into the glass.

"More," he said.

"You just want to kill the pain, not put yourself into a coma." But she filled the glass to the halfway mark and handed it to him.

"I hate to waste the expensive stuff on a gunshot wound."

"Go ahead. I haven't exactly been celebrating much lately." She tapped out three aspirins. "These will help."

Never taking his eyes from hers, he tossed back the aspirin, brought the glass to his lips and drained it in three gulps. Landis watched, fascinated as he shuddered, then set the glass back on the table.

Leaning against the sofa back, he closed his eyes. "Give this a minute to kick in, will you?"

She looked down at her scant first aid supplies, praying she could get through this without making the wound worse than it already was.

"Okay. Let's get this over with." Grimacing, he unbuttoned the shirt, wincing as it came down over his shoulder.

Careful not to get too close, Landis peeled back the bandage he'd applied after his shower. The moment the wound came into view her stomach did a slow-motion somersault. She wasn't squeamish, but the sight of the bruised flesh and gaping wound made her feel light-headed. "I'm sure this isn't what you want to hear, but I flunked basic first aid.''

"You're not going to pass out on me, are you?"

"Don't be ridiculous."

A chuckle rumbled in his throat. "From the looks of you, I'd say the jury's still out on that. Maybe you ought to sit down. That floor's hard as hell, and I don't have the strength to pick you up."

"I'm not going to pass out."

He didn't move as she rounded the sofa and set the peroxide and antibiotic cream on the end table. "Hold this." She handed him the gauze. "And be quiet. I need to concentrate."

Unable to avoid it any longer, she looked closely at the wound. It was no longer bleeding, but the gash was deep, the flesh jaggedly cut. She could only imagine how painful it was. "Hand me a section of gauze," she said.

He opened the wrapper and held it out for her. "Am I going to live?"

"That depends on how much pain you can take."

"On a scale of one to ten, it's already a nine."

"So we've got some room to work with." Saturating the square of gauze with peroxide, Landis drizzled it over the wound. His quick intake of breath told her it stung, but he didn't flinch. She repeated the procedure several times until the peroxide stopped foaming. As gently as possible, she applied some of the antibiotic ointment.

"Hurt?" she asked.

"No worse than the day you walked out of my cell for the last time." A fine sheet of sweat coated his forehead. "On a scale of one to ten, that was definitely a ten."

Her hands stilled, but she didn't look at him. A day didn't go by that she didn't remember the look on his face when she'd left him standing in his cell, looking like the ground had just caved in beneath him. Aside from burying her brother, it was the hardest thing she'd ever had to do.

"This isn't a good time to dredge up the past, Jack."

"Another hour and I'll be gone. We won't get another chance."

She felt his gaze burning into her, but she focused on the bullet wound, realizing with dismay the mass of damaged flesh was easier to look at than those accusing eyes of his. "Maybe that's best for both of us."

"Maybe it's time you looked a little deeper. Maybe it's time somebody put Duke in prison for what he did to Evan. For what he did to us. For God's sake, Landis, what we had…"

The tube of antibiotic cream slipped from her hand and fell to the floor. Exasperated, she cursed and dropped her hands to her sides. Her heart pounded, and she couldn't keep her mind from racing with the possibilities of what he was saying. "Damn it, Jack, if you want me to get your shoulder bandaged, you're going to have to shut up."

Turning his head slightly, he glanced down at the wound. Landis didn't miss the slight paling of his face. "I'm going to need some more of those aspirin."

She hesitated, knowing she was going to cause him real pain when she tried to join the jagged edges of the wound. "You need stitches, Jack. I'm not sure I can butterfly this. I don't want to hurt you."

"Ah, come on, Red. You've already ripped my heart out. This ought to be a breeze."

She glanced sharply at him, but his eyes were closed. He had an incredibly sensuous mouth for a male, and she suddenly remembered how many times that mouth had kissed her, how good he was at it….

He shifted slightly, and the shirt fell open the rest of the way. Her eyes did a slow, dangerous sweep, skimming over his magnificent chest, the dark sprinkling of hair, and the rounded pectoral muscles. The towel was knotted just below his navel and she could see the flat stretch of his belly, the thickening of hair...

"Your hands don't look too steady, Red."

She jolted, jerked her gaze back to his. "Bullet wounds make me nervous."

"Maybe it's the convict making you nervous."

"I don't think so."

He stared at her, making no move to close the shirt, one side of his mouth curved into a knowing smile.

Struggling to keep her hands from shaking, she withdrew three long sections of first aid tape from the dispenser. She then placed a sterile gauze pad over the wound. Sweat moistened her forehead as she stretched the first piece of tape tightly over the gauze, effectively pulling the edges of the wound together.

Jack winced and cut loose with a curse. "Jesus..."

"I'm sorry."

"Hurry up," he ground out between clenched teeth.

Holding her breath, she secured the second length of tape, trying in vain to ignore his groan of pain. Oh, dear God, when was Aaron Chandler going to arrive?

By the time the bandage was in place Landis was shaking all over. A dime-size stain of fresh blood marred the gauze. The injury would leave a tremendous scar, but at least it wouldn't get infected. Sighing with relief, she stepped away, aware that her legs were rubbery.

Jack slumped against the back of the sofa with his eyes closed. He cradled his left arm as if it were broken. His face was pale and drawn and his strong jaw had finally stopped clenching. She watched him for several minutes. Slowly, his breathing returned to normal. His hands, which had been fisted in pain, relaxed. The furrow at his brow smoothed out. At least he wasn't hurting anymore.

Surprising herself, she raised her hand and touched his

lean cheek the way she'd done a hundred times in the months they'd been involved. The stubble of his beard felt rough and unfamiliar beneath her fingertips. She could smell his clean, masculine scent. Memories stirred uncomfortably inside her. She stared at him, remembering, hurting, regretting and wishing things could have turned out differently.

"Why can't I hate you for what you did?" she whispered.

Chapter 4

By the yellow light of the banker's lamp in her study, Landis scrutinized the brief she'd spent the last hour hammering into her computer. It was a technique she'd developed in her first year of law school, and the habit had stuck with her. Whenever she was perplexed by a case she could usually work things out by outlining the facts, the points of contention, the supporting evidence and analyzing it. Ironically, the one time she desperately needed logical conclusions, her system failed her. How was she supposed to concentrate when the man convicted of murdering her brother was sleeping upstairs in her guest room?

Cursing the memories and emotions for getting in the way, she slipped her reading glasses on to her nose and stared at the screen. On the first page she'd organized the data indicating Jack's guilt, which consisted of a multitude of damning physical evidence, namely his service revolver and a $50,000 bank deposit, both of which conceivably could have been planted. In addition, two witnesses had placed him at the scene of the crime. A fellow cop had testified that he'd heard Jack and Evan arguing just days earlier. None of the evidence was conclusive in itself but combined it was compelling as hell.

Lower, she'd listed the prosecution's portrayal of what happened that night, including his version of motive, means and opportunity. It hadn't been difficult for him to convince the jury Jack had killed his partner to cover up his own illicit dealings, which included bribery, extortion and racketeering. The truth of the matter was he looked guilty as sin.

Landis composed a few of her own theories based on what Jack had told her. At the bottom of the page the name Cyrus Duke stood out in stark black and white followed by a question mark. To anyone else, the case might have looked cut-and-dried. A cop on the take who'd murdered his partner to keep his crimes from coming to light. But Landis wasn't just anyone. She was an assistant prosecutor. She'd once known Jack well. She'd been his lover for the better part of a year. She'd known his mind and his heart. And in her own heart she suddenly knew there was nothing cut-and-dried about the case.

The thought was not a comforting one.

Taking into consideration Jack's background in law enforcement, his street smarts and keen intelligence, the case against him was almost *too* neat. There was no way he would have made some of the mistakes that had convicted him. Jack would have covered his tracks well.

"So why didn't you?" she whispered.

She considered his actions after his escape from prison. Would a guilty man risk his newfound freedom chasing down a known criminal who'd proven himself untouchable even to the police? Was it her own wretched conscience that was bothering her? Or maybe it was her father's ghost that wouldn't let her see this case in black and white.

Dropping her face into her hands, Landis let out a weary sigh and acknowledged the headache at her temples. She refused to believe Evan had been involved with Cyrus Duke. After what their father put them through twenty years earlier, she just couldn't believe Evan would put himself—or his family—in the same position.

But if not Evan, then whom?

She jolted when the doorbell sounded, telling her Aaron Chandler had arrived. Relief poured through her that she would no longer have to deal with Jack alone. Leaving her study, she walked briskly to the foyer, checked the peephole and opened the door.

Aaron Chandler stood on the porch looking like a cross between a drug lord and a high-dollar gigolo. The Italian suit and expensive wingtips lent him an air of sophistication. But the ponytail, the gold earring and his lack of physical stature, did little to further the image. Landis had learned early in life that looks could be deceiving, so she refrained from making judgments based on first impressions. She didn't know the man personally, but as an attorney herself she was well aware of his reputation.

Despite his height, people noticed when Aaron Chandler walked into a room. Judges respected him. Hostile witnesses opened up to him. Juries invariably trusted him. His fellow lawyers feared him—especially prosecutors facing off with him in the courtroom. He took on cases that left other defense attorneys quaking in fear. The high-profile cases. The controversial cases. He thrived on visibility, debate and victory. On the rare occasion when he *did* lose a case, it was rumored that he was a consummate sore loser and prone to temper tantrums.

Landis had stopped being intimidated by facades a long time ago. Personally, she didn't care for the kind of dark brilliance Aaron Chandler brought to the profession. It didn't matter to him if his clients were guilty or innocent.

In a game where winner took all, a little detail like justice was inconsequential.

"Jack always swore Lady Luck was a redhead." Brandishing a thousand dollar smile, he extended his hand.

She returned the handshake, regarding him with a combination of professional respect and personal disdain as he stomped the snow from his shoes and walked into the foyer. "It seems Jack has been incorrect quite often recently," she said.

Chandler looked around the cabin as if he were in the market for a summer home—and hers didn't quite fit the bill. Landis watched as his eyes traveled to the first aid supplies she'd left on the end table to the French door where a piece of cardboard covered the broken pane. A quiet shrewdness rested easily behind his wire-rimmed bifocals, and she found herself immediately on guard.

"Not bad for an assistant prosecutor." He winked at her with a sort of fatherly wisdom he didn't quite manage, then leaned closer as if to let her in on a much-coveted secret. "But I'm sure you know the real money is in defending the private sector."

She shrugged. "Not every lawyer is motivated by money."

"There's nothing wrong with earning a good salary."

"I guess that depends on what you have to do to earn it."

"Touché." Looking thoroughly amused, his gaze traveled from the dining room to the staircase, then back to her. "I've heard you're good. If you ever want to cross over to the other side, give me a call."

Landis had met enough people like Aaron Chandler in her lifetime not to be flattered. No wonder Jack hated lawyers. "My legal brilliance aside, Mr. Chandler, I'd say you have a rather large problem on your hands this evening."

"Ah, yes, our mutual friend." His brows snapped together. "I'm afraid he's jumped out of the frying pan and into the flame this time, hasn't he?"

"You've got to talk him into turning himself in."

"He's innocent, you know," he said, eyeing her over the tops of his bifocals.

"All of your clients are innocent."

"Just as all of your defendants are guilty?"

"Innocent until proven guilty," she corrected. "I'm sure I don't need to inform you that Jack LaCroix was found guilty in a court of law."

"Unjustly, I'm afraid. Where is he?"

"Upstairs in the guest—"

"I'm right here." Jack's baritone voice cut through the air like a lance.

Landis and Chandler turned simultaneously to see Jack moving gingerly down the stairs.

After only an hour of sleep, the improvement in his appearance amazed her. He was still pale, but the sharpness had returned to his eyes. He watched them with the caution of an animal that knew it was being stalked. On reaching the foot of the stairs, he walked toward them.

Landis couldn't take her eyes off him as he approached. His very presence seemed to suck all the oxygen from her lungs. Six feet, four inches of lean muscle, bad attitude and one of the most complex personalities she'd ever encountered. He'd put on his clean prison issue trousers and shirt, and she was keenly aware of the way the fabric lay over hard-as-rock muscle.

Chandler extended his hand when Jack reached them. "You're the last person I expected to do something so incredibly stupid."

Grimacing, Jack accepted the handshake. "You're the last lawyer I expected to lose my case."

"We won't lose the appeal."

"No offense, but I didn't want to stick around to find out."

Landis watched the exchange, telling herself she was doing the right thing. She couldn't harbor a fugitive. Jack was better off with his lawyer. Maybe Chandler could talk him into giving himself up.

"Your lack of patience has landed you in a heap of trouble this time," Chandler said. "You made the evening news."

"Lead story?" Jack asked.

Chandler shook his slicked-back head. "They gave the lead story to a big warehouse fire in Provo."

"Can't say I'm disappointed."

"Possibly armed and very dangerous—or so they said. A witness claims to have seen you with Elvis on board the Burlington Northern near Brigham City."

One side of Jack's mouth quirked. "Hell of a guy, that Elvis."

Annoyance rippled through her that the two men could be so casual about such a grave situation. "Elvis sightings aside, gentlemen, I think you should be using your collective brain power to figure out how you're going to rectify the situation." She looked at Jack. "We know the only smart thing for Mr. LaCroix to do is give yourself up."

Jack met her gaze unflinchingly, his eyes dark and indecipherable as he studied her. "I didn't risk my life breaking out of prison just to give myself up, *Ms.* McAllister." He used the formal title with a hefty dose of sarcasm. "I plan to use what little time I have as a free man to prove I didn't kill my partner. Then I'm going to nail the bastard who framed me." He looked at Chandler. "I need a car, some clothes and some money."

The attorney snorted. "I'm sure you're familiar with the term aiding and abetting. Does the word disbarment mean anything to you?"

Landis's heart rate sped up. She couldn't imagine Chandler agreeing to aid and abet a convicted murderer—even if it was his own client. "You can't operate outside the law, Jack," she said. "Every law enforcement agency from here to the Canadian border is looking for you."

Jack raked a hand through his hair, wincing with the sudden movement and cutting loose with a curse.

"He's been shot," Landis explained.

Shock flashed across Chandler's face. "*Shot?* My God, man, you need to see a doc—"

"What I need is some bloody cooperation!" Jack shouted.

Shaking his head, the attorney studied him. "You look dead on your feet. You can't afford to jeopardize your health on a wild-goose chase that will do nothing but earn you another ten years in prison."

Jack scowled. "For the record, Chandler, my health doesn't mean a whole hell of a lot if I'm going to be spending the rest of my life behind bars."

Chandler set his hand on Jack's shoulder. "Landis is right. You can't operate outside the law. The police have itchy fingers when it comes to cop killers. As your attorney, the only advice I can give you is to let me handle this through the appeal process."

A cynical laugh escaped Jack. "I hate to break your heart—not that you have one—but my faith in the legal system is a little shaky at the moment. I'll take my chances with the hounds and bullets before I let myself get railroaded again."

"Just how do you plan on proving your innocence when I couldn't?" Chandler looked ruffled.

"Did you bring me a change of clothes?" Jack asked, dodging the question.

Chandler sighed. "There's an overnight case in the car. I'll merely add the cost of the clothes to your final bill."

"What about money?" Jack asked.

Chandler looked as if a gas pain hit him. "I've got a couple of hundred on me—"

"That'll do."

The attorney looked at Landis over the top of his glasses. "Are you two...?"

"No!" Landis blurted, dismayed that Chandler had jumped to that conclusion. She didn't even want to think about what else he may have assumed. "I don't want any part of this." She felt the heat of Jack's stare on her, but she maintained eye contact with Chandler. "I don't want him here, Aaron. As of right now I'm washing my hands of the entire situation. You're taking him with you or I'm calling the police."

Blowing out a breath of frustration, Chandler frowned at Jack. "Does she know?"

Jack shook his head. "I tried. She doesn't believe me."

Landis didn't like surprises. Judging from the men's expressions, she had the feeling this one was going to be a doozy. "Believe what?"

Jack's gaze swept to Landis. "Chandler is close to getting proof that Evan was taking money from Duke," he said quietly.

She couldn't have been more shocked if he'd pulled out a switchblade and slashed her. For a moment she could only stare, first at Jack, then at Chandler. She forced herself to breathe.

"What kind of proof?" she asked in a voice that sounded much calmer than she felt. All she could think of was that Evan wasn't here to defend himself. That Jack was a desperate man. And that Aaron Chandler would do anything to win a case.

"I'm working on getting his bank records subpoenaed," Chandler said. "The proof is there. We'll get the subpoena."

Her lawyer's mind clicked into place. "Money can be planted."

"Why didn't I think of that?" Jack said dryly.

Chandler frowned. "Not if we can prove Evan had been depositing and withdrawing for quite some time."

She was aware of Jack's eyes burning into her, as hot as lasers. Was this another brilliant legal maneuver by the illustrious Aaron Chandler? Or had her brother followed in their father's footsteps and taken a very dark secret with him to the grave?

"Why didn't the police do that?" she asked.

"Because they thought they had their man," Chandler said.

"I'm sorry, Landis," Jack said. "I'm not trying to make Evan out to be the villain, but I'll do what I have to in order to clear my name."

Landis risked a look at him. "Even if you're able to prove Evan was taking bribes, it doesn't prove your innocence," she pointed out.

"No. But it does give the courts cause to have another look at Jack's case," Chandler said. "We'll get a retrial."

Releasing the breath she'd been holding, Landis stepped away from the two men, her head spinning. She thought of the brief she'd drafted and realized everything Jack had told her was plausible. She felt betrayed. By her own heart. By the brother she'd loved. And now by the system upon which she'd based her career.

"If you believe Evan's bank records will reopen your case, why didn't you just wait until your appeal came up?" she asked.

"The retrial isn't even on the docket. It could be months from now," Jack said. "Someone already tried to put an ice pick between my ribs. The corrections officers weren't too concerned." He shrugged. "Sooner or later, one of Duke's thugs would have gotten me. He's got people in the prison system. Even incarcerated, he knew I could make trouble for him.''

The thought of Jack dying in prison for a crime he hadn't committed shook her with unexpected force. She grappled for the cool distance of the lawyer she was. But it was the woman who felt the pain.

''Look,'' Jack began, ''I'm not going to waste any more of my life waiting for some lawyer or judge or jury to decide my fate. I'm innocent, Landis. If anyone can find the evidence to support the truth, it's me. I'm a cop. I know what to do. I've got contacts. I've sure as hell got the most at stake.''

She didn't want to believe any of it. But a traitorous part of her heart jumped with a hope she didn't want to define. ''You're going to get yourself killed,'' she said.

''That's a risk I'm willing to take.''

Landis looked deeply into his eyes, searched his gaze. For what she wasn't sure. He stared back at her, his eyes clear and filled with a hard determination. God, how could he look at her like that and not be telling the truth?

Suddenly overwhelmed by the weight of the question, frightened by the terrible new suspicions roiling inside her, Landis stepped away from him. ''I think you should leave now. Both of you.'' She looked away, unable to maintain eye contact. She wasn't sure what her eyes would reveal. Uncertainty. Regret. There were so many feelings battling inside her she felt as if she were about to come apart at the seams.

Jack turned to Chandler. ''I need a minimum of forty-eight hours. I'll need a few hours to recuperate. I'll spend the rest of the time digging. I've got a few leads to check out.''

Groaning, Aaron removed his glasses and pinched the bridge of his nose. ''Do you have any idea what you're asking me to do?''

"I'm asking you to do the right thing." Jack's jaw flexed with tension. "You know I won't come up empty-handed."

Chandler scrubbed a hand over his jaw and shot Landis a sage look. "Are you going to refrain from speaking to anyone about this? Namely the D.A.? I can do without getting disbarred."

Landis risked a look at Jack. The reckless light was back in his eyes. He looked dangerous as hell and…hopeful. She wasn't sure why, but that made her sad. Maybe because she knew what it was like to hope for something that would never be. "I'm going to forget tonight ever took place," she said.

Chandler turned to Jack. "I'll give you forty-eight hours to come up with some evidence to clear your name. After that time, and whether or not you've been successful, you will turn yourself in. Understood?"

Jack grimaced. "All right."

The attorney continued. "I'll drop you at my summer cottage near Soldier Summit south of Provo. It's secluded, so you won't have to worry about neighbors. There should be some canned food and firewood. I keep an old pickup out back. Both the truck and the cabin are yours for forty-eight hours."

Jack started to speak, but Chandler cut him off. "I can count the number of people I trust on one hand. You're one of them, Jack. But don't cross me. If you don't call me so I can arrange for you to turn yourself in within the allotted time, I'll deny this conversation ever took place, and I'll do whatever I have to in order to protect myself." His eyes swept from Jack to Landis. "Agreed?"

Jack nodded.

"Let's get this show on the road." Chandler extended his hand to Landis. "It was a pleasure, Ms. McAllister."

She gripped his hand, but couldn't shake the feeling that

she'd just made a deal with the devil. "I don't approve of your methods."

Chandler smiled. "No offense, Ms. McAllister, but I don't give a damn if you approve of my methods or not." Without another word, he turned and walked out the front door and into the falling snow.

She stared after him, keenly aware that Jack was standing just a few feet away. Even without looking at him, she knew he was watching her. She felt his gaze like a physical touch. Knowing she couldn't put off the inevitable, she turned to him.

"This is…crazy," she said.

He shrugged. "There's no other way."

Landis wished she had an argument, but she didn't. She didn't know what to say, what to feel. If he were innocent…

The reality that he was leaving, that she would probably never see him again should have pleased her. This was the moment she'd been waiting for. She could wash her hands of him. Strangely, the only thing she felt was a new concern for his safety and a boatload of regret.

"Be careful," she said.

He glanced out the door. Beyond, Landis heard Chandler's Mercedes start. She knew she should turn around and walk away before she did something impulsive. Before Jack did something impulsive. But neither of them moved.

"I know you don't want to hear this," he began, "but you and I have some unfinished business."

"No, we don't."

"You can deny it all you want, but I'm not buying it. Judging from the way you're looking at me, neither are you."

"It's not the first time you've misjudged me. I want you to leave."

He started toward her. "That's not what your eyes are telling me."

Landis knew he was going to kiss her an instant before he moved. Dread and a unsettling pang of anticipation skittered through her. Her heart went wild in her chest. She could feel the tempo of it in her pulse. The heat of it streaking through her veins. Her brain screamed for her to turn and run, but her legs refused the command.

He crossed the distance between them in two strides. His eyes were level and cool and focused on her with an intensity that sent a shiver through her. She jolted when his hands closed around her biceps.

"Jack…"

He didn't ask for permission. One instant she was rigid and on the brink of running. The next she was flush against his hard-as-steel body and all the oxygen was being sucked from her lungs. She was still trying to get her brain around the idea of his touching her when his mouth came down on hers.

The contact went through her like a jolt of electricity. Her gasp of protest came out as a sigh of pleasure. His lips were warm, demanding, and devastatingly clever as they claimed her mouth. He'd always known how to kiss, how to tease her mouth into submission, how to drive her crazy with wanting. He was doing it now in a war of give and take, and it was a battle she was quickly losing.

Desire crashed through her, an avalanche tumbling down a mountain, gaining momentum and crushing everything in its path. She'd forgotten what it was like to be kissed by Jack LaCroix. To have her mouth possessed by his, her senses heightened to a fever pitch. He kissed her with a no-holds-barred sexuality that scrambled her thoughts and left her trembling and disconcerted as hell.

Before even realizing she was going to respond, her arms went around his neck. She could feel him trembling, feel the tension in his muscles. He smelled vaguely of soap, her shampoo and his own unique brand of masculinity. Growling low in his throat, he wrapped his arms around her, pinning her against him until they were chest to chest, thigh to thigh, body to body.

A shudder went through her when she discerned the hard ridge of his arousal against her belly. She closed her eyes against the knowledge that he wanted her, against the disturbing knowledge that she didn't have the strength to pull away. She told herself it didn't mean anything. It couldn't mean anything. Not to him. Certainly not to her.

But her body had never been able to lie when it came to Jack. Her breasts grew heavy and full. She wanted to deny it, but she could feel the ache in her womb. The sudden dampness between her legs. She tasted need and frustration, not sure if it was his or her own. For a wild, fleeting moment, the world around her ceased to exist. She was aware only of Jack, his mouth against hers, his body straining to get closer.

Every nerve ending in her body jumped when he tested her with his tongue. Her intellect told her not to let this go any further. She knew how easily she could get swept up in his kiss. But the protest in her throat came out as a moan when he slid his tongue between her teeth. Vaguely, she was aware of his hand at the back of her head, the other at the small of her back. She wanted to pull away before this tumbled completely out of control. Instead, she responded with the kind of wanton abandon she didn't know she possessed.

The kiss shattered her resolve not to feel. Emotion and intellect tangled with physical sensations. Dangerous, forbidden thoughts thundered through her, frightening her with their unleashed power. All the while his mouth worked dark magic on hers. Like a mind-altering drug that left her head reeling, her body aroused, her senses crying out for more,

As quickly as he had assailed her, he broke the kiss. Landis blinked at him, aware that his hands gripped her upper arms, that they were both breathless and shaking and shocked as hell.

"You taste the same," he growled. "Better than I remember."

Landis didn't trust her voice to speak. She was shaking on the inside. On the outside. And every place in between. Even as she cursed him, cursed her own weakness, another wretched part of her wanted just one more taste of that unforgettable mouth.

"This doesn't change anything," she managed after a moment.

One side of his mouth curved. "It changes everything."

"I can't let it mean anything."

"You're not in charge of the way we feel." Dropping his hands from her arms, he backed toward the open door.

"Maybe not, but I know right from wrong. This is wrong."

"Go ahead and believe that if it's what your conscience needs. But we're not finished with this. Not by a long shot." He reached the door, looked back at her. Finality stabbed through her as she realized this was probably their final goodbye. She couldn't bring herself to say it, but she wished him well.

He crossed the threshold.

She whispered his name, wanted desperately to say something about fate and forgiveness, but it was too late. Instead she stood there with her heart pounding, her body on fire, and watched him disappear into the darkness like a phantom.

Chapter 5

Landis jerked awake to the sound of the doorbell. She bolted upright, disoriented, vaguely aware of the gray light slanting in through the window above her bed. The first thought that hit her befuddled brain was that the police had come to her door with questions about a certain escaped convict.

Scrambling out of bed, she slipped on her robe and hit the floor running. Her feet barely touched the steps as she ran down the stairs. Heart pounding, she reached the foyer and looked out the peephole, half expecting to see a dozen deputies standing on her front porch. Relief bubbled through her when she found only her younger brother, Ian, looking boyish and handsome in his crisp blue uniform.

Reassuring herself that no one could possibly know about Jack's illicit visit the night before, she opened the door and hefted her best smile, hoping it looked genuine. "Ian," she said breathlessly.

"Hi, Landy." Leaning forward, he kissed her cheek then stepped back as if to get a better look. "I woke you."

"It's okay. I...overslept."

"Late night?"

"I was...working on a case," she said quickly, wondering suddenly why he'd stopped by. "Come in."

He stepped into the foyer. "I don't have to be at the station until ten." Looking at her oddly, he swept by her then turned to face her. "Not working today?"

The question seemed casual, but Landis knew her younger brother well enough to know there was nothing casual about the question—or the visit. A jab of trepidation shot through her. "I took the day off. Still reveling in my big win from yesterday, I guess."

"I heard. Congratulations. You're building quite a career for yourself." An affectionate grin softened his expression. "Got time for a cup of coffee with your kid brother?"

"I always have time for my kid brother."

Ian followed her to the kitchen and seated himself at the table. It was the same chair Jack had used the night before, Landis remembered, trying to ignore the nervousness spearing through her. Her mind raced with explanations for her brother's visit as she scooped coffee and filled the carafe. Could Ian possibly know Jack had been to see her?

"So what brings my favorite brother all the way from Salt Lake City to Provo on such a cold morning?" To hide her anxiousness, she busied herself with the creamer and sugar.

His hesitation sent another bolt of tension to her already tight nerves. "Did you know Jack LaCroix escaped from prison two days ago?"

"I heard it on the news yesterday." Concentrating hard on keeping her hands steady, she reached for the carafe and poured two cups of coffee. "Why do you ask?"

"Did you know Aaron Chandler well?"

Her gut clenched at the mention of Chandler. Walking to the table, she shoved a cup in front of him then took the chair across from him. Ian was beginning to make her very skittish with his line of questioning. "I know of his reputation, but I've never met him."

Ian reached for his cup. "Chandler was found dead in his office this morning."

Shock jumped through her with such force that she jolted. "Oh my God. How did it happen?"

"He took two .38 slugs in his chest." He stirred his coffee, studying her with his watchful cop's eyes as if he suddenly found her every move fascinating. "Ballistics aren't back yet, but one of the detectives told me it was Chandler's own gun. His paralegal told the cops he keeps it in his desk drawer. You know the kind of scum he defended."

Because her hands were shaking, Landis didn't pick up her cup. "Do they have any suspects?"

"This isn't official yet, but one of the detectives told me there was an overnight bag found at the scene."

A deep, gut-wrenching fear clamped around her chest. She stared at her younger brother, knowing what he was going to say next and dreading it with every fiber of her heart.

"What was in the bag, Ian?"

"A set of prison-issue clothes. The lab hasn't confirmed it yet, but they think the clothes were the ones LaCroix was wearing when he escaped. They'd been washed, but there were traces of blood. Lab boys are typing it as we speak. They'll run DNA. I'm sorry, Landy, but you know they'll get a match."

She barely heard the words over the relentless pounding of her heart. The only thought that registered was that Jack was a suspect—and she knew he couldn't have done it. Aaron Chandler had called her from his office in Salt Lake City *after* dropping Jack at his summer cabin in Soldier Summit some forty miles away. Her lawyer's mind accepted the possibility that Jack could have driven to Chandler's office at some point during the night and shot him, but deep down, she knew Jack wasn't responsible.

"I'm sorry, but I thought you should know," he said.

"It's okay." Unsure what her expression was revealing to her brother, she started to rise only to knock over her mug. She looked down to see coffee spread over the table-top. "Damn."

Ian rose and crossed to her, his expression concerned. "Easy sis." He took her hand, squeezing it gently. "Jesus, Landy, you're shaking. Are you—"

"I'm fine. I just...need to get this cleaned up." Easing her hand from his she walked on unsteady legs over to the counter and tore off several paper towels.

"I know you and LaCroix had a thing. I know how hard you've worked to get over him. I'm sorry he's putting you through this again."

"Jack and I have been finished for a long time."

"I hope someone takes down that son of a bitch. He's hurt our family enough."

Landis closed her eyes against the quick slice of pain. Ian had taken Evan's death particularly hard. Afterward, he'd made no effort to hide his hatred for Jack. Ian wore that hatred like a medal, proudly and with conviction. She wondered how he would react if he knew she'd offered Jack a few hours of refuge the night before. If he knew she'd kissed him and liked it...

"Dirty damn cop. Gave up his partner—"

"Don't." Landis picked up her cup and moved away, needing a moment to gather what little composure she had left. She didn't want to lie to her brother. Ian didn't deserve lies. But, she couldn't tell him the truth. Aside from the killer, she was the only person who knew Jack hadn't murdered Chandler. But how could she come forward without incriminating herself?

"Don't what? Remind you of what a scumbag he is?"

Landis carried her cup to the sink and rinsed it. "I don't need to be reminded, Ian. But my relationship with Jack ended a year ago."

"Why am I getting the impression that you're not too terribly upset that he's out of prison?"

"Because you're letting your need for revenge cloud your judgment."

"He murdered our brother, for chrissake. He turned Casey into a widow and left our nieces without a father. How can you stand there and defend the bastard?"

Landis felt sick inside. Cold to the bone and scared to her core. In her mind's eye she could see the way Jack had looked at her when he'd walked out the door. She'd spent half the night ruminating everything he'd said. By dawn, she'd decided the only thing left for her to do was delve into his case herself.

The decision startled her, sent her heart into a wild somersault. "I'm not defending him. I'm just trying to sort through the facts objectively and deal with it the best way I can."

Ian looked at her the way a teacher might look at a baffling, recalcitrant child. "Look, sis, half the cops down at the precinct stood by LaCroix when he went to trial. They stood by him because they liked and respected him as a cop. But after all that evidence… You know how cops feel about cop killers."

From a family steeped in law enforcement, Landis knew firsthand. She was also aware of how cops reacted when one of their own was taken out by a traitor. The thought sent a wave of fear vibrating down her spine. Jack may as well have a price on his head.

She turned to her brother, searched his features. "Ian, what if he was somehow framed? What if there's information out there that never came to light during the trial?"

"Oh, Landy, for God's sake…"

"I mean it. What if someone in a position of power wanted him to take a fall? What if…what if there were cops involved?"

Anger darkened his young features. "What the hell are you talking about?"

Oh, God, how could she tell him what she suspected without incriminating herself? Ian was a straight arrow. As much as he hated Jack, he would probably take whatever she told him directly to his superiors.

"I don't want things to get ugly, Ian."

"Things got ugly the day he put a bullet in my brother."

"The last thing anyone needs right now is for the police to get caught up in revenge," she said. "You know how I feel about due process."

He made a sound of disgust, then bent his head and pinched the bridge of his nose. "Holy smoke, Landy. You're still hung up on him."

"No, I'm not."

He gave her a hard, incredulous look. "I wanted you to know LaCroix might be in the area. He's armed and extremely dangerous. If you see him, call the police. Call me. I don't have to tell you what he's capable of." He set his coffee cup on the table. "I've got to get to the precinct."

Landis stared at him. More than anything she wanted to tell her brother that Jack wasn't responsible for Chandler's death, but logic stopped her. It would only make things worse if she rushed in before thinking the situation through fully. As an attorney, she knew the value of silence.

"I'll call you later," she said.

After casting her a long, lingering look, Ian started for the door. Halfway there, he stopped and turned to face her. "You'd tell me if he came around, wouldn't you, Landy?"

She stared at him, trying desperately to keep her voice even. "Of course I would."

At the door, Ian paused and glanced out across the snow-covered landscape. ''Without help, he won't make it far. I'm surprised he's been able to elude law enforcement this long. The feds will be getting involved pretty soon. One way or another, I guarantee they'll have him in custody within twenty-four hours. Not even an animal like LaCroix can disappear without a trace.''

He sprinted through the darkness, branches tearing at him like claws. Cold rain soaked his clothes and chilled him to the bone. Behind him, he could hear the relentless baying of the hounds.

He had to reach her before it was too late. He knew she was just ahead. If only he could find her. If only he could see her face. Touch her flesh just one more time. He was so close he could smell her. He could see her silhouette through the trees and fog. Landis...

The crack of a rifle splintered the air. He braced for the impact of the bullet, the hot streak of pain. But neither came. Then he saw her. Running. Reaching out to him. Falling... Bleeding... Oh, dear God. Landis...

Jack bolted upright, the sudden movement wrenching a sound from him when his shoulder objected. Trembling and disoriented he looked quickly around to get his bearings, saw the sparsely furnished bedroom, realized he was in Aaron Chandler's cabin. Safe, he thought. At least for now.

Cursing the bastard who'd shot him, he lay back against the pillows and let out a long, shaky breath. He listened as the frantic beating of his heart returned to normal, felt the nightmare recede back into the darkness.

''Jesus.'' He sat up and eased his legs over the side of the bed. Dizziness swirled in his head, but quickly leveled off. He needed more sleep, but knew there wasn't time. Judging by the light coming in through the window, it was probably midmorning already. He would have to make do with his physical condition as it was. A shower, some coffee, a handful of aspirin, and he would be on his way.

He was in the process of stepping into the jeans Aaron had brought him when a knock at the front door sent a rush of adrenaline through him. There were only two people in the world who knew where he was, and he wasn't expecting either of them. Unless maybe one of them had called the cops…

Wishing he had a gun on the outside chance Cyrus Duke had somehow located him, Jack crept silently down the hall, then peered into the living room. Heavy drapes covered the front window. Stealthily, he moved through the room to the door and peered through the peephole.

Surprise rippled through him when he saw Landis standing on the front porch ankle deep in snow and looking breathtaking in the thin morning light. Her flame-colored hair was pulled into an unruly ponytail. Silky tendrils framed cheeks that were blushed with cold. Her eyes were wary and alert and very troubled.

Jack opened the door. ''What the hell are you doing here?''

''Using a real lack of judgment.'' Looking once over her shoulder, she sighed. ''This is probably the stupidest thing I've ever done.''

''Well, hell. Maybe we could start a club.'' His eyes traveled to the gravel drive where her Jeep was parked in six inches of new snow. ''Are you alone?''

''Of course I'm alone.''

''Were you followed?''

''I don't think so.''

''You don't *think* so?''

''Look, I didn't see anyone, but I'm not used to this cloak-and-dagger routine, so could you cut me some slack?'' Looking flustered and annoyed, she put her hands on her hips, inadvertently opening her coat.

Jack knew better than to look, but his eyes took on a life of their own and skimmed down the front of her. He saw a soft sweater draped over curves he had no right to be noticing at a time like this. Snug jeans hugged nicely rounded hips and slender thighs. For a redhead, she looked damn good in hot pink and fuchsia.

"Can I come in?"

He dragged his gaze to hers, forcing himself to forget about the hidden riches that lay beneath those layers of wool and silk. Opening the door, he stepped aside. "How did you find me?"

Barely sparing him a glance, she brushed past him and entered the cabin. Jack tried to ignore the thread of pleasure that sifted through him when he caught a whiff of her scent. The sweet familiarity of it made him remember the kiss, the way she'd felt in his arms the night before....

"Chandler's name was on the mailbox," she said.

"Was?"

She reached into her bag and handed him a rustic piece of wood with Chandler's name etched on to it. Jack looked at it, realized it was the decorative panel from the mailbox.

"I had to break it," she said. "You probably shouldn't stay here long."

Baffled, he took the piece of wood from her and set it against the wall, suddenly very curious as to why she had come. "You want to clue me in to what the hell's going on?" Checking the driveway one more time to make sure she hadn't been followed, Jack closed the door.

Landis walked to the dining room table, then turned to face him. "I need to know what time Aaron dropped you off here last night."

An alarm went off in his head. For the life of him he couldn't figure out why she would show up now after practically throwing him out of her place the night before. "He brought me here directly from your cabin.'' He shrugged. ''Maybe around midnight or so. Why?''

''What did you do after he left?''

''Did you have a brainstorm during the night or did you come here simply because you enjoy giving me the third degree?''

''Believe me, enjoyment doesn't enter into the picture.'' She sighed. ''Answer the question, Jack. It's important.''

''I crashed. You know the condition I was in when Aaron and I left your place. I didn't wake up until about five minutes ago.''

''You're sure?''

He laughed, but heard the tension in his voice. ''How could I not be sure?''

She stared hard at him, her emerald eyes large and turbulent. ''How long did Aaron stay?''

''Long enough to show me the woodpile and where the keys to the truck are kept.'' Growing uncomfortably chilly without his shirt, Jack started toward the bedroom.

''Did you go anywhere after he left?'' Her boots clicked smartly against the floor as she trailed him. ''Where are you going?''

''I hate to put a damper on your fun, Counselor, but my patience is a little too thin this morning for a game of Twenty Questions.'' Jerking his flannel shirt off the bed, he turned, barely avoiding a collision with her. Not sure if he was relieved or disappointed, he moved past her, praying Aaron had coffee in the kitchen. He was desperate for something hot and black and chock-full of caffeine. As much as he didn't want to admit it, her questions were beginning to make him nervous.

''While we're playing Twenty Questions, you want to tell me why you're here?'' He swung open a cabinet door and began to rummage. ''The last time we talked, I believe you were under the impression that I was a murderer and belonged in prison with the rest of the scoundrels you spend your days putting away.'' Spotting a jar of instant coffee, he breathed out a sigh of relief and reached for it. ''Or did you come to your senses and realize I'm an innocent man after all?''

''Jack…''

''Or maybe it was that kiss that brought you back for more.''

''Stop it.''

He turned to her and for the first time since she'd breezed into the cabin and started barking out questions, he noticed the anxiety etched into her features. ''What's going on, Landis?''

Visibly shaken, she walked to the small table and lowered herself into a chair. Her eyes were large and dark when they met his. ''Aaron Chandler was murdered last night.''

The words registered like a slap. He recoiled as the repercussions penetrated a brain that didn't want to believe. In the months Chandler had been his lawyer, they'd spent quite a bit of time together. Jack had come to respect him. He'd come to like him. Had the circumstances been different, he might even have called him a friend. He couldn't believe he was gone. For several long seconds he could only stare at her, speechless. Aaron Chandler had been his last chance. The appeal had been filed. The framework for his defense had been laid. With Aaron's murder, all of it had gone up in smoke….

''Are you sure?'' he heard himself ask.

She nodded. ''I'm sorry.''

Jack couldn't believe it. Couldn't believe fate would snatch away the last remnants of hope. His last chance for a future.

On an oath, he turned away and strode to the window, stared through the dirty glass at the frozen landscape beyond. All the while desperation clawed at his throat like a bloodthirsty animal. He felt sucker-punched and sick to his soul. He couldn't believe Chandler was dead, couldn't believe the timing of it.

"That brings my defense to a grinding halt," he said.

"I'm sorry, Jack, but…it gets worse."

He turned from the window and looked at her. "What do you mean?"

"The police found your prison clothes in Chandler's office."

He felt a jolt, didn't know if it was physical or emotional, but it was powerful enough to immobilize him. "Chandler was supposed to get rid of the clothes."

"Evidently, he hadn't done that yet."

A terrible new realization dawned. "I'm a suspect." He laughed, but it was a hoarse, humorless sound. "Jesus."

"I thought you should know."

Outrage and a damnable sense of helplessness surged inside him. He tasted bitterness at the back of his throat and felt the dark pull of a new and frightening suspicion burgeon. Raising his fist, he brought it down on the counter hard enough to send the jar of coffee crashing to the floor.

"Jack, please…calm down."

Her words barely registered. He couldn't believe Chandler was dead. A year ago, he would have laughed at the absurdity of the situation. Today, he knew firsthand how cruel fate could be.

He wanted to lash out. At the system. At whomever had engineered this latest frame-up. He knew better than to take his fear and anger and frustration out on Landis. But she was the only person within reach.

"Are you going to jump on the bandwagon the way you did the last time?" he snarled. "Or maybe you've already called the Salt Lake County sheriff's office. Hell, Landis, if you really want to put a feather in your cap, maybe you should have called the media. I can see the headlines now.

'Lady Justice Single-handedly Nabs Cold-blooded Cop Killer.'''

She came out of the chair. "It was against my better judgment, but I came here to help you."

The words hung between them like a rain-laden storm cloud waiting to burst. Willing his temper to cool, Jack turned away from her, strode to the counter and leaned. "How was he murdered? When did it happen?"

"He was shot and killed in his office last night."

"You said they found my clothes at the scene?"

"Yes."

"How did you find out about it?"

"Ian came to the cabin this morning to tell me."

A bitter laugh escaped him when he thought of Evan's younger brother. "I'll bet he was frothing at the mouth to get at me."

"Don't take this out on Ian," she snapped. "None of this is his fault."

"He thinks I'm low enough to murder my own partner," he said with disgust. "He won't have a problem believing I killed Chandler." Struggling to regain control of the emotions banging around inside him, Jack turned from the window and gave her a hard look. "Was he able to convince you? Do you think I killed my own lawyer in cold blood?"

"Chandler called me last night," she said. "*After* he dropped you here."

Jack wasn't an emotional man, but the words shook him hard. The surge of relief that followed was so powerful he had to look away, uneasy with the notion of her seeing just how desperately he needed her to believe him. "That puts you in a rather precarious position, doesn't it?"

"Yes, it does." Her hands shook as she tucked a wisp of hair behind her ear. "I'm not sure how I want to handle this yet."

"You're the only person—aside from the murderer—
ho knows I didn't kill Chandler."

"Probably."

"In order for you to exonerate me, you would have to
criminate yourself. I guess the question is how far are
ou willing to go to vindicate the man accused of murder-
g your brother?"

Her gaze met his. "I think we both know the only sane
ing for you to do is turn yourself in."

"How many times do I have to tell you? Turning myself
is not an option," he snapped.

"How can you possibly hope to clear your name when
very cop from here to the Canadian border is looking for
ou?"

"If I turn myself in, it's over, Landis. I'm a dead man.
don't have a choice but to do this."

"I can help you. I mean, legally. Jack, damn it, I'm a
wyer."

Hope jumped through him that she would offer to help
m, but he quickly shoved it back. He was tired of hoping
d then having that hope wrenched away. "Look, clearing
y name will be more difficult without Chandler, but I can
it. If I go back to prison, it won't happen."

"You can be protected in prison."

"That's crap and you know it."

"I can prove you didn't murder Chandler."

Jack met her gaze steadily. "A good prosecutor will
int out that I could have taken Chandler's truck, driven
his office after he talked to you, murdered him, then
ove back here."

"That's barely plausible."

"So is my murdering Evan, but look what happened."

"Jack, the evidence was compelling...."

"Screw the evidence! You know I didn't murder Chan-
er," he growled. "If there was any doubt in your mind,

you wouldn't be here. You're just covering your bases be
cause you're afraid of what might happen between us
you let yourself believe me.''

He didn't miss the quiver that ran the length of her befor
she turned away. He stared at her arrow-straight back, th
rigid set of her shoulders and wondered what it would tak
to bow that steadfast resolve—and make her believe him

''This isn't about us,'' she said. ''It can't be. Damn it,
don't want it to be.''

Coming up behind her, he put his hands on her shoulder
''You know I didn't murder Chandler, Landis. And yo
know I didn't murder Evan. Ancient history aside, that
why you're here, isn't it?''

The scent of her hair drifted lazily through his brai
teasing him with memories he was insane to think of nov
Memories that would do nothing but hurt him. Her shou
ders felt small and delicate beneath his hands. But he kne
there was nothing fragile about Landis McAllister. She bo
the weight of the world on those shoulders with a tenaci
that spoke volumes about the force of her personality ar
her competence as a lawyer.

''I'm here because you involved me. Because I'm tryir
to do the right thing. Because I need to know the truth.'

He desperately wanted to believe she'd come to him fe
other reasons, too. Reasons that had nothing to do wi
Evan or Chandler or the fact that he'd spent the last ye
in prison. But Jack knew wishing for impossibilities wou
only make an already difficult situation infinitely more di
ficult.

He'd spent too many hellish years in foster homes, livir
with families that hadn't really wanted him, to believ
wishes could make a difference. He'd spent the better pa
of his childhood yearning for what could never be, and a
that wanting hadn't done a damn thing except mak
him hurt.

He was through with hurting.

"If the circumstances were different, I would agree with ou about turning myself in, Red. But there's someone pull-ng strings from the inside. Maybe from the top. I can't ght that. I can't survive it." With his life on the line and esperation knocking at his door, Jack knew he'd had no hoice but to take the situation into his own hands.

She turned to him, her troubled gaze searching his. "At ome point I'm going to have to go to the police with what know."

"Your going to the police will do nothing but put you n some very hot water."

"I didn't do anything wrong."

"You aided and abetted a fugitive from the law."

"You didn't give me much choice."

"You lied to the police, Landis. For God's sake, get al!"

"My going to the police will vindicate you from Chan-ler's murder."

"Maybe. But what about Evan's murder? I hate to point his out to you, but in my mind that is the bigger issue of e two."

Moving away from him she walked over to the counter nd pressed her fingers against her forehead. A breath shud-ered out of her. Jack hated seeing her so shaken. Hated ven more that he cared. He tried reminding himself that he'd walked away from him when he'd needed her. But t the moment the knowledge wasn't enough to make him el anything less for her.

"Look," he began, "neither of us needs any more trou-le in our lives. If we do this my way, you won't have to ontend with a black mark on your sterling reputation, and won't have to go back to prison for a crime I didn't ommit."

She choked out a humorless laugh. "You're forgetting

that you no longer have a lawyer, and that every law en
forcement agency in the state is looking for you."

"I'm a cop." He shrugged. "I can elude them for a fe
days."

"A few days?" She glared at him. "And then what?"

"I'm going to find the son of a bitch who killed Evan."

"You're going to do that when no one else has been abl
to? When not even your lawyer could do it?"

"Chandler might have been a legal whiz, but he wasn
a cop. I'm a detective. I know how to work this."

"*Were* a detective."

"At this point that title is semantics. I'm talking abou
finding hard evidence."

"Okay, Super Cop, define hard evidence."

He rolled his shoulder, wondering how much he shoul
tell her. Would she react as a tough prosecuting attorney
Or would she react as the woman who'd once bared he
soul to him? "I've got a few leads."

"That's not very specific."

"I need to talk to a couple of my old snitches. One c
Evan's snitches."

"That's *it?*"

He stared hard at her, debating, keenly aware that if sh
turned on him his one and only chance would die. "I'
need my file from Chandler's office."

"Oh, that's brilliant." She put her hands on her hips. "I
that weren't such a bad idea, I'd laugh!"

"Damn it, Landis, he was close to getting some har
evidence on Evan."

"Let me get this straight," she said. "Your brilliant pla
is to question some lowlife snitches and break into you
attorney's office? Oh, excuse me, your *dead* attorney's o
fice, which is now a crime scene? That's genius! Wh
didn't I think of it?"

"I can do without the sarcasm."

''I can do without a dead convict on my hands. Jack, your plan is weak and certifiable. Chandler's office is going to be crawling with cops!''

''You got a better idea?'' he shouted.

She stared at him, her eyes wide, color riding high on her cheeks. ''There's nothing in that file that's worth dying for.''

''I'm going to prove I didn't kill Evan. Then I'm going to nail Duke. For what he did to Evan. For what he did to us. Either you're with me or you're not. I think it's high time you made up your mind.''

Chapter 6

The ultimatum unnerved her. Of all the things he could have demanded, that was the most difficult. To ally herself with Jack now would be to admit she believed him innocent. Not only of Aaron Chandler's murder, but of Evan's. The repercussions of that were almost too enormous to absorb.

She couldn't bear to believe he'd spent the past year in prison for a crime he hadn't committed. She didn't want to think that she'd walked out on him when he'd needed her so desperately. That he'd been innocent all along. That she'd been so terribly wrong.

Pressing her hand to the knots in her stomach, Landis turned away from him and walked into the kitchen. She felt sick inside and more uncertain than she'd ever felt in her life.

"What's it going to be, Red?" he asked.

She'd always known Jack LaCroix wasn't for the faint of heart. There was nothing easy about him. He could be uncompromising and unreasonable and stubborn as hell. He bent the rules until they broke. Pushed the limits until the boundaries changed. He embraced risk, courted danger and laughed in the face of authority. He was all of the things she was not. But the combination of those things had attracted her like a moth to a flame....

Raising her chin, Landis met his gaze, praying he didn't see the emotions twisting her heart into knots. "I'll help you," she said.

"That's not an answer."

"That's all you're going to get."

Eyes flashing dangerously, he stepped so close to her she could feel the heat emanating from his body, feel the anger coming off him in shimmering waves. "You can't have it both ways," he said.

His eyes slashed at her with dizzying intensity. She couldn't look away as he moved even closer, overpowering her with his presence, his anger, the raw sexuality that was so much a part of him.

Automatically, she stepped back, hating it that she'd lost ground. A tactical error on her part, but she was smart enough to know when she was outgunned. "You've convinced me your case warrants looking into," she said breathlessly.

A smile whispered across his mouth. "Well then in that case maybe I ought to level with you about what Chandler might have in his office."

The hairs at the back of her neck began to crawl. "What are you talking about?"

"I'm talking about Chandler having information that could exonerate me."

"What kind of information?"

"He was always vague, never told me who his sources were, but he led me to believe he had information that would clear me."

"Why didn't he use it, for God's sake?"

"Because he didn't get this information by going through the proper channels. It was relatively new information he'd only recently come upon, and he was waiting for court orders, subpoenas to come through so it would be official and admissible in court."

"How do you know all of this?"

"Chandler liked to walk on the wild side occasionally." Jack shrugged. "And he liked to brag about it."

"But he was going to use whatever information he had to exonerate you?"

"So he said." He grimaced. "Maybe that's why he was killed."

She tried not to react, but felt the color leach from her face. "You make it sound like a conspiracy."

"Maybe it is." His voice was deadly and soft. "In any case, I need to get into Chandler's office. Then I'm going to make Duke wish he'd never heard of Jack LaCroix."

Turning away from him, Landis strode to the counter to stare out the window. Jack was the only person in the world who could make such an outrageous and dangerous plan sound reasonable—and then proceed to convince her it was a good idea.

"If you turn yourself in and retain me as your lawyer, I can subpoena Chandler's files," she said after a moment. "I can subpoena witnesses. I'll help you, Jack. I promise."

"I'm flattered by the offer, but I'm finished with going by the book."

"You'll only destroy what's left of your life—"

"My life has already been destroyed. I'll do whatever it takes to get it back." One side of his mouth curved. "Besides, what's a little felony B & E when you're already facing life in prison?"

"That's not funny." Needing to move, Landis paced the length of the kitchen. She didn't like feeling trapped. Not by Jack. Not by her own sense of right and wrong, especially when the line between the two was so thin. "I'm not going to let you involve me in this cockamamie scheme of yours."

"Are you willing to let justice slide on this one, Counselor?"

"We're not talking about justice, we're talking about breaking the law."

"So you're willing to overlook the occasional glitch in the system, even if a man's life is on the line? My life?"

His words pierced her with the proficiency of a bayonet. Landis stopped pacing and looked at him. Logic warred with her heart as she recognized the lay-it-on-the-line desperation in his expression. He was the only human being she'd ever known who could make her feel so acutely with nothing more than a look, a gesture, or the tone of his voice. She didn't want to see fear or desperation when she looked into those clear, dark eyes. She didn't want to see hope, or longing, or the kind of pain she could only imagine in her worst nightmare. But she saw all of those things when she looked at Jack.

The realization that she was going to help him shook her badly, made her realize exactly what she was risking. The career she'd devoted her life to. Her freedom. Maybe even her life.

Groaning, she lowered her face to her hands. "Do you have a death wish or do you merely want to ruin my life, too?"

"Quite the contrary on both counts." A smile touched his mouth. "As much as you don't want to hear this, I'm starting to like you again."

Her heart fluttered wildly. She felt as if she'd stepped into a bog of quicksand and was being sucked down inch by inch. "I can't deal with you when you say things like that."

"Yeah, well, I'm afraid you'll have to take me as I am. What's it going to be?"

It hurt to gaze into the depths of his eyes and see the glimmer of hope for a future that was shaky at best. It hurt even more knowing he was going to risk his life to do it. "All right. We'll go to Chandler's office. I'll help you find—"

"I go in to Chandler's office alone. All I need from you is to help me sort through the files and all the legal mumbo jumbo."

"You won't know where to find what you need. I know how paralegals and lawyers keep things filed."

"I'm not taking you with me."

"It's not your decision," she snapped. "You involved me in this, damn it. If I'm going to help you, I'm going to do it my way."

"I thought you drew the line at aiding and abetting?"

"An assistant prosecutor having personal knowledge of a suspect's innocence would qualify as mitigating circumstances."

"You're a tough cookie, Red."

"Just mildly insane."

He looked away, his expression going serious, his jaw flexing. "A year ago I would have cut off my own hand to keep you out of this kind of situation."

Landis didn't miss the bitterness in his voice. It was obvious he didn't want her involved—at least when it came to burglarizing Chandler's office. That he would acquiesce so easily made her realize just how desperate he really was.

"With my help, we can be in and out of Chandler's office in a matter of minutes," she said. "It's the logical decision."

Jack brooded, his expression as telling as anything he might have said as he stared out the window.

The water on the stove came to a boil. Thankful for the

diversion, Landis made two cups of coffee. All the while her mind ran the gauntlet of obstacles they faced. Jack was the most wanted fugitive in the state. Chandler's office was now a crime scene; it would be extremely difficult to gain access to his files. Not to mention the fact that if she went into Chandler's office with Jack she would be breaking the law.

Picking up their cups, she met Jack at the dining room table. "Why did Duke have Evan killed?"

Jack settled into the chair across from her. For an instant he looked tired and older than his thirty-eight years. "I think Evan wanted out from under Duke. When he became more of a liability than an asset, Duke had him shot."

She digested the information, her heart aching. If Jack was right—and God help her she was beginning to believe he was—the fact that Evan had wanted out of the situation was something she hadn't considered. The thought of her brother trapped in such a dangerous and compromising situation—even of his own doing—devastated her. It must have been terrible for him. The shame of betraying his profession. The fear that his wife and two little girls would be harmed. Having a sister who worked in the D.A.'s office...

"When Evan threatened to take everything to the D.A, the bastard had him shot in that warehouse."

Landis stared at him, her mind grinding through the words, picking apart the logic. It would have been easier not to believe him. The alternative was too terrible to contemplate.

"Why didn't this information come out during the trial?" she asked. "If Chandler knew about this, but didn't use it in court, he did you a grave injustice."

"I didn't know about any of this until about six months ago."

"You were in prison six months ago. How did you—"

"I bunked with Duke's ex-head of security, Jimmy Beck.

We shared a cell for about six weeks. Not a bad chap considering he broke kneecaps for a living.''

He said the words lightly, but Landis didn't miss the glint of fury in his eyes. She didn't want to think about the kind of people Jack had been forced to live with while he'd been in prison. Granted, he knew how to handle himself. He was strong both physically and mentally, yet an entire year in such a terrible place, especially if he were innocent, had to have worn his armor very thin.

''Beck said Duke had ripped him off. He had a bridge to burn.'' Jack shrugged. ''He talked to me.''

''Will Beck testify on your behalf?'' she asked.

He gave her a hard look. ''Someone slipped a knife between his ribs while he was in the shower room. He's dead. Two inmates came after me the next day, but I fought them off and got away.''

Landis didn't allow herself the luxury of flinching. She didn't want to think about how close Jack had come to being murdered. ''Exactly how do you plan to go after Duke?''

''I won't know until I see Chandler's file.''

''What if there's nothing there?''

''We'll deal with it when and if it happens.''

She thought about it for a moment, her head spinning. ''Did Beck tell you anything else?''

''Enough to get him killed. That's all you need to know.''

For the first time she realized he hadn't told her everything. The thought angered her. ''This is not the time for secrets, Jack. If I'm going to lay it on the line for you, I deserve to know everything.''

''I've told you everything that matters. You know too much and you could become a target, too. If you're not already.''

His answer chilled her. "Okay. How do you propose we get into Chandler's office?"

"Crime techs will have finished collecting evidence by tonight. We'll have to get into the building. Past any security officers they've got posted. Then we've got to get into the suite."

She rubbed at her temple. "In case you missed that day at the academy, breaking and entering in the state of Utah will get you two to five years in the pen."

Never taking his eyes from hers, he reached into the breast pocket of his flannel shirt. "Why break in when I have a key?"

Landis groaned at the sight of the key dangling from a purple rabbit's foot. "How on earth did you get that?"

"Let's just say I borrowed it and leave it at that."

"You took it from Chandler. The night he came here to pick you up." She had a very bad feeling about this. "Entering a crime scene and tampering with evidence is a serious offence, Jack."

A smile brushed the corners of his mouth. "Only if you get caught."

But Landis knew getting caught was just the tip of the iceberg when it came to all the things that could go wrong.

Landis parked the Jeep curbside and shut down the engine. Steam billowed from a nearby storm gutter, giving the winter landscape a surreal edge. Next to her, Jack sat quietly, his eyes riveted to the sleek, eight-story structure a hundred yards away. Around them, the night was quiet and so cold she could hear the frozen tree branches snapping together in the brisk westerly breeze.

Providence Legal Tower was located in an upscale office park just outside Salt Lake City. Nestled amongst stately lodge pole pines and low-growing juniper bushes, it was the kind of building that bespoke of prestige, money and high rollers. The kind of place Landis had imagined herself in as a child, when her dreams had been as big as the Utah sky.

She and Jack had spent the afternoon poring over his hand-drawn blueprints of the tower and drinking cup after cup of wretched instant coffee. They would enter the building via the loading dock at the rear, then take the freight elevator to the penthouse. Chandler's firm encompassed the entire floor.

A shiver rippled through her as she studied the building. A shiver that had nothing to do with the single-digit temperature outside—and everything to do with the fact that she was scared out of her wits.

"I guess Aaron didn't mind high rent." She tried to make her voice light, but her throat was too tight to manage it. She hated being scared. Especially when Jack seemed so calm.

She jumped when his hand covered hers. "High rent hell. Chandler owned the building."

His eyes were dark, shimmering pools in the semidarkness. She could just make out the cut of his jaw, the shape of his mouth, frowning at her, and she realized the calm was a front to cover nerves that were as taut as hers.

"You're shaking," he said.

"It's cold."

"You'd be an idiot if you weren't afraid." He squeezed her hand. "And I'm a son of a bitch for involving you."

The words tugged at her with unexpected force. "This isn't the time to start second-guessing the decision we made. Okay?"

"It's not okay." Cursing, he leaned back in the seat. "I'm not going to do this."

"Jack—"

"I'm going in alone. I want you to drive over to the mall, turn around in the parking lot, then come back. Take your time, but don't stop. Don't do anything to draw attention to the Jeep. Meet me back here in twenty minutes.''

Landis stared at him. It would have been easy to say yes. The last thing she wanted to do was walk into that building with him. But she'd never been able to take the easy way out, especially when the easy way wasn't the right way. "No," she said. "I'm going in, too. That was our agreement."

"I don't give a damn about the agreement. It was wrong of me to involve you."

Turning away from him, she looked through the windshield at the building and felt her insides turn to jelly. The fear was so thick inside her, she could taste it at the back of her throat, feel it vibrate through her body with every pulse of her heart. But when she thought of Aaron Chandler, gunned down because of his legal brilliance; when she thought of Evan, whose life had been snuffed out so ruthlessly; when she thought of the man sitting next to her with his very life on the line, she suddenly realized she wanted to get her hands on whatever information Chandler had every bit as badly as Jack did.

He reached out and brushed the backs of his knuckles against her cheek. "If anything happens, I want you to drive to Ian's house and tell him everything."

"I'm going in."

"Come on, Red. For God's sake, don't get stupid on me now."

"You can insult me until you turn blue, but I'm going in that building with you."

"If things go wrong—"

"Things aren't going to go wrong." She searched his face, hoping he couldn't see the fear in hers. "Damn it, Jack, we have a plan. It's a good one. I can help you do this."

"No."

Knowing he was willing to sacrifice his agenda to keep her safe only made her more determined to follow through. "I've got to do this. If not for you, then for Evan. For me."

Cursing, he flung open the Jeep's door and got out. For a long minute he stood facing the wind, looking at the building hulked against the night sky. She could tell by his body language that he was angry. But she couldn't help that. She only hoped he was able to put it aside long enough to get this done.

"All right," he said after a moment. "Come here."

Adrenaline danced in her belly as she got out of the Jeep and crossed to him. She didn't expect him to take her hand, but was glad when he did. Sticking to the shadows, he led her at an easy jog across the parking lot toward the loading dock at the rear of the tower. At the corner of the building, they stopped. Her legs trembled, but she didn't know if it was from the sudden exertion or the fear pumping through her.

Jack peered around the edge of a Dumpster. "It's clear."

The next thing Landis knew, she was being pulled up a concrete ramp toward a double set of scarred wooden doors. Behind them, a delivery truck's engine rumbled. The smell of diesel fuel filled the air. Jack's hand tightened on hers as they approached the doors. Beyond, light filtered through a single window.

"If we run into anyone, smile." He looked quickly from side to side. "Try to look like you know where you're going, and we won't be stopped. These guys are here delivering supplies and picking up recyclables."

"Of course they're not going to concern themselves with an escaped con and a lawyer-turned-felon," she muttered.

Taking Jack's cue, she kept her eyes straight ahead and followed him through the double doors. Despite the frigid temperature, Landis broke a sweat beneath her coat. Two men wearing coveralls and yellow work gloves maneuvered a dolly stacked with corrugated boxes. One of them looked right at her, and she smiled. He smiled back and continued down the hall without pause.

"The freight elevator is to the right.'' Jack led her around a corner where the battered doors of the freight elevator loomed into view. After punching the up button, he turned to face her. For an instant he looked like the old Jack she'd once known. He was breathing hard from the run across the parking lot. His dark hair was windblown, his eyes alight with determination. She wondered if his senses were humming as keenly as hers....

She jolted when the elevator bell chimed. The doors slid open. Her heart skittered when Jack set his hands on her shoulders and ushered her inside. He punched the button for the eighth floor, and they began the slow ride up.

"The suite should be deserted,'' he said. "Chandler wasn't the trusting type so he kept most of his files locked up in his office. I figure we'll start there. But he's also got a file room. That could take some time.''

"What if the police confiscated your file for evidence?''

"Proper legal channels take time.'' Jack poked impatiently at the floor button. "It'll take a couple of days for the detective assigned the case to get a warrant. Lawyers are pretty good at tying things up.''

"Or expediting if it's in their own best interest.'' She hated to think that they'd risked so much for nothing.

The elevator halted on the eighth floor. The doors opened to a long hall. Landis stepped out of the car and looked around. Recessed lighting cast muted light onto plush blue carpeting. Abstract paintings set into intricate gold leaf frames adorned the walls. She headed toward a particularly intriguing painting that looked startlingly like a Dali abstract. "I've been to art shows less interesting than this.''

Her pulse jumped when Jack's hand settled around her arm and pulled her in the opposite direction. "This way.''

A moment later they were standing outside the mahogany and beveled glass doors of Chandler & Associates. Yellow crime scene tape stretched across the front like a sentinel, daring them to enter.

"Is there an alarm?" Landis asked.

Jack fished the key from his pocket. "Yeah, but I know the code."

"How?"

"Chandler and I spent a lot of time in his office before my trial. All I had to do was watch him punch in the numbers."

"That's convenient."

"I thought so, too."

"How do you know someone didn't change the code?"

"I don't." He slid the key into the lock, twisted.

She held her breath, let it slide between her lips when no alarm came.

Ducking under the tape, he stepped into the suite. "Piece of cake."

Landis followed him inside. "Good thing we had that rabbit's foot."

"Keep your gloves on and don't touch anything." He closed the door behind them. "Chandler's office is in the back."

The smells of lemon wax, paper dust and recirculated air wafted over her as they walked to the rear of the suite. The ambience of the office reminded her of her own cramped office in the Utah County courthouse, and an odd sense of homesickness swept through her. She wondered if she would get the chance to go back.

"The door's locked."

She glanced up to see Jack studying the lock on a paneled wooden door. "Can you pick the lock?" she asked.

"I'm a cop not a burglar."

"What are we going to do?"

"Improvise." Taking several steps back, he gathered himself then lunged forward and landed a kick at the door. Wood splintered. The door swung open, banging hard against the wall.

"That should alert at least one security officer," she said.

Giving her a dark look, Jack entered the office. "Let's make this quick."

Landis followed him into the office. Even in the dim light she couldn't help but notice the opulence of Chandler's inner sanctum. Carved teak paneling. Exquisite paintings. Floor-to-ceiling glass comprised the east wall. In the daylight the vast span of glass would offer a stunning view of the mountains.

Removing a small penlight from his pocket, Jack strode purposefully to the desk. Landis trailed behind him, noticing the fingerprint powder on the desktop. A chill raced through her when she recalled that Chandler had been murdered in this very office the night before. Unlike some of her counterparts, she wasn't comfortable at crime scenes, especially violent ones. Morbid curiosity wasn't part of her persona. Though sometimes the criminals she prosecuted were violent, the courtroom had a way of distancing one from the actual crime. There was no blood, or injuries, or death to contend with. Just facts. That was the way she preferred it.

"Here's the file cabinet."

She started at the sound of Jack's voice. Coming up behind him, she watched him tug at the drawer. "Locked." He rapped his hand against the lock. "Of course."

Anxious to get out of the office, Landis looked quickly around for a makeshift tool with which to pry open the drawer. Spotting the wood-handled umbrella next to the coat tree, she pointed and started for it. "What about that?"

He illuminated the umbrella with his penlight. "You're getting good at this breaking and entering stuff."

"Maybe it's the company I keep." Landis took the penlight from him and started toward the umbrella. She was halfway there when something dark on the floor gave her pause. Using the penlight, she illuminated the shadow—and everything inside her froze. Blood, she realized. A large puddle had soaked into the carpet. Flecks of it marred the lower part of the wall.

Revulsion swept through her. She could smell the blood now, a dull, sickening odor that sent her stumbling back. "Oh, God."

Vaguely, she was aware of the penlight tumbling from her hand. In a small corner of her mind, she heard Jack curse. She backed away from the blood. She needed distance and fresh air. The smell... Oh, God, the smell. If she didn't get away, she was going to be sick.

Putting her hand over her mouth, Landis stumbled across the room. At the far wall, she set her hand against the floor-to-ceiling bookcase and leaned, taking deep breaths.

"Easy."

She jolted when he set his hands on her shoulders and guided her over to the sofa near the door. "I'm sorry you had to see that."

"I'm okay," she said. "Damn it, I'm okay." But even as she said the words a cold sweat broke out on the back of her neck. Her face felt hot. "I just need some air." She worked frantically at the buttons of her coat.

"Sit."

She didn't have to be told twice.

"Are you sick?"

Unable to speak because of the clenching in her stomach, she shook her head. "Just get what you need so we can go."

"Take a couple of deep breaths for me, okay?"

Landis obeyed. Slowly, the nausea passed. She became

aware of his hand at her nape, where his fingers gently massaged her tense muscles.

"I should have realized how this would affect you," he said.

"God, Jack, they cut him down like an animal." Raising her head, she looked at him. "Seeing that...what they did to him...makes this real to me. The violence of it." She shivered. "Maybe I needed to see it."

"No one should ever have to see something like that."

"Duke has got to be stopped."

"You're not going to get an argument from me."

Embarrassed that she'd come so close to losing it, wanting to forget the incident and get on with the task at hand, Landis rose—only to find herself standing toe to toe with him. His hands were on her shoulders. His eyes were uncomfortably direct and focused intently on her, as if she were a puzzle he couldn't quite solve. His hard mouth was sculpted and pulled into a frown. His five o'clock shadow made him look dangerous in the semidarkness. And for an insane instant she found herself thinking about the mind-numbing kiss they'd shared the night before.

She stared at him, aware of her heart beating a hundred miles an hour, her mind running a fast second. Only she knew her quickened pulse had nothing to do with what she'd seen, and everything to do with the man standing so close she could smell his masculine scent.

"You should try listening to your instincts sometime." His voice was slow and thick. "Might be interesting for both of us."

Realizing the situation was an inch away from veering into dangerous territory, she shrugged off his hands and turned away. "Let's just get the file so we can get out of here."

Growling low in his throat, Jack turned away and picked up the umbrella. Wordlessly, he strode to the cabinet and drove the metal tip into the space between the drawer and the lock. Wood splintered, and the sound was as loud as a gunshot in the silence of the suite. An instant later the drawer rolled open, revealing a row of legal files. "Bingo," Jack said.

Landis quickly located Jack's file, which was as thick as her arm, then began rummaging for others. "There's nothing under Duke," she said. "Maybe we could check the file room."

"Too risky. Let's get the hell out of here." Tucking the thick file under his arm, Jack started for the door.

She followed him through the office and into the reception area. "No security guards in sight," she said.

"Yeah, well, if they decide to crash our little party, it's every man for himself."

The file under Jack's arm rustled softly as they jogged down the hall. "I can't believe we pulled this off," she whispered.

"Don't strain your arm patting yourself on the back just yet. We still have to get out of the building."

But Landis was on a high and barely heard the words. "It's the first thing that's gone right since you showed up at my door."

"The story of my life. Keep your voice down."

At the freight elevator, Jack punched the down button, looked nervously over his shoulder, then punched the button again. "Come on, damn it."

Landis's mind had already jumped ahead to the file they now had in their possession when the sound of a slamming door sent her into a panic. "What was th—"

Her words were cut short when Jack slapped his hand over her mouth. "Our worst nightmare," he whispered and shoved her into a nearby alcove.

Chapter 7

Jack figured he knew better than most what it was like to be a fox faced with being ripped to shreds by the hounds or a fatal leap off a cliff. He was quickly learning he didn't much care for the feeling.

Next to him, Landis peeled his hand from her mouth, her back pressed against the wall and her face the color of new snow. "What do we do now?" she whispered.

"We hide." Clutching the file in one hand, he grasped her arm with the other and hauled her toward a restroom door. "Get inside."

"What about the elevator?"

"We're cut off. We walk back into the corridor and we're going to have a close encounter with someone who's probably going to know we shouldn't be here." He opened the door and shoved her through it. "For once in your life, don't argue."

"This is the men's room."

"You got a better idea?"

"No. I mean, yes." She bit her lip. "Jack, we're trapped in here. We're eight stories up. How are we going to get out?"

"I don't know. We'll wait them out. Just…get in the stall, damn it. Hurry."

Ignoring her protests, he guided her to the last stall. "Step up on the commode." He didn't like bullying her, but he didn't have time to finesse. Under the circumstances, he couldn't think of another way to make her obey. Landis had never been one to take orders. He figured he could apologize for pushing her around later—hopefully not from the inside of a jail cell.

He was about to go in search of the yet-to-be-identified intruder when the door to the men's room opened. Praying the commode lid was strong enough to hold their combined weight, Jack quickly closed the stall door, set the lock and stepped up with Landis.

Every sense on high alert, he listened as the door banged shut. The intruder walked in, whistling an old rock and roll song. Jack stood perfectly still, barely breathing. Landis stood in front of him facing the same direction, her rear end snugged up against him. He could feel her trembling, hear her breaths coming short and fast.

He put his mouth close to her ear. "Shhh."

Two stalls down, he heard the rustle of clothing, then the unmistakable sound of a zipper being lowered. More whistling, then a steady stream as Mr. Zipper relieved himself.

Holding the file with one arm, Jack wrapped the other around Landis. Just until she calmed down, he told himself. Until she stopped trembling…

But in the next instant, the only information his brain processed was that her backside was pressed snugly against his pelvis. That she smelled like heaven. That she was warm, soft and curvy—and his body had taken notice of all those things. His blood heated and rushed directly to his groin. He desperately needed to move away from her, but couldn't risk making any noise. Cursing silently, Jack closed his eyes and hoped Mr. Zipper didn't linger.

But closing his eyes only heightened his other senses. The scent of her hair reminded him of what it had been like to make love with her. Made him remember the sweetness of her kisses. The storm in her eyes right before she surrendered. How she fought to maintain her control when he was taking her apart piece by piece…

The logical side of his brain knew that now was not the time to lose himself in the past or indulge in the sheer pleasure of holding her. But his pulse was racing. Only the pounding of blood through his veins had nothing to do with the intruder—and everything to do with the woman he held in his arms.

The knowledge that all the old feelings were still there, that they hadn't changed in the year he'd been locked away stunned him. Intellectually, he knew there was no future for them. His life was in shambles. In contrast, she was on her way to the top. He lived from hour to hour with little hope for a future. She had her sights set on a future that didn't include a convicted murderer. But God help him, none of those things mattered when he was touching her.…

The sound of running water drifted through his brain. Landis was still trembling, but her breathing had slowed. Shifting slightly, Jack lowered his mouth to her ear. ''Easy,'' he whispered.

Surprising him, she tilted her head as if to give him better access to the sensitive area just behind her ear. She'd always liked to be kissed there, he remembered, and set his mouth against her flesh. The urge to devour was overpowering, but he knew better than to get carried away at a time like this. After all, he was only trying to keep her calm.

The sound of paper towels being yanked from the dispenser reached him through the haze of pleasure. Her hair felt like silk against his cheek. He breathed in her scent. The sweetness of it intoxicated him, numbed him to the dangers of getting distracted at a time like this. But he was crazy for her, would have sold his soul for a kiss…

She felt incredible against him. Temptation tormented him, tearing down the barriers of control. When she sighed, something inside him broke loose. Pulling her tightly against him, he set his mouth against her neck. The taste of her flesh hit his system like an addictive drug, and all he could think was he wanted more. That he wanted it now or he would die.

He ran his tongue over her flesh, tasting, wanting, needing with an intensity that blinded him to the dangers of what he was doing. He trapped the tender flesh of her earlobe between his teeth and nibbled, letting her feel his teeth. She made a soft sound and he pressed against her, knowing she could feel the hard length of his arousal, a part of him not caring.

The restroom door opened and closed. Jack waited, his body humming with tension, his sex heavy and uncomfortable within the confines of his jeans. He was trying to decide how to handle that when Landis elbowed him hard enough to knock the air from his lungs.

''What the—'' His left foot slipped off the seat. An instant later they went down in a tangle of arms and legs. Jack twisted in midair to keep himself from falling on top of her. The file flew from his grasp, papers scattering about like leaves in a gale. He landed hard on his back with Landis on top of him.

''What the hell are you trying to pull?'' she growled.

Jack scrambled to his feet. ''You'd better hope whomever was just in here didn't hear the racket,'' he snapped.

Without looking at her, he strode to the door and eased

it open an inch. Relief trembled through him when he found the hall empty.

Landis stalked up behind him. "You were out of line."

"I was trying to keep you from losing it," he said. But he was as furious with himself as he was with her.

Noticing the papers from his file scattered on the floor, he stooped and began shoving them into the file. One more mistake like that and he could kiss his freedom goodbye for good.

"I wasn't losing it," she said.

"You were shaking and hyperventilating and if I hadn't distracted you, you would have gotten us busted."

"I wasn't the one who was breathing hard."

He shot her a killing look. "Oh, that's real funny."

He wanted to ask her if she'd hurt herself in the fall, but his pride wouldn't let him be nice. Damn her. And damn his attraction to her. He had no business acting like some irresponsible schoolboy with a bad case of hormones when both their necks were on the line. What the hell was he thinking allowing himself to get sidetracked when she'd made her feelings crystal clear?

Stuffing the last of the papers into the file, Jack stalked to the door, pushed it open and peeked out. "Let's get out of here."

He left the restroom without looking back. He heard her behind him, but he didn't slow down. He was halfway to the freight elevator when she caught up with him. "You need to get some very important rules clear in your head, LaCroix."

Annoyance rippled through him that she felt the need to reprimand him. What did she expect? Didn't she realize what she did to him?

"Don't push me, Red." He punched the down button.

"I'm talking about setting boundaries, Jack. I'm talking about your having a little respect."

The elevator doors rolled open. Ignoring her, he stepped inside, punched the down button. "Now isn't the time to discuss this."

"If we're going to work together on your case, we've got to talk about this. We can't go back to the way we were. I don't want that. And, damn it, I can't handle it when you—" Landis poked his chest with her index finger, hard enough to make him wince. "Would you *listen* to me?"

It didn't hurt, but it made him mad. Closing his eyes, he rubbed his hand over his face and silently counted to ten. The last thing he wanted was a lecture on male decorum from the woman who was the object of his darkest fantasies. "I'm listening."

"These are the rules, Jack. No innuendo. No touching. No kissing. I won't tolerate that kind of conduct."

"I guess that means you're not going to sleep with me."

"That's not funny."

He didn't think so, either. "Tell me something, Red, do these rules work both ways? I mean, hell, you kissed me back last night. Wasn't that breaking one or two of those rules?"

She made a sound of exasperation. "What did you expect me to do when you had your tongue shoved down my throat?"

"Push me away?"

"You know, Jack, you're making this a lot more difficult than it has to be."

"Consider yourself forewarned, Landis. The next time you kiss me like that I'm not going to be thinking about rules."

"Just because I'm helping you do this doesn't mean the situation between us has changed." Turning away from him, she punched the down button again.

An angry, unsettled silence ensued. He knew it was childish, but it ticked him off that she'd gotten the last word. It ticked him off even more that she was right. He might be attracted to her. He might even have feelings for her that went a hell of a lot deeper than the flesh. But Jack had been around the block enough times to know when he was facing a losing proposition. A relationship was out of the question. Sex would have been nice—but he knew Landis would never open herself up like that. Where he was going, emotional baggage would do nothing but weigh him down. The only question that remained was how in the hell he was going to keep his hands off her in the interim.

The delivery men were gone when they reached the ground level. Ignoring Landis as best he could, Jack made his way down the corridor and through the doors to the loading dock. He couldn't believe they'd actually pulled off mission impossible. Something that felt vaguely like hope stirred in his chest, making him realize just how badly he'd needed a lucky break.

Stepping into the frigid night air, he drew a deep breath, feeling better than he had in months. "What were you saying about the dangers of breaking and entering?" he asked Landis when they reached the bottom of the concrete ramp.

"We're lucky Chandler didn't have security cam—"

"You there! *Halt!*"

The command hit him like a cattle prod. Jack glanced over his shoulder, saw a uniformed security officer jump off the loading dock and start toward them at a determined clip. "Put your hands where I can see them!" the officer shouted. *"Now!"*

"What do we do?" Landis asked.

"Run." Clamping his hand around hers, Jack hurled himself into a dead run. They blew through deep snow and a shallow ditch, covering the ground at a dangerous speed. But twenty yards back, the security officer was closing in on them at an alarming speed.

"Stop or I'll shoot!"

A gunshot split the air. Shock and a healthy jab of fear streaked through Jack. Praying the officer had only fired a warning shot, Jack forced Landis ahead of him, keeping himself squarely between her and the gun. "Faster!"

An instant later her hand was ripped from his grasp. He looked back to see her plow headlong into the snow. His first thought was that she'd been shot.

The world stopped. Horror and fear splintered inside him. *"Landis!"*

"I'm...okay."

Relief shook him when she scrambled to her feet. But the terror clung to him when he took her hand and dragged her into a reckless sprint. He looked back at the officer, caught a glimpse of blue uniform through the trees. The cop was so close Jack could hear the bark of his police radio.

"Run, damn it!"

Twenty feet from the Jeep, he let go of her hand. "The keys!" Behind them, the cop shouted another command. Landis tossed the keys. Catching them in one hand, Jack hit the button to unlock the doors and headed for the driver's side door.

Another shot rang out. Fear stabbed through him again when he heard the tinny *thwack!* of a bullet penetrating the Jeep. *Damn stupid rookie.* Yanking open the door, he lunged inside. Landis slid on to the seat next to him. "Get down!" he shouted, forcing her head down with his free hand.

Through the windshield, he saw the security officer drop to one knee and raise the gun. Jack twisted the ignition key. The engine turned over. Slamming the shifter into gear, he floored the accelerator. The Jeep's wheels spun, then jumped forward and hurled them into the night.

Landis fought for breath as she huddled on the passenger side floor and listened to the gears slam into place. Her heart beat like a drum in her ears. Every muscle in her body trembled uncontrollably as she dragged herself onto the seat.

"Oh my God." For the first time in a long time, she felt like putting her face in her hands and weeping. With relief. With the sheer joy of being alive. With the unsettling knowledge that she had crossed a very dangerous line.

Jack negotiated a turn, glanced in the rearview mirror, then tossed her a quick, concerned look. "Are you all right?"

"You mean other than the fact that I probably just ruined my life? Hey, I'm just peachy."

"Were you hit, damn it?"

She looked down at her snow-covered coat, half-expecting to see a bullet hole in the fabric. "No bullet holes. That's a good sign, I suppose."

"I guess that means we won't be able to compare scars."

What she and Jack had just survived was the kind of thing that happened in Arnold Schwarzenegger movies—not in real life, certainly not in her predictable, wonderfully dull life. Well, her former wonderfully dull life. All that had changed the night Jack LaCroix walked into her cabin and turned her world upside down.

The laugh that escaped her contained an edge of hysteria. "I've finally wigged out. I knew it was going to happen sooner or later. I should have known it would involve you."

Jack grimaced. "I'm sorry I put you in that situation. I shouldn't have let you come. I shouldn't have dragged you into this."

Landis didn't miss the lines of strain in his face or the tight set of his mouth. His eyes went repeatedly to the rear-view mirror, to the road, to her. Always back to her. She watched as he raked a trembling hand through his hair, and she suddenly knew she wasn't the only one who was scared.

"You didn't drag me into anything," she said quietly. "I came of my own free will."

He cut her a hard look. "I manipulated you. I used you."

"Jack, we made it out. We're okay."

Cursing, he rapped his palm against the steering wheel. "I nearly got you killed!"

Jack wasn't prone to emotional outbursts. He was distant and aloof and damn hard to read most of the time. Even during the dark days of his trial, when he was fighting for his life, he'd done it with a cool stoicism. She knew that stony facade had to do with his childhood. That he'd learned to deal with the pain of being shuffled from foster home to foster home by locking his emotions down tight. But she knew he felt things deeply, that he bled just like everyone else.

Landis had seen a glimpse of his emotional side only once in all the time she'd known him. The night Evan died he'd opened up to her. They'd held each other and cried that night. They'd never discussed it since, but she'd never forgotten it. She knew there were plenty of emotions buried deep inside him. That he would show them now gave her pause.

"Everything's going to be all right," she said firmly.

He shot her a sideways glance, his jaw flexing. She wanted to know what was going on inside his head, but knew him well enough to know he wouldn't say.

"You don't think he made out the license plates, do you?" she asked after a moment.

He shook his head. "I switched your plates with the ones on Chandler's truck before we left the cabin."

"You think like a criminal."

"Keeps you one step ahead of the bad guys. That's what made me such a good cop."

The wistful tone of his voice struck a chord within her. And with sudden clarity, she realized the full scope of everything he'd lost. That he'd endured so much hardship, so much unfairness—and never lost hope—touched a place inside her that was battered and raw. A part of her ached for him because she was finally beginning to understand what the last year had done to him.

Closing her eyes, she leaned against the seat and tried to shut off her mind. But her mind refused to obey. She wasn't exactly sure when it happened, but she no longer believed Jack had murdered Evan. He might cross lines and push limits, but she knew deep down he wasn't capable of murdering his partner. Maybe that was why she'd risked everything going into that office with him tonight. Maybe because a small part of her thought she'd owed it to him.

Troubled by the repercussions of that, she looked out the window and watched the lights and mountain terrain fly past. She could no longer deny the connection between them. A connection that hadn't been severed by time or circumstance. And she knew it was long past time for her and Jack to have a serious talk. Not about Evan or Cyrus Duke or the dangerous situation they were embroiled in. But about the bond between them.

She found it ironic that of all the things they needed to discuss, their relationship was the one that frightened her the most. Jack had made it clear that he wanted her on a physical level. But a one-night stand with an escaped convict wasn't an option. Even if he were able to prove his innocence, Landis refused to give her heart to a man who would hand it back to her in pieces.

The only question that remained was how she was going to keep that from happening.

It was 1:00 a.m. when Landis and Jack arrived at Chandler's cabin. A full moon cast pearlescent light over crystalline snow, illuminating the mountains to the east. The temperature hovered around zero, and Landis felt the chill all the way to her bones.

Anxious to get a look at the file, she sat at the table and opened the file while Jack built a fire. She spent ten minutes organizing police reports, court transcripts, witness statements and general correspondence. The appeal documents were stored neatly inside a smaller brown folder. Setting the other paperwork aside, she put the appeal file in front of her and began sifting through it.

It was obvious Aaron Chandler and his army of paralegals, interns and junior attorneys had been working fervently on Jack's case. Like her, Chandler had been a perfectionist. His work was thorough and succinct, trademarks of a good lawyer.

Jack approached the table with two mugs. "Coffee?"

Absently, Landis nodded, her attention focused on the documents in front of her. It felt good to be back on familiar ground. She was much more comfortable with legal documents and court exhibits than she was with breaking into buildings and dodging bullets.

"What exactly do you hope to find in this file?" she asked.

Putting his elbows on the table, Jack rubbed his hands over the dark stubble of his jaw. He looked worn out, she thought, and wondered how long he could keep this up. How long would he try before giving up on clearing his name and making a run for it?

"The last time I met with Chandler," he said, "he was working on getting copies of wires from a bank in Salt Lake City to an account in the Cayman Islands. The Cayman account was in Evan's name. The checks were coming from Duke's restaurant payroll account."

"Evan was too smart to put an account in his own name," she said.

"I'm just telling you what Chandler told me. I haven't seen any of the statements or transaction docs myself."

"If they exist."

"Why would Chandler lie?"

"I don't know." She sighed in frustration. "It's not like his case makes a whole lot of sense to begin with."

"A lot of what happened in the last year doesn't make sense."

"It seems like the more we dig, the more confusing this mess becomes."

The intensity of his gaze unnerved her. She told herself it was because she was tired. Because Jack was in deep trouble and she didn't know how to help him. But she saw the question in his eyes. A question she had no desire to answer.

"You know I didn't murder Evan, don't you?" he asked quietly.

Not quite sure how to respond without venturing down a very dangerous path, Landis looked down at the document in front of her, hating that she couldn't meet his gaze. "I've seen enough to know your case warrants looking into."

"That's not an answer."

"It's the only answer I've got." She saw a flash of anger in his eyes an instant before she looked away. It bothered her that she couldn't hold his gaze. But she didn't want him to see the uncertainty she knew her eyes would reveal.

She blew out a sigh. "When was your last meeting with Chandler?"

"A couple of weeks ago. He came to the prison. We went into an interview room. He updated me on my case and stayed for about an hour."

"Did he actually show you any of the evidence he had on Evan?"

Jack's eyes hardened. "No. But he assured me he was

close to proving Evan had taken money from Duke. Tha
one of Duke's men had pulled the trigger. Landis, for God'
sake, Jimmy Beck told me as much before he got stabbed
to death in the shower.''

Reaching into her bag, she extracted her glasses and
shoved them onto her nose. "I want to go through every
thing. Every piece of paper. Notes. Documents. Billing
hours. If there's a grocery list in this file, I want to see it.'
She felt his gaze on her, but she didn't risk looking at him
He was watching her too closely, and she was still feeling
the remnants of adrenaline. The combination was doing a
number on her ability to concentrate.

"Hopefully, he wasn't the kind of lawyer who kept ev
erything in his head," she finished.

"When did you start wearing glasses, Red?"

Annoyed that she was suddenly concerned with the way
she looked, Landis set the file aside and glared at him ove
the rims. "They're reading glasses, and I got them the las
time I went to the eye doctor." Her voice was firm, bu
she felt like squirming beneath his scrutiny.

"You look really good in them," he said.

She knew better than to be flattered. But she was. Ridic
ulously so. "We don't have much time, Jack. It's late, and
we've got about four hours of paper to go through. I'
appreciate it if you'd just—"

"Shut up and get to work?" One side of his mouth
pulled into a smile.

She couldn't help but grin back. "Well, yeah."

"Yes ma'am."

Landis handed him a stack of paper, then set to work
She tried to concentrate on the documents in front of her
but her attention kept drifting to Jack. She watched him
covertly as he peeled off his coat and draped it over th
back of his chair. Elbows on the table, he opened the file
and began to read. The hard-edged desperation she'd seen

the day before had been replaced by cool determination. Even with the cut above his eye and the bruise on his cheek, he was attractive. He was tall and lean, and it was damn near impossible for her not to notice how good he looked in the flannel shirt and faded jeans. She'd forgotten a man could look that good.

Unhappy with the direction of her thoughts, Landis rose and refilled her cup. At the table, Jack scowled at a particularly complicated-looking legal document. *He still looks like a cop,* she thought. A career-minded detective hell-bent on solving a case. Taking in the tough facade, she never would have guessed his life was the one on the line. Or that the odds of the situation working out in his favor were slim to none.

Worse, however, was the knowledge that she cared a lot more than was wise—and there wasn't a damn thing she could do about any of it.

Chapter 8

"Nobody said this was going to be easy." Jack slid the last document into the file, shoved away from the table, and rose. Needles shot up his calf where his leg had fallen asleep. His shoulder ached dully where the bullet had grazed him, keeping time with the headache thundering behind his eyes.

Across from him, Landis lowered her face into her hands and rubbed her eyes. "That appears to be the theme we've been keeping."

Jack watched her flame-colored hair cascade down and felt the familiar tightening in his belly. She'd worked alongside him through the night, guiding him through some of the more complicated legal documents. Her knowledge and attention to detail impressed him, and he couldn't help but think if he ever needed a lawyer, he wouldn't mind having her in his corner.

Too bad she was the prosecutorial type.

He stretched and looked out the window. It was still

dark, but dawn was only a couple of hours away. Exhaustion and frustration and the very real fear that he wasn't going to find the proof he needed to clear his name taunted him with renewed vigor. They'd gone over every piece of paper with a fine-toothed comb right down to Chandler's documented telephone conversations and handwritten notes. After risking their lives breaking into the lawyer's office, the file had yielded exactly zilch.

The disappointment came with a vengeance, a rabid animal tearing into him with sharp teeth. He hated feeling so hopeless. But he was getting damn tired of hitting brick wall after brick wall.

Landis leaned back in her chair and sighed. "There's no proof of anything in this file. There has to be another one that we missed."

"Even if there is another file, we're not going to be able to get our hands on it," he said. "Not after what happened. Chandler's office is going to be locked down tighter than a prison."

"Maybe the police confiscated it. Maybe Chandler was working on it and took it home—"

"We're running out of time."

"Maybe I could go to the presiding judge and—"

"I need to get some air," he cut in, sudden anger at the situation making his voice sharper than he'd intended.

"Look, I know you're frustrated, but—"

"That's not the right word for what's going on inside me right now."

"Jack—"

"For God's sake, Landis. You're a prosecutor. You know good and well what I'm facing. Think about it!"

Her expression turned fierce. Never taking her eyes from his, she rose and approached him. "If there's something to be found, we'll find it. You have to believe that."

"Forgive me if I don't share your optimism right now." Snagging his coat off the chair, he started for the door.

"Jack?"

He didn't answer, didn't even pause as he crossed through the mudroom. He needed a few minutes alone. A few minutes where he didn't have to sit across from a woman who made him want all the things he knew he could never have.

He went out through the back door. The cold sank in all the way to his bones, but he welcomed the diversion. Anything was better than the hopelessness and utter bitterness churning inside him. He walked to the old pickup parked beneath the carport a few yards from the cabin. Because he didn't want to go back inside any time soon, Jack figured now might be a good time to see if it ran.

Climbing into the truck, he stuck the key in the ignition and twisted. The motor groaned like a sick cow. Cursing, he pumped the gas and tried again. On the third try the engine sputtered to life. White exhaust billowed into the cold air.

He should have been relieved that at least he had transportation. But the knowledge did little for his frame of mind. If the truck was registered, the police would soon know about it—if they didn't already. If luck was on his side, he figured he had another day before they started looking for it.

He sat in the truck and watched the moon set over the jagged line of trees to the east, and tried not to think. He tried not to think about the injustices that had been inflicted upon him. Of what those injustices had done to his life.

It seemed as if he'd spent his entire life on the outside looking in. As a young orphan, all he'd wanted was a family to love him. To be like other kids, with parents that cared. But shuffled from family to family, Jack had learned the sting of abandonment at a very early age. Then along came police officer Mike Morgan and his wife, Pat. Two good people who'd taken in a troubled boy and turned his life around.

Mike had taught Jack how to be a man. He'd taught him what was important in life. Family. Career. Love. Mike had taught Jack not only how to give love, but how to receive it. Mike had believed in him when no one else had. Jack had worked hard for that love, even harder for Mike's respect. Sitting in the truck with the world crashing down all around him, he wished like hell Mike were alive today to tell him what to do.

He watched a silver cloud skid past the moon, and his thoughts shifted to Landis. A dangerous topic considering the electricity that snapped between them every time they were within shouting distance. He'd known he would have to deal with his feelings for her sooner or later.

It was then that Jack realized that Landis was at the root of his despondency. As hard as he'd tried not to let her get to him, she had, like a sliver of bamboo being shoved slowly under a fingernail. She was the best thing that had ever happened to him. She'd influenced his life in ways she would never know, pulled him back from a dark edge when he'd needed it badly. Landis was decent and kind and still saw that indelible line between right and wrong; she still believed in doing the right thing. She represented light and laughter and proved to him that good still prevailed over evil.

Jack had known she would help him. He'd known she would risk everything to do it. And just as he'd known it was wrong of him to manipulate her and drag her into this mess, he'd done it anyway. He'd used her. He'd just about gotten her killed.

He couldn't ask her for anything more.

As much as he needed her—as desperately as he wanted to be with her—he knew that asking her to do more was a line he would never cross. He had to send her away. Before he ruined her life. Before she got hurt.

The thought cut him with unexpected sharpness. The pain that followed came so hard and fast that for a moment he couldn't breathe. A week ago when he'd been lying in his cell planning his great escape, he'd believed fate would cooperate, that he could make it happen.

Reality had proven him wrong.

The best he could hope for was a safe trip through Mexico to a country where nobody spoke English. There weren't extradition laws in Colombia. He'd give himself another twenty-four hours. If he couldn't turn up any solid evidence, he'd drive the truck as far south as it would take him and try like hell not to think of all the things he'd left behind.

The cabin smelled of coffee and burning pine when he entered. He hung his coat on the rack in the mudroom. Mild surprise rippled through him when he found the kitchen empty. He walked into the main room fully intending to tell Landis to get in the Jeep and forget she'd ever seen him. But the moment he caught sight of her curled on the sofa, his mind blanked.

She'd loosened her hair at some point, and it spread out in a halo of shimmering silk. Her lashes lay dark and thick against her pale complexion. He noticed the dusting of freckles on her nose, and a rush of affection engulfed him. She'd always disliked her freckles. He couldn't imagine why when they charmed him so completely.

His eyes traveled to her mouth and a different kind of tension quivered through him. Her full lips were slightly open and wet. The memory of the kiss they'd shared the night before drifted through his mind and he went instantly hard. He remembered every sigh, every touch, every subtle shifting of hips with stark clarity. It hadn't gone unnoticed that in the end, she'd wrapped her arms around him and kissed him back.

The sudden need to touch her, to run his fingers through her hair, to hold her lovely face in his hands and kiss her mouth was as powerful as his need for his next breath. But because he couldn't do any of those things, he simply stood there, aching for her, and put every detail to memory because he knew that all too soon it would be all he had left.

Jack didn't want this to go any further. It was bad enough wanting her on a physical level. But to care for her was something else altogether. He didn't want his emotions getting in the way of what he had to do.

He closed his eyes against a sudden, wrenching pang of loneliness. As much as he wanted to go to her, as much as he wanted to touch her and lose himself in the soft warmth of her body, he knew that for sanity's sake he couldn't. He wouldn't do that to her. Wouldn't do it to himself.

Logic told him to wake her and send her back to her cabin right now. But the part of him that wasn't feeling quite so logical wanted just one more night. Acquiescing to that stronger side, Jack walked into the bedroom, pulled the quilt and pillow from the bed and carried them to the living room. He covered Landis with the quilt, then eased the pillow under her head.

He had every intention of going back into the bedroom. Of climbing into the cold, empty bed, and getting some badly needed sleep. But his willpower failed him. Kicking off his boots, he lay down beside her. Hands laced behind his head, he watched the fire flicker against the ceiling and tried to concentrate on the dull pain in his shoulder, on all the things he needed to do the next day. But nothing could take his mind off the sweet ache of being so close to her. Of feeling the soft warmth of her body next to his.

He didn't know why he was subjecting himself to this.

But for a few short hours, he would be with her. And in the morning, he would tell her goodbye for the last time.

Fog rolled over the casket like a billowing, white blanket. Landis watched as two police officers donned in full dress uniform folded the American flag in a neat triangle and handed it to Evan's widow. Her two nieces stood quietly by their mother's side, their young faces confused and streaked with tears.

The twenty-one gun salute shattered the morning air until Landis thought the blasts would never end. Her mother's high-pitched keening punctuated the profound silence that followed. Across from her, Jack LaCroix stood stone-faced, his dark eyes never leaving the glossy wood coffin.

Only when the lid panel of the casket began to open did she realize this wasn't how she remembered Evan's funeral. Horror engulfed her when the silhouette of a man inside the coffin came into view through the swirling fog. No, Evan, she thought. It couldn't be her brother who now sat bolt upright within the plush interior of that dreadful box. Evan was dead.

Her heart thudded painfully as she strained to identify the impostor. A break in the fog revealed a man with dark hair, steel-blue eyes, an angular face that would have been handsome if not for the glint of cruelty. Recognition dawned, followed by a flash of disbelief. Cyrus Duke...

Her blood ran cold when his eyes met hers. She saw evil in the depths of his gaze, felt it grip her like a clawed hand. Shock enveloped her when he raised the pistol and leveled it at her chest. When he grinned, she suddenly knew he was going to pull the trigger. He was going to kill her. That he would enjoy it.

Landis turned to run, but her legs seemed to be weighted. A scream bubbled up from inside her. She braced for the hot punch of agony in her back. The blast deafened her.

Her scream echoed in her head as pain streaked up her spine. Oh, God, she didn't want to die—

"Landis!"

Heart pounding, she fought the hands that held her.

"Easy. It's me." Jack's voice cut through the fog.

Landis jolted awake. The scream in her throat died as the nightmare receded. Awareness of her surroundings rushed in to calm her. She was in Aaron Chandler's cabin. On the sofa. With Jack. She must have fallen asleep....

Shaken and embarrassed, suddenly aware that he was leaning over her, touching her, Landis pulled away and sat up. "I'm okay," she said quickly.

"You cried out."

His hands gripped her biceps. His fingers were warm and incredibly reassuring against her chilled flesh. For a crazy instant, she wanted to lean against him and let him hold her. It had been such a long time since anyone had held her. Since Jack had held her.

Knowing they were dangerous thoughts at a moment like this, she shook off his hands and pulled away. "Just a nightmare," she said.

"Must have been a bad one."

She remembered the hot punch of the bullet in her back and shivered. "It was...vivid. I never dream like that."

"The last couple of days have been stressful."

Slowly, her nerves began to steady. "I didn't mean to scare you."

"I'm not the one who's scared." When she shot him a look he added, "you're still shaking."

Because she didn't want him to know just how rattled she was, Landis rose and walked to the hearth without looking at him. The room had grown cold during the night, so she tossed a log onto the embers. Thin light floated in around the heavy drapes, and she realized with mild surprise that it was dawn.

"You want to talk about it?" he asked. "Sometimes it helps."

She looked over to see him folding the quilt he must have covered her with at some point during the night. His hair was tousled, and he had that disheveled look about him usually brought on by a rude awakening. His jaw badly needed a razor. He shouldn't have looked appealing, but he did.

"What would really help," she said, "is a break in your case."

He crossed to her. She tensed when he reached out, jolted when he set his hands on her shoulders. "I don't think that's going to happen, Red. I think you know it, only you don't know when to give up."

A tremor went through her, but she knew it had nothing to do with the cold or the nightmare and everything to do with the way he was looking at her, the warmth of his touch, the finality of his words. "It's too early in the game to give up."

A wan smile touched his mouth. "I'd wanted to talk about the other thing before you go, but I think we both can agree that it's best if we don't at this point."

Landis wasn't sure which part of the statement to challenge first, so she went with the safest. "I'm not going anywhere."

"If you're smart, you'll get in the Jeep and forget you ever saw me."

"In case you've forgotten, we're trying to keep you out of prison."

"The only way for me to avoid going back is to run." He brushed his fingers against her cheek. "I think what we're really trying to do here is figure out what the hell's going on between us. Figure out if there's anything left. If it's worth pursuing one more time."

Her heart began to pound. "There are more pressing issues that need to be dealt—"

"I see it in your eyes, Landis. I feel it in the way you
tremble. In the way you avoid getting too close to me.
There's something between us, damn it, whether you're
willing to admit it or not."

Holding her gaze, he glided his hands gently up and
down her arms. The contact was whisper soft and so incredibly intimate it raised gooseflesh on her arms. Her
breasts tightened, but she swore it was because of the cold.
There was no way she was going to let his ministrations
get to her. She was far too cautious to let this moment get
out of hand or lead to something she would regret.

But he was standing too close; she was feeling too much.
An explosive combination that would lead to disaster if she
allowed it.

"I see the wheels spinning in your head," he whispered,
"but I don't know what you're thinking." Raising his hand,
he brushed a strand of hair away from her face. "What
wars are being waged inside you, Landis? Which side is
going to win?"

"I'm thinking about mistakes," she said, but the words
were little more than puffs of air.

"Making them?" His mouth curved sensuously. "We're
damn good at it."

"Avoiding them."

"Some mistakes are worth it, don't you think?"

"Most just hurt."

"No pain, no gain. Isn't that what they say?"

"I don't see how I could gain anything by messing up
my life. Helping you is one thing. Getting involved with
you again is something else altogether." She could feel
every nerve in her body vibrating, feel the intensity of his
gaze all the way to her bones.

"You're already involved with me." He leaned closer,

his hands skimming over her shoulders, down her sides, his thumbs brushing the outsides of her breasts. "That's why you're trembling. That's why I can hear you breathing. Why I see all that heat in your eyes. What else is going on inside you?"

Realizing he was about to kiss her, annoyed with herself because she was an inch away from letting him, Landis stepped back. "Don't do that," she snapped. "Don't toy with my emotions like that, damn it. That's not fair."

Making a sound of frustration, Jack stalked over to the kitchen window and looked out. Landis held her ground near the sofa, trembling, aware that she was breathing hard, that her nerves were snapping like a lit fuse.

"You're right," he said. "That wasn't fair. For either of us."

"Jack, I know you've been alone for a long—"

"That doesn't have a thing to do with what's going on between us," he cut in.

"There can't be anything between us."

"Wishing for something doesn't make it so."

She sighed, unhappy with the situation, unhappy with herself for having come so close to making a mistake that would further complicate an already complicated situation.

For several tense minutes the only sound came from the crackle of the fire. Then Jack turned to her, closed the distance between them. "I did some thinking last night," he began. "It's only a matter of time before the cops find out about this place. I don't want to be here when they show up."

Surprise and regret and a shimmer of pain punched her hard enough to take her breath. Staring at him, she realized the one thing she didn't feel was relief. "I was going to go through your file again. There are other avenues we can explore."

"I'm out of time, Red. We're out of time." He grimaced

''I want you to drive back to your place. I'll leave it up to you whether or not you go to the cops. If you do, I'd appreciate it if you tell me now so I have time to get out of the state.''

She swallowed hard at the jumble of emotions his words elicited, struggled to stay focused on the matter at hand. ''If I talk to the police, it will only be to tell them what I know, that you're innocent.''

A smile whispered across his features. ''I'm flattered you would do that for me, but I think we both know it's going to take a hell of a lot more than your word to make them believe you.''

''You're innocent,'' she said.

Crossing to her, he reached out and set his hand against her cheek. ''Your saying that means more to me than you'll ever know. But it doesn't change anything.''

The realization that he was sacrificing his chances of clearing his name to protect her went through her like an electric shock. ''You're trying to protect me.''

''And not doing a very good job of it.''

''I don't need your protection.''

His dark eyes ran the length of her, lingering at her breasts, her hips, but he didn't move toward her. ''You need protection from me.''

''I can handle you.''

''Maybe this time. But what about next time? I think we both know there will be a next time. And we both know it's going to lead to a mistake we can't take back.''

''I know better, even if you don't.''

''I'm a man, Landis, and I've got my sights set on you. You can put any kind of spin on that you want, but we both know I'll eventually get inside you.'' His eyes burned into hers. ''You give me a chance, and I'll take what I want from you without a thought as to what it will do to you.''

His face was grim as he snagged her coat from the chair

and started toward her. "That's why you're going to leave now."

The earth tilted beneath her feet, and she struggled hard to keep her footing. "If you retain me as your lawyer I'll be protected by attorney-client privilege."

"If I were the scoundrel you seem to think I am, I might take you up on that." He retrieved her purse from the dining room chair. "But I'm not." He thrust the coat at her. "Put on the damn coat."

"Jack, there's still a possibility you'll be cleared."

"There's an even bigger chance I'll get railroaded back to prison. That you'll get disbarred from practicing law. Is that what you want?"

She didn't accept the coat. "I'm not leaving things like this."

"You don't have a choice. Neither do I."

Landis wanted to tell him it didn't have to end like this, but she couldn't speak. Things were happening too fast, like a movie speeding along in fast forward and she didn't know her next line. She knew it would be professional suicide for her to get more deeply involved in his plight. She didn't even want to think about what it would cost her on an emotional level. But it would destroy her to walk out that door.

"I'm not leaving," she said. "I'm already involved. I'm going to finish this."

Never taking his eyes from hers, he flung her coat and purse on the kitchen table. Her heart beat madly in her chest when he crossed to her, his face set with anger. "You're not being very smart about this."

She stepped back, surprised by the extent of his anger. "I'm handling this the only way I know how."

"You're making a mistake that's going to cost you everything. I don't want to be responsible for doing that to you."

He didn't stop when he reached her, but crowded her, sent her back several steps until her back hit the wall. "I'm not going to let you intimidate me."

"Is that what I'm doing?" He smiled darkly. "Intimidating you?"

"You think you can drive me away by behaving like an idiot."

"Or maybe I think this is one mistake that just might be worth it."

He didn't ask for permission when he took her mouth. The bold contact stunned her. She felt herself stiffen in shock, then the spark of pleasure ignited and burst into a roaring flame. Heat engulfed her, burning her from the inside out. Growling low in his throat, he wrapped one arm around her and pressed the full length of his body against hers. She could feel the hard ridge of him against her belly. Her own arousal came swiftly and with stunning power. A short fuse that burned close and hot. She felt one of them trembling, but for the life of her she couldn't tell if it was her or him.

He kissed her, then tilted his head and whispered her name. "Damn it, you make me want you."

Closing her eyes against the accusation in his words, the threat in his voice, she put her arms around his neck. He smelled of soap and the out of doors and healthy male. Her senses drank in the scent of him, the feel of him. The hard length of his body against hers. The bristle of his whiskers against her cheek. The harsh sound of his breathing. The insistence of his mouth as it coaxed hers into submission. All of it laced with an underlying redolence of male hunger.

Slanting her head back, he deepened the kiss. Erotic pleasure skittered through her when his tongue probed her mouth. Landis opened to him, tested him with her own tongue, loving his taste and the silky texture of his mouth. She could feel the need pounding deep in her womb.

Warmth pulsing between her legs. Need churned inside her, an urgent mix of heat and desperation and a sweet ache that grew with every beat of her heart.

Jack broke the kiss momentarily and whispered something in her ear, but Landis was beyond hearing, beyond understanding. His erection nudged her belly, a steel rod she could feel through their clothing. The knowledge that he wanted her should have brought her to her senses—she knew this could never come to fruition. But the raw truth of it thrilled her, ignited a flame she'd thought was dead.

Body to body, he kissed with the urgency of a man driven by the most fundamental of needs. He moved against her without finesse. She absorbed him, wanting with a fierceness that was frightening in its intensity. Somewhere in the back of her mind an alarm wailed. An alarm that warned of an impending mistake. But she silenced it with ruthless precision.

He cursed her, kissed her and then savaged her mouth. She should have been shocked, by his words, by the violence of his need. But she wasn't any of those things and kissed him back with an abandon she'd never before known.

Impatient hands fought with the fabric of her sweater, pulling and tugging in their search for flesh. "I need to touch you," he whispered. "Now."

His hand slid between them and with a clever flick of his wrist, the clasp of her bra opened. Landis barely had time to gasp when without preamble he cupped her breasts. She jolted hard when his fingertips brushed over her sensitized nipples. She felt the zing of sensation all the way to her core. Her knees went weak when he molded her flesh with his hands. She'd known desire before. She'd known desire with this man. But it had never been anything like the sensations assaulting her now.

Raw lust splintered through her. Insanity descended, hijacked her intellect and she let it go without a fight. His hands went to the small of her back. He bent to her, kissing her throat, whispering words beyond her understanding. His mouth left a wet trail over her collarbone, then lower to the valley between her breasts.

The last of her control tumbled away when he took her nipple into his mouth. She cried out as intense pleasure crashed through her. She arched, felt her body flexing and contracting, knew she was seconds away from a freefall. He suckled greedily. Vaguely, she was aware of his hand flat against her belly. The warmth of his fingertips sliding beneath the waistband of her jeans. She could feel her body pulsing. The need clenching at her. His hand slid lower, and she wondered if he could feel the beat of her blood against his palm.

She knew better than to let this go any further. The words to end it were on the tip of her tongue. But the pleasure was like a mind-altering drug, destroying the last of her judgment. When his fingers met the crisp curls at her vee, she opened to him. She knew it was foolish, knew she would pay dearly for it, knew he would hurt her. But for the first time in her life, she didn't care about any of those things.

She cried out when he slicked his finger over her, into her. "Jack…"

Fever built inside her as he began to stroke. Tremors wracked her body. Heat burned her from within, running through her veins like lava. Her body gripped him. Intellectually she fought what she knew would happen next. Emotionally, she cried out with the pain she knew this would bring her. But physically, she took everything he offered, and wanted more.

"Jack…I can't."

"Yes, you can," he whispered. "For me…let go."

The power of what she felt for him awed as much as it

frightened. It was too much. It was too good. It was a mistake.

Her body didn't care.

He stroked her, moving within her, sending her higher and higher. He took her to the limit, then over the edge and into a wild, tumbling freefall. She relinquished her control. He stole the rest like a thief in the night.

She cried out his name when the climax struck her. He whispered hers in answer. Once. Twice. She closed her eyes against the intensity of the moment, against the keen sense of vulnerability that followed.

Jack kissed her deeply. "I've dreamed of touching you like that a thousand times," he whispered. "God, Landis, I've missed you...."

She couldn't speak. A hundred emotions pulled her in a hundred different directions. She felt as if he'd taken her apart cell by cell. As if she would never be put back together the same way.

His arms were still around her, locking her against him. Vaguely, she was aware of him tugging at her jeans with his free hand, trying to get them down. All she could think was that this wasn't what she'd intended to happen. That it would be wrong to let this go any further.

He leaned close to kiss her again, but she turned her head. "No."

"Why not?"

She tried to pull away, but he tightened his grip, held her in place. "Landis..."

She broke free of his grip and stepped back. "I can't do this."

Heat glittered in his eyes when he raised his gaze to hers. He was breathing hard, his nostrils flaring with each inhale. She could see a hint of moisture on his forehead. He stared at her, looking perplexed, angry and frustrated as hell.

Only then did she realize she was crying. Hot, humiliating tears that squeezed through her lashes to scald her cheeks. Her chest was so tight she couldn't explain herself even if she knew what was going on in that foolish heart of hers.

"What's wrong?" She could hear the anger in his voice, but he made no move to go to her. "Did I hurt you?"

Feeling horribly vulnerable, Landis closed her eyes. "Damn it."

"I don't know what I did wrong."

"You didn't do anything wrong. I did." Shaken, she stepped back, hoping the distance would help clear her head. It didn't.

"Maybe you should have left when I told you to," he growled.

It took every ounce of strength she possessed to look him in the eye. "I can't let...what's between us muddle things, Jack. If I'm going to help you, I've got to stay focused. I can't stay focused when you—" She stopped cold, realizing she didn't want to finish the sentence.

He contemplated with a gaze so cold it chilled her. "Next time I won't give you the chance to change your mind."

"You never used to be self-destructive."

"Yeah? Well, you never used to be a tease. Looks like we've both changed."

Anger flashed, but she didn't let herself react. She knew his crude words and biting tone were a result of frustration and fear, so she let it roll off her.

"I don't need you here, messing with my head," he said.

An instant before he turned away, she saw the bitterness in his eyes. She hated the way it looked on him. Jack had never been bitter. Even after twelve years on the police force—and another year spent locked away for a crime he hadn't committed—he'd never lost hope. Until now.

"If you run, where does that leave you?" she asked.

"That leaves me a free man."

"The police will never stop looking for you. You know that. Damn it, Jack, you won't be free until you—"

Cursing, he spun on her. Anger flared in his eyes. In two steps, he was upon her. She gasped when his fingers closed around her upper arms. "It's over, Landis! As much as I wanted this to work out, as much as I want to get inside you, this isn't going to work. I can't stay here. I'm out of time. Out of options. And so are you. Now get the hell out!"

"I know what you're doing," she said, but her voice shook. "And it's not going to work."

She saw pain in his eyes an instant before he crushed his mouth to hers. There was no tenderness in the kiss, only a deep, smoldering violence that unnerved her. Rage tore through her that he would treat her with such utter disrespect. Breaking free of his grip, she drew back to strike him, but Jack was too quick. He braceleted her wrist and squeezed hard enough to make her wince. "Forget about me! Get on with your life!"

He released her with such force that she stumbled back, shocked to her core, pain breaking open inside her. "Don't do this."

Without looking at her, he walked to the sofa and picked up her coat. From the kitchen chair, he snagged her bag and brought both into the living room and thrust them at her. "Go back to your safe little life, Landis."

The words went through her like a lance. Contempt was the one thing she hadn't expected from Jack.

He pressed her purse into her hands. "Go home, pack a bag and stay with Ian for a few days. You'll be safe there until I can get out of town. Don't do anything stupid."

He didn't even look at her as he muscled her toward the door. Without preamble, he swung it open and shoved her onto the porch hard enough to make her stumble. Incensed, she spun, ready for battle. But the look in his eyes stopped her. She'd never seen such anguish. Such regret. Her anger faded as quickly as it had assailed her.

"You don't have to do this." Knowing he was going to slam the door in her face, she reached out and pressed her hand flat against it. "Don't—"

A hollow thud went through the door. Landis yelped when splinters of wood jumped out at her. Something hot bit into her cheek. Shock ripped through her when she looked at the door and saw the bullet hole.

Only then did she realize someone was shooting at her.

Chapter 9

Heedless of his own safety, Jack reached for Landis and hauled her inside. "Get down!"

"The police?" she asked.

"Cops usually don't shoot the hostage." He slammed the door, bolted it, then turned to her, his eyes wild. "Are you hit?" A wave of cold, hard fear thundered through him when he saw the blood on her cheek. "God, you're bleeding."

Eyes wide with shock, she raised her hand to her cheek.

Without waiting for an answer, he dragged her away from the door and into the main room, then turned her to him. Swiftly, he ran his hands down her coat, looking for holes or, God forbid, blood. When he found nothing, he raised his hand to her cheek and touched the well of blood with trembling fingers. "A chip of wood must have grazed you."

She frowned at the blood on his fingers. "Jack, if that wasn't the police, then who was it?"

''We're not going to stick around to find out.'' Taking her hand, he pulled her through the kitchen and mudroom and out the back door. ''The truck,'' he said and hauled her into a dead run toward the carport.

''Why are they shooting at us?''

Jack didn't want to voice what he was thinking. He didn't want to think about who might be taking potshots at him. He sure as hell didn't want to think about who might be taking potshots at Landis. ''Let's just concentrate on getting out of here alive for now. If that's who I think it is, we've got about two seconds before all hell breaks loose.''

Their feet pounded through snow as they crossed the driveway toward the detached carport a few yards away. ''Get in the truck, then get down on the floor. You got it?''

''You don't have to tell me twice.''

Jack reached the truck first and yanked open the driver's side door. Landis lunged inside, then slid across the seat. He heard a gunshot from inside the cabin, realized at least one gunman had gained entry. He jammed the key in the ignition and twisted. The engine coughed and sputtered. ''Come on, baby.''

He tried again and the engine turned over. Ramming the shifter into gear, he popped the clutch. The truck jumped forward. Realizing they would be directly in the line of fire if he used the driveway, Jack braced himself and sent the truck down the steep embankment toward the road below.

''Hang on!'' he shouted.

A muffled pop sounded over the scraping of rock against the underside of the truck. A hole the size of a dime blew through the windshield. Jack watched in horror as a thousand white capillaries spread across the glass. Swearing, he cut the wheel and stomped the gas pedal to the floor. The truck bounced wildly as it barreled down the embankment. Relief flitted through him when the ground leveled and the tires grabbed pavement. Spewing gravel and snow, he wrested the truck onto the highway and sped north.

For several minutes the only sound came from their heavy breathing. Eyes glued to the rearview mirror, Jack pressed the accelerator to the floor and watched the speedometer climb to ninety.

"Are they coming after us?" Landis's voice was high-pitched and unsteady.

"I don't know. I don't see them." But he knew they would sooner or later. He jerked his gaze away from the rearview mirror to assess her. "Are you all right?"

Large, dark eyes contrasted sharply with her shock-paled face. "Who the hell was that, Jack? Why are they shooting at us?"

Residual fear shuddered through him at the sight of blood on her face. He would never forget the instant when he thought she'd been shot. Dear God, he would never forgive himself if something happened to her because of him. She was too good to die a senseless, violent death. He hated it that he'd involved her, hated it even more that she was in danger because of him. Because he hadn't had the strength to send her away when he should have.

Shoving the thoughts aside for now, Jack glanced over at her. "I'd lay odds those goons were sent by Duke. I don't have to tell you what he's capable of."

He wanted to reach out and touch her, but knew that would only make things worse. If he wanted to keep her safe, he had to stay focused.

"Why would Duke's men be shooting at us?"

"That's what I've been trying to tell you, Landis. He knows I've talked to people who can finger him. Even if I'm not successful, he knows I'm going to at the very least raise some questions. He's got cops and judges on his payroll. He knows I know his little secret, and he wants me out of the picture." Jack thought about Duke knowing about Landis and grimaced, his stomach turning nauseous. "Now he knows about you, too, Landis. That puts a whole new spin on this mess."

She turned in the seat to face him. Only she didn't look scared. She looked fierce and determined as hell. "I don't like getting shot at."

"Yeah, well, I don't like it much, either."

"We can't let him get away with this."

"Unless you've got an M-16 in your sock, we don't have much choice at the moment."

"The night you came to my cabin, you said you could offer up Duke. I want to take you up on that. I want him."

"That offer no longer stands."

"I want in on this," she said. "Don't try to lock me out."

Jack checked the review mirror, then exited the highway and headed toward the suburb where Ian McAllister lived. "I'm taking you to Ian's. You'll be safe there."

"I don't want to go to Ian's."

Jack didn't respond.

"Ian hates you. He'll call in his cop buddies before you even get through the front door. For God's sake, he thinks you killed Evan."

Jack checked the mirror again, then negotiated a turn. "I'll drop you curbside—"

"Take me back to my cabin."

"Stay away from your cabin!" he shouted. "After what just happened, it's not safe."

"Your dropping me at Ian's isn't going to keep me from what I need to do to make this right."

"For God's sake, you're stubborn." Swearing, he rapped his fist against the steering wheel. "I never should have come to you."

"You didn't have anywhere else to go. You knew I was in a position to help you. Jack, I can still help you."

"Don't fight me on this, Red." He glanced over at her, looked into her pretty green eyes and tried not to think about how hard it was going to be to walk away from her. "One day, you'll thank me."

"I'll hate you if you shut me out of this."

Jack said nothing.

"I'm not going to sit on the sidelines and let Cyrus Duke get away with murder. Has it even crossed your mind that maybe I want to nail Duke as badly as you? You're not the only one who's got a stake in this. For God's sake, he murdered my brother!"

"I'll take care of Duke." He wasn't sure how he was going to do it, but he was going to stop the bastard. There was no way in hell Jack could leave the country and give an animal like Duke a chance to get his hands on Landis.

She reached out as if suddenly realizing the turn his thoughts had taken. "Jack, please don't do anything crazy."

He winced when her fingers closed around his forearm. The unexpected touch went through him like a hot needle. Longing and regret swept through him with a fierceness that left him raw and shaking inside. He risked a look at her, knew too late it was a mistake. A fierce protectiveness rose up inside him. And he swore that no matter how badly he wanted her, he wouldn't let her get sucked into this mess any more than she already was.

"Jack, my God, you're shaking," she whispered.

He looked away, concentrated on the road, on the rearview mirror. "You've already aided and abetted, Landis. How many more charges do you want levied against you?"

She looked down at her hands, then back at him. "There are extenuating circumstances—"

"That won't save you from being disbarred. If you don't walk away right now, you can forget about ever practicing law again. Hell, you might even do hard time."

"I don't believe that."

"Oh, for chrissake! Your Jeep is at Chandler's cabin. He's dead. They think I killed him. It's common knowledge you and I have a history. Do you actually believe the police don't know we're together? Come on!"

Pressing her hand against her stomach, she looked away. Jack hated seeing her go pale, hated even more knowing he was the reason for it. But he couldn't let this go on. As desperately as he needed her help, as badly as he wanted to be with her, he couldn't let her ruin her life.

"What about you?" she asked after a moment. "Somewhere mixed in with all that honor and gallantry is a man's life. A man who's innocent and doesn't have anyone to help him."

That she would fight so fiercely to help him when he'd done everything in his power to drive her away moved him a hell of a lot more than he wanted it to. But then Landis had never been one to back down from a fight. That was one of the things he'd always loved about her. She fought for what she believed in until the end.

That was little consolation knowing this was a battle neither of them would win.

He took the backstreets to the subdivision where Ian lived, then drove around the block twice. When he was certain no one had followed him, he parked down the street from the tidy Spanish-style house and shut down the engine. When he ran out of things to do, he turned in his seat to face her.

She returned his gaze with stoic silence. Her eyes were huge within the pale frame of her face. He hated seeing the pain etched into her every feature, hated even more knowing he was responsible for putting it there. But he knew what the alternative held and decided he would rather hurt her now than let her get any more involved—or risk her being marked by Duke.

"Tell Ian everything," he began. "Tell him what I told you about Duke. About Evan. Tell him Duke tried to kill you this morning. Tell him you need police protection."

"I will, but I'm not sure he'll believe me. He's going to think I'm too...involved to see things clearly. I mean, because of our history."

"You have to convince him, Landis. This has gone beyond my trying to prove my innocence. I never thought Duke would go after you." He felt the words like barbed wire twisting inside him. "Ian might hate me, but he's your brother. He's a cop. He'll keep you safe."

"What are you going to do?" she asked.

"I think it's best that I don't tell you that."

She glanced out the window, blinking rapidly. "I'm not giving up on your case. You can run all you want. But I'm not going to give up."

He knew it was foolish, but hope jumped through him at the words. But it was tempered by the knowledge that every shred of hope he'd had in the past year had been taken away from him. He figured they both knew there wasn't a whole lot she could do to help.

Clamping his jaws against the rise of emotion in his chest, he forced a smile. "No regrets, okay?"

She reached for the door handle. "This isn't over."

He didn't intend to reach for her. But one moment her hand was on the handle. The next he was pulling her across the seat and into his arms. Tears shimmered in her eyes when her gaze met his. Her mouth was slightly open and wet, but she didn't fight him. He cupped her face, taken aback by her loveliness, and put the picture she made to memory, knowing that soon it would be all he had.

"One more thing," he said and lowered his mouth to hers. Pleasure crashed through him on contact. He told himself it was just a goodbye kiss, but knew that was a lie. His brain ordered him to pull back and regroup, but the command never made it to his body. He wanted to say something, but there were no more words left inside him. Just an edgy need that he could no longer ignore, and the knowledge that he was no longer in control.

Wrapping his arms around her, he deepened the kiss, testing her, tasting her, letting his mouth linger over hers. The sweetness of her kiss devastated him. The taste of her tears shattered the last of his resolve. He deepened the kiss, vaguely aware of her hands on his shoulders, her scent surrounded him like a drugging fragrance. He breathed in deeply, let it intoxicate him.

A moment later he broke the kiss and eased her to arm's length. He waited for his vision to clear, then slid back behind the wheel. "I'll wait here until you get inside."

The hurt in her eyes cut him. Jack looked away, hating it that he couldn't meet her gaze. He heard the door open. The truck rocked gently as she stepped out. He jolted when the door slammed. He felt her departure like a stake through his heart.

As he watched her walk to the front door, he felt his priorities shifting, changing. No longer was his goal merely to clear his name. His number one priority now was to protect Landis from Cyrus Duke. Prison. South America. Escape. None of those things seemed as important now that she was in danger.

And with that knowledge came the dark realization that he didn't have anything to lose.

Landis should have known her younger brother would be angry with her. Still, she hadn't expected such an icy reception when she'd shown up at his front door shaking and bleeding and trying like hell not to fall apart. Once he'd made certain she wasn't seriously injured, he'd transformed from worried brother to hardnosed cop and started asking questions. Questions Landis had absolutely no desire to answer.

"You've been with him, haven't you?" Even out of uniform, he looked like a cop. Standing in the kitchen doorway, he glared at her with eyes that were as hard and cold as ice. "Jesus, Landy, I can't believe you would do something so stupid."

Heart pounding, she paced the length of the living room, barely noticing the Christmas tree or the silver-and-blue garland strung along the mantle of the hearth. Her hands were shaking so badly she could barely hold the cup of coffee he'd offered between the bursts of questions and hard, concerned looks. Her nerves wouldn't stop jumping. She was exhausted, yet she couldn't sit still. She couldn't think straight. Every time she tried, all she could think of was Jack.

She should be thankful he hadn't allowed her to make a mess of her life. That he'd brought her here where she was safe and among family. That he was finally out of her life for good. The truth of the matter was she'd never felt more despondent in her life.

"Are you going to talk to me?" Ian asked.

"I haven't decided yet."

He shook his head as if in exasperation. "You look like you've been to hell and back."

She stopped pacing and looked at him. She *felt* as if she'd been to hell and back. Now, she was stuck in purgatory because she knew a man she cared for deeply was innocent of a heinous crime. She knew he was either going to flee the country or get himself killed. The fear and frustration were eating her alive because there wasn't a damn thing she could do about it.

Ian crossed to her, took her by the shoulders and guided her to the sofa. "Jesus, Landis, you're shaking. Sit down before you fall down."

She sank onto the sofa. He eased the cup from her hands and set it on the coffee table. "I'm going to get the first aid kit for that cut on your face. You sit here and pull yourself together. Then I'm going to ask you some questions, and I damn well want some answers." He disappeared into the hall.

Dreading the conversation ahead, Landis picked up the cup and drank some of the coffee, not caring that the caffeine had her nerves snapping like frayed wires. She didn't want to lie to Ian. He didn't deserve lies. But Landis knew how much he hated Jack. She didn't think there was much of a chance that she would be able to convince Ian he was innocent.

"What happened to your face?"

Landis looked up to see him walking toward her with a first aid kit in hand. She was pondering how to best explain to her brother that she'd been shot at when he turned to her, put his forefinger beneath her chin and angled her face toward him, his lips peeling back in a snarl as he cleaned and bandaged her cut. "Did that son of a bitch do this to you?"

"Of course not! Jack wouldn't—"

"I can't believe you're defending him! I can't believe you let him get to you. Landy, for God's sake, he could have killed you. Look what he did to Evan!"

"Ian, listen to me. Jack didn't hurt me. Someone took a shot at me when I leaving Chandler's cabin."

"The police know you've been with LaCroix. They found your Jeep at Chandler's place. They're going to have a hell of a lot of questions for you."

A quiver of fear went through her. A terrible sense of helplessness overwhelmed her when she realized the situation was spiraling out of control. "Ian, I need for you to calm down and listen to me."

Releasing her, he leaned back against the sofa and

scrubbed a hand over his face. "You've put me in a hell of a position."

"I haven't told you anything, Ian. You're assuming—"

"You're here, and I haven't called the detective who's running the case. I know you're aiding and abetting—not to mention sleeping with—a convicted murderer!"

"I'm not—"

"Damn it, Landy, I can't believe you threw it all away for him."

"Jack didn't do it, Ian. He's innocent. The gun. The money. All of it."

"Oh, for crying out loud! You don't really believe that, do you?"

"Someone tried to kill us this morning, Ian. The bullet that barely missed me wasn't my imagination."

"So LaCroix has some enemies. Maybe Duke thinks he's going to turn over on him. He's dangerous, Landy, and you need to stay away from him. Am I getting through to you?"

"Jack saved my life this morning!"

That stopped him, but only for an instant. "You don't know him as well as you think you do. Evan trusted him and look what happened. I'm warning you. Stay the hell away from him."

"If you won't help me, then I'll find someone who will. Or I'll do it myself."

"Do *what?*"

"Help him clear his name."

He threw up his hands and looked to the heavens as if in utter exasperation. "He's brainwashed you."

"He has not!"

Lowering his head, he pinched the bridge of his nose, then shot her a hard look. "Where is he, Landy?"

Landis stared back. "I don't know."

"I'm asking you as a cop, not your brother. You'd better level with me."

"I told you. I don't know."

He stared at her as if incredulous. "I can't believe you would lie to me about this."

"That's the truth."

"Yeah, well, here's a news flash for you. I'm not going to let you throw away your life." Face set with anger, Ian rose from the sofa and strode to the kitchen.

Heart pounding with sudden uneasiness, Landis followed him as far as the doorway, watched as he picked up the phone and punched in numbers. "Who are you calling?" she asked.

"A lawyer. For you. Then the three of us are going to drive down to the police department and you're going to tell the cops everything you know about LaCroix. Hopefully, your cooperation will salvage what's left of your career and keep you out of jail."

"Damn it, Ian—"

"You can thank me later."

She was about to say more, but someone must have come on the line because Ian turned his back to her and began to speak. She heard him ask for Jason Bellamy, a well-known defense attorney, and her insides turned to jelly. God, he was serious about this. He was going to turn her in.

Landis listened, shaking inside, hurt to her core that her brother would do this to her. That he would discount everything she'd said. That he would betray her.

You don't know him as well as you think you do.

Ian's words rang uncomfortably in her ears. She thought of Jack, of what he was trying to do single-handedly and against insurmountable odds and suddenly knew she couldn't let Ian do this to her. She loved her brother, but he was wrong about Jack. She was willing to bet her life on it.

Spotting the keys to Ian's SUV on the coffee table in the

living room, she crossed to it and looked down at them. Over her shoulder, she could hear Ian on the phone, arranging the time and place for them to consult with the attorney. *I'm sorry, Ian,* she thought and picked up the keys, gripping them tightly to keep them from jingling.

Never taking her eyes from him, she backed toward the door, opened it, and slipped quietly out.

Chapter 10

Landis parked Ian's SUV in the rear lot of the Utah County courthouse and sat inside for ten minutes trying to muster the courage to go inside. The courthouse was usually deserted on Sunday, but if she was wanted for questioning about Jack, she didn't want to run into a coworker—or a cop.

She tried not to feel guilty about what she'd done to her brother. He was going to be furious with her—and rightfully so if she wanted to be honest about it. But there hadn't been another way; he certainly hadn't left her an alternative. She only hoped he didn't come after her—or, God forbid, turn her in to the police.

After leaving his house twenty minutes earlier, her first instinct had been to return to her cabin. But with Cyrus Duke's goons taking shots at her, she didn't want to risk it. For the same reason, she couldn't go to her mother's house in Ogden. The last thing she wanted to do was endanger her family. And so she'd driven to her office in

Provo. A place that had always been her refuge. Her salvation.

The only place she felt safe at the moment.

All she needed was a place where she could sort through everything that had happened, look at all the information she had on hand and decide what to do next. She wanted to have another look at Jack's case—from a lawyer's perspective, not a woman in two miles over her head and sinking deeper with every moment she spent with him. She had a copy of the transcript from his trial. She could go over it again, look for things she'd missed. She could poke around on the Internet and see if she could drum up anything useful. She also had the home phone number for one of the junior attorneys who'd worked with Aaron Chandler. He was more of an acquaintance than friend, but she could give him a call and try to garner some information about Jack's case. Hopefully, it wasn't common knowledge that she and Jack had been together.

Using her access card, Landis entered through the employee entrance at the rear of the courthouse. She barely noticed the beauty of the old building as she headed at a brisk clip toward the bank of elevators off the lobby. Her heart beat out a steady rhythm as she rode to the second level. The doors slid open, and she peeked into the dimly lit hall. Finding it deserted, she jogged to her office a few doors down, the heels of her boots clicking smartly against the marble floor.

She used her key to unlock her door and went directly to her computer. As the machine booted, she absently paged through the mail in her inbox. She was pulling up her contact information on her computer when she came to the nondescript brown envelope at the bottom of the stack. It caught her attention because there was nothing on it except her name. No return address. No postage. It hadn't been sent via interoffice mail.

Curious, she opened it, found herself looking at a computer disk. She was about to set it aside, when the label caught her eye: Jack LaCroix. Puzzled, she looked inside the envelope for a note, but found nothing.

Turning back to her computer, she shoved the disk into the drive, then double clicked on the single file. The drive whirred. Holding her breath, she watched as her word processing software opened a single-page document.

Dear Landy,

I've probably already met an untimely demise, probably a violent one, but don't grieve too much. I knew what I was getting into. Of course, I never meant for things to go this far. I never meant to hurt you or mom or Ian. Lord knows I never meant to hurt Casey or the kids. Believe me when I tell you I'm sorry.

Now that I've got that out of the way, I suppose you're waiting for the really tough stuff. Unfortunately, I've got plenty. You probably know by now that I was on Cyrus Duke's payroll. Biggest mistake I ever made, but you know what they say about hindsight. Landy, I'm not the only cop on Duke's payroll. In the last two years Jack LaCroix has accepted over $200,000. In return, he allowed Duke's drug cartel to operate unencumbered by the Salt Lake City P.D. I wanted to come clean, but Jack was dead set against it. I know you're crazy about him, sis, but he's bad news. Stay away from him. He's dangerous.

I left this disk with the last person I trust. If something happens to me, you're supposed to get it. I hope you get it in time. Being the terrific prosecutor you are, I know you'll do the right thing and take this to the D.A. no matter how painful.

In closing, watch your back. I love you always.

Evan

The words tumbled over her like an avalanche, cold and smothering and devastating. By the time she read the last sentence she was fighting tears. Of disbelief. Of frustration. Of pain. She looked for a date, realized it had been written two days before Evan was murdered.

Shaken, she stood abruptly and stared down at the monitor. Denial reared up inside her followed by a sharp sense of betrayal that cut her to the quick. *"No,"* she said, rapping her fist against her desk.

Heart thrumming steadily against her breast, she sank into the chair and lowered her face to her hands. She felt sick. As if a giant hand had reached into her and was twisting her heart into knots. But as much as she wanted to just sit there and cry, she knew it wouldn't help. She'd learned a long time ago that tears never helped anything.

She thought of Evan and felt the knife of betrayal cut a little more deeply. *I wanted to come clean, but Jack was dead set against it.* It hurt that her brother had betrayed her, that he'd betrayed the system he'd sworn to uphold and followed the tainted legacy of their father. But it hurt even more to think that Jack might have done the very same thing. That he'd lied to her, used her. That she'd been gullible enough to put everything on the line for him.

"Oh, God, Jack," she whispered. The pain was like a torrent inside her, flowing swift and deep. A river flooding its banks, threatening to drown her.

She didn't want to believe Jack was somehow involved with Duke. But like before, the evidence was in stark black and white and damning as hell.

Landis knew the disk could be a fake. Anyone could have written it and brought it to the courthouse. With her name written boldly on the envelope, the mailroom would have eventually delivered it to her even if it hadn't come from the post office.

But from whom had the disk come? What would they

have to gain by sending it to her? Why not the attorney who'd prosecuted the case? And why had they waited until now?

No matter what the answer to the questions, the fact remained that she was going to have to deal with it. At some point she would have to take it to the police, maybe even to the D.A., if only to have it disproved.

Or added into evidence.

The thought filled her with a dread so cold, she felt frozen inside.

But even as she pondered her options, a dark new suspicion crept into the backwaters of her mind. Something about the disk didn't feel right, like a piece of puzzle that wouldn't quite fit into the mold. Forcing her lawyer's mind into place, she tried to put the letter's appearance into legal terms. The timing of it disturbed her more than anything. Evan had been dead for more than a year. Why would someone wait until now to bring it to her? Why would Evan use a disk instead of a handwritten letter? Was it possible the disk was part of the setup Jack had been referring to? If so, who was responsible? Cyrus Duke?

The questions pounded at her relentlessly, but she didn't have an answer for any of them. If Jack were guilty and had $200,000 stashed in a bank account somewhere, why was he in Salt Lake City? Why were Duke's thugs trying to kill him? Why was Jack a threat?

On an emotional level, even faced with the damning statement on the disk, Landis couldn't believe he was a cold-blooded murderer. Not the man who'd used his own body as a shield when the security officer had shot at them at Chandler's office. Not the man who'd saved her life when Duke's thugs had stormed the cabin. Not the man who kissed her like there was no tomorrow.

She stared at the monitor where the ugly words taunted her. For a crazy moment she considered deleting the file.

Simultaneously, a jab of shame cut her, reminding her of the clear dividing line between right and wrong. It was a line she swore she would never cross. Even knowing how damaging the disk would be to her personally, to her family, to Evan's memory—and to Jack—Landis knew she wouldn't be able to live with herself knowing she'd destroyed possible evidence.

She thought about her father and shuddered at the situation she now found herself in. As a child, she'd believed in Reece McAllister; she'd given him a child's unconditional love and trust, only to have him betray her in the worst way a child could be betrayed. That she'd laid everything on the line for Jack—a man who seemed every bit as ambiguous as her father—shook her badly.

Shoving the troubling thoughts to the back of her mind, she set her fingers against her temples and rubbed where the headache had broken through. She was reaching for the phone when the door to her office swung open. Adrenaline jolted her as she imagined a slew of police officers bursting in to arrest her.

Her heart stopped dead in her chest when Jack appeared in her doorway.

Jack knew the instant he looked into her eyes that something had changed since he'd last seen her. In his years as a cop he'd seen shock enough times to know she was perilously close to it. The bandage on her cheek stood out against a complexion that was several shades too pale. Her clothes were in disarray. She looked dead on her feet. Worse, she looked on the verge of bolting.

"How did you get in?" she asked.

"I caught the paralegal on the second floor coming in to do some transcription." Looking over his shoulder, he stepped into her office and closed the door behind him. "Why the hell aren't you with Ian?"

She contemplated him, a doe about to be mowed down by a speeding eighteen wheeler. "How did you know I was here?"

"Process of elimination." He cursed. "I had a feeling you wouldn't stay put."

"Ian knows we've been together."

He grimaced. "I'm sure he's not happy about it."

"He thinks you're a killer. He thinks I'm insane."

The calm in her voice belied everything he saw. Her hand rested on the desk in front of her, but he could see her fingers trembling.

"I'm not crazy," she said.

"I know." Unable to stop himself, he started toward her. Uneasiness rippled through him when she tensed. The anxiety inside him darkened, like a storm cloud filled with violent winds and drenching rains.

She raised her hand, as if to stop him. "Don't come any closer."

He halted, but it cost him. The need to touch her was like a living thing inside him. As vital as the next beat of his heart. He was so close to her he could smell the clean scent of her hair, the soft scent of her flesh. "I want to know why you're pale and shaking and staring at me as if you just realized I'm Jack the Ripper," he said.

"The situation is out of control, Jack. The police want to talk to me about you. I'm pretty sure Ian has already talked to them. He's already been in contact with a defense attorney for me. I've put him in a terribly compromising position—"

"And he's covering his ass."

"He cares about me."

"If he cared about you he wouldn't have let you out of his sight."

"I didn't give him much choice."

He frowned at her, his eyes narrowing. "What did you do? Steal his SUV?"

"Something like that."

He scrubbed a hand over his jaw. "Jesus, Landis…"

"Why are you here?"

"Because I figured you wouldn't stay with Ian if he started giving you flack about me." His eyes burned into hers. "Because the more I thought about it, the more certain I became that if Duke gets the chance he's going to come after you."

"Duke doesn't want me. He doesn't even know who I am."

"He knows exactly who you are. And he knows you're the weakest link to me."

Across the desk from him, Landis shivered. "God, I hate this."

"I'm not going to let him hurt you."

"You're not going to have a say in the matter if you're in prison." Her eyes flicked to the computer screen, then back to him. "I think you need to see this."

Something in her tone made his nerves go taut. Rounding the desk, he turned to the computer, read quickly. Dread twisted inside him with such force that he felt dizzy. "Where did you get this?"

"It was delivered here to my office anonymously, sometime in the last two days."

"That's convenient as hell." Jack studied her, hating the question he saw in her eyes, hated even more the uncertainty he saw in her expression. "In case there's any question in your mind, Evan didn't write that," he snapped.

She stared at him for a long while, her gaze level and direct. "I figured that out all by myself."

The words struck Jack so hard for a moment he couldn't speak. He stared at her, felt something inside him shift and freefall. He wasn't an emotional man, but hearing those words, knowing she believed in him after everything that had happened undid him as nothing else could have.

On an oath, he set his hands against the desk, leaned and closed his eyes against emotions dangerously close to the surface. He knew Landis was watching him, knew she was wondering what the hell was the matter with him. But for the first time in too many years to count, he was overcome.

"Jack?" She reached out, set her hand against his cheek. Her palm was incredibly soft against his face.

He drew a breath, let it out slowly, felt the emotions clenching his chest ease. When he raised his gaze to hers, her eyes were soft and compassionate.

"I didn't want to believe it about Evan, either," he said quietly. "But there's no other explanation."

He laid his hand against hers, then turned his head slightly and kissed her palm. There were a hundred things that needed to be said. Issues that needed to be addressed. Wounds that needed to be healed. But Jack knew now wasn't the time for any of those things. If he wanted to clear his name before the world came crashing down around them, he was going to have to keep pushing, keep moving and pray to God he and Landis lived long enough to deal with everything that stood between them.

"Any idea how this disk was delivered to you?" he asked after a moment.

"There's no return address." She handed him the envelope. "It was probably dropped off at the courthouse."

"Or delivered by someone who has access to the courthouse," he said. "Security is relatively tight here. Not just anyone could waltz in and drop this in the mailroom."

He saw the wheels begin to spin in her mind. "You think it was a cop?" she asked. "An officer of the court? Who?"

"Someone who wants me out the picture and thinks they can use you to help them."

"I'm going to be honest with you, Jack. The disk is

damning. You and I know Evan didn't write it, but it will still need to be disproved officially. We're going to have to deal with it."

"Yeah, well, one disaster at a time, Red. Okay?"

"I don't know what to do next," she whispered.

Jack heard the fear and uncertainty in her voice. He felt the same two emotions coiling inside him. But he knew what they had to do next. What *he* had to do. Something he'd hoped he wouldn't have to resort to, but now realized it was his last hope. A last hope that was dangerous as hell and probably wouldn't garner him anything but a bullet for his trouble. That was the reason he couldn't tell Landis, why he couldn't take her with him. That presented another problem he wasn't sure how to resolve. He didn't know how to keep Landis safe. He couldn't leave her here. He couldn't take her back to Ian's. It wasn't safe for her to go back to her cabin. He didn't want to endanger her mother by taking her there.

Turning to the window, he looked out at the parking lot beyond and wondered how much time he had before the police caught up with him. He knew the moment was inevitable, sensed the sand pouring through the timer at an alarming speed.

He turned to Landis. "I'm going check you into a hotel."

"You mean us, don't you?"

He nodded, telling himself lying to her now was the only way to play this. "We'll be safe for a while. Maybe we can come up with a plan." And once he was gone, he'd already decided to contact Ian himself and explain to him that Landis was in danger. Hopefully, her younger brother would be able to put his hatred for Jack aside long enough to do the right thing and keep his sister safe.

"Give me a dollar," she said.

He laughed, but it was a hard, rough sound. "Not a chance."

She crossed to him, put her hand on his arm. "If you retain me now, it will protect both of us from possible problems down the road."

"You mean if we get busted and get a starring role in the trial of the century? No thanks."

"I'm getting pretty tired of you fighting me every step of the way." Never taking her eyes from his, she leaned close and slid her hand into the pocket of his jeans.

Jack met her gaze unflinchingly, keenly aware of her fumbling inside his pocket for the money Chandler had given him. She was so close he could smell the clean scent of her hair. See the sprinkling of freckles on her nose. The sheen of moisture on her full mouth. He wondered what it would be like to lean forward and touch his mouth to hers. He wondered if she would kiss him back.

He endured the contact with stoic silence, aware that his body was reacting, that he wanted her, that there wasn't a damn thing he could do about either of those things.

Quickly, she fished out a roll of bills, pulled out a five and stuffed the rest back in his pocket. "You've now retained me as your legal counsel. As your lawyer, I'm protected by client-attorney confidentiality."

"I know the law," he growled. "If you think that's going to protect you from an aiding and abetting charge, you've got another thing coming."

"I know our criminal justice system isn't perfect. But I still believe in it. I believe it is fair."

"Unless someone tips her scales in the wrong direction."

"We're the good guys. That's got to mean something or that law degree hanging on the wall is useless. Jack, I need for it to mean something."

"Sometimes the good guys lose," he said.

"Not this time."

Staring into the emerald depths of her gaze, he wanted badly to believe her. But Jack knew firsthand just how fickle Lady Justice could be. He knew she could be a ruthless bitch with a cold heart and a twisted sense of fairness. He'd been on the receiving end of that fickleness too many times in the past year to trust her now.

He only hoped that when all was said and done, Landis received a hell of a lot more mercy than had been shown to him.

Landis felt almost human after a hot shower and Jack's promise of Chinese takeout. Wrapping herself in the hotel's complimentary robe, she stepped out of the tub and looked in the mirror, cringing at the sight of her pale complexion and the dark smudges of fatigue beneath her eyes.

But even more glaring than the physical traces left on her body was the knowledge that she was no longer the same person on the inside. She'd ceased to be the idealistic, ambitious young prosecutor she'd been before Jack had shown up at her cabin. Her life had been forever changed, and she would never again look at the world in quite the same light.

The criminal justice system upon which she'd based her career had failed her. She now stood squarely on the wrong side of the law. Like her brother. Like her father before her. The irony of that burned.

To make an already catastrophic situation infinitely worse, she could no longer deny her feelings for Jack. Feelings that were so tangled she feared she might never sort through them. Caring for Jack was like a wild ride on a roller coaster, the kind with hairpin curves and dangerous speeds and a very rickety track. And yet every time she looked into his eyes and saw the man beneath the tough facade—the man who had been hurt and betrayed—she felt herself sliding down a very slippery slope.

Too exhausted to ponder the questions burgeoning inside her, she wrapped her hair in a towel and stepped out of the bathroom. At the table, Jack unpacked their take-out food and soft drinks. In spite of the physical and emotional strain of the past two days, he looked calm and in control and undeniably handsome in his flannel shirt and snug-fitting jeans. His hands were steady as he arranged plastic utensils.

Glancing in her direction, he smiled. "Nothing fancy, but it's hot. I hope you still like egg rolls and fried rice."

She didn't miss the concern in his eyes, and hoped she didn't look as jittery as she felt. "Hot mustard?"

"You bet."

Landis approached the table and took the chair across from him, aware that his eyes followed her every move. She wanted to talk to him, about the case, about what was going on between them, but didn't have the slightest clue where to begin. She had absolutely no idea what the next twenty-four hours would bring. She didn't even know if they would be alive that long. Cyrus Duke had made it abundantly clear that he wanted them dead. The manhunt would undoubtedly intensify in the coming hours....

"You're pale as a sheet, Landis. You need to eat." Jack shoved a plate heaped with food toward her.

"Yeah, well, flying bullets and cryptic messages from the dead wreak havoc on a girl's appetite." She wasn't hungry, but because it had been nearly twenty-four hours since she'd taken in any food, she reached for her fork.

"What do we do now?" she asked.

"I'm going after Duke."

She choked out a laugh of disbelief, but she had the terrible suspicion he wasn't kidding. "Maybe we could just march up to Duke's front door. When he comes out, you hold him while I punch him. We'll coerce a confession out of him, and then hightail it out of there before his armed bodyguards blow us to pieces."

His silence and deadpan expression raised the hairs at the back of her neck. ''Jack, exactly how do you plan on going after Duke? He wants you dead. He's brutal and wealthy and powerful as hell. He lives in a fortress and surrounds himself with bodyguards and corrupt politicians—''

''And corrupt cops,'' he interjected.

''You're not even armed.''

''Ah, Counselor, where's that pit bull mindset I used to know and love?''

Setting her fork down, she glared at him, aware that her temper was heating. ''Maybe I'm just smart enough to know when I'm outmanned and outgunned.''

''Outmanned and outgunned, maybe. But not outsmarted.'' One side of his mouth curved. ''Do you know who Pete Boyle is?''

''The computer hacker? Of course I do. Everyone knows—'' She stopped. ''Why are we talking about Pete Boyle?''

''Because he's part of this.''

''You could have mentioned that sooner.''

Jack rolled his shoulder, and Landis got the distinct impression that he hadn't told her about Pete Boyle for a specific reason. She wondered what it was. ''I'm all ears,'' she said.

''Two years ago Pete Boyle was convicted of writing corporate sabotage and sentenced to three years. He and I had the breakfast and lunch shift for a couple of months. Hell of a guy for a crook. Makes a mean parsnip and carrot soup.'' Jack shrugged. ''But Pete didn't adjust to prison life very well. He's scrawny. Wears glasses. Didn't know how to protect himself from the thugs, you know?''

''I'm getting the picture.''

He broke an egg roll in half. ''In any case, I helped him

out of a couple of tight spots. Saved his ass once or twice. Kept the gangs off him.''

''So where are you going with this?''

''Pete liked to talk, Landis. He's just a kid. Not even twenty-two years old. Throwing names around was his only power. He was always hoping it would be enough to keep the predators off him.'' His eyes glittered when he looked at her. ''I protected him, but I didn't do it for free. And he told me all kinds of things about Cyrus Duke.''

Her pulse kicked as the repercussions of what he was saying registered in her brain. ''What things?''

''When I was a cop, it was common knowledge that Duke is paranoid with sociopathic tendencies. I think one of the reasons we could never nail him for anything boiled down to the fact that he's incredibly cautious in every aspect of his business. He pays top dollar for security and any other toys that help keep him on top of the game.''

''Tell me something I don't already know,'' she said dryly.

''So when it came time for Duke to get a new computer system, he didn't trust the job to just anyone. No way. Only the best for Cyrus Duke. So he hires Pete Boyle, hacker extraordinaire.''

Her heart pinged against her ribs. ''Bingo.''

Jack's mouth curved. ''Pete spent a month setting up a state-of-the-art computer network for Duke, about a month before his conviction. He linked Duke's home to his downtown office to his restaurant. He installed e-mail, high-speed Internet access, Palm top connection, wireless for his notebook, the whole nine yards. No expense was spared.''

''Jack, do you know what's on the network?''

''Some of it. For example, I know his tax and financial data are on there. Payroll for his restaurant.''

''Anything we can use?''

''I thought we might be able to do something with the

list of government officials who are close personal friends.''

Landis's heart began to pound in earnest. ''Oh my God.''

Jack's eyes sparked like black diamonds as he regarded her. ''Pete gave me passwords and security codes. At the time, it was a personal security thing for him. I mean, he was scared spitless that Duke would murder him after he did all that work, so he walked away with a little insurance policy.''

''Master key login ID and password.'' Landis had heard the term while reading about a case involving a hacker in another state. ''It's where a master login ID and password overrides any other password programmed in to the operating system.''

''Not bad for a lawyer.''

''Where are they? Do you have them written down? What?''

He tapped his temple. ''I have them in a very safe place.''

''This could be the break we've been praying for.'' For the first time in a long time, hope burgeoned in her chest. ''Why didn't you mention this sooner?''

Without answering, Jack went to the door and engaged the security lock. Landis waited, excited and impatient. When he didn't answer, she tried again. ''So? What do we do now?''

''We wait.''

''*Wait?*'' That wasn't what she'd wanted to hear. ''Why would we wait when, after all this time, we finally know his weak point?''

''I know patience has never been one of your virtues, Red.'' He turned toward her. ''But for my plan to work, I have to wait until after dark.''

She stared at him, an edgy anticipation building inside

her. "You're not suggesting we break into Duke's mansion, are you?"

He cut her a dark look. "I'm not suggesting we do anything."

"Jack, that's insane. Suicidal—"

"You got a better idea?"

"Maybe we could play Russian Roulette out on the Interstate, for God's sake! Our chances of surviving might be a little better."

He leaned back in the chair, stretched his long legs in front of him and contemplated her in the most unnerving way. She endured his scrutiny in stoic silence, but she sensed the shift in his mood, felt the heady zing of nerves that followed. And for the first time since they'd arrived, she realized just how small the hotel room was.

"In any case," he said, "it looks like we have a couple of hours on our hands. Any idea how we might spend them?"

Trying hard not to look as rattled as she felt, praying he didn't notice that her legs were shaking, Landis rose and began stowing their used plates back into the bag with ridiculous neatness. "I thought we could discuss exactly how you plan to get us in and out of Duke's mansion without our getting killed."

"Or maybe we could use this time to clear the air," he said quietly. "There are some things I'd like to get off my chest, Landis. Some things I don't want to go unsaid."

"Jack—"

"Damn it, Landis, if you've got the guts to break into Cyrus Duke's mansion, why the hell don't you have the guts to talk about us?"

Chapter 11

Jack might have smiled if the situation hadn't been so serious. He found it ironic—and so very like Landis—that the thought of breaking into a drug kingpin's mansion didn't scare her half as much as talking about what had happened between them one year ago, what was happening between them now. But he'd known how she would react. He'd been counting on it, in fact.

As much as he hated manipulating her, he knew it was the only way to keep her from making one demand he would not allow. He had no intention of letting her anywhere near Cyrus Duke or his mansion.

"This might be our last chance to clear the air," he said after a moment. "I think it's time we did."

He didn't miss the flash of panic in her eyes as she took the chair across from him. He'd seen that panicky look before—the day she'd walked out of his cell for the last time—and it gave him a bad feeling in the pit of his stomach.

"This isn't a good time to talk about...us," she said with outward calm. "The last couple of days have been... intense. Emotions are high. I, for one, am not thinking straight."

"You don't have to be thinking straight to listen." He could see the pulse point above the little mole on her throat quivering like a frightened bird. She might have everyone else fooled with that detached-lawyer facade, but he knew the woman hidden beneath the reserved exterior was shaking inside. He knew her heart was hammering. Knew if he took her hand her palm would be wet.

It would have been smarter for him to have slipped out the door while she was in the shower. But Jack had never claimed to have command of his better judgment when it came to Landis. She was his greatest weakness, his greatest strength. And at this moment he would sell his soul for just a few more hours with her.

He wasn't even sure what he was going to say. While part of him wanted to breach the subject of their relationship, the more logical side of his brain warned him to steer clear. She'd hurt him badly the day she walked out of his cell. He'd bled for months, a dark bitter flow he hadn't been able to stanch. And while he had no qualms about manipulating her to keep her out of harm's way, he would never again let her get anywhere near his heart.

Jack had learned at a formative age to keep people out, to keep his emotions under lock and key, his heart off limits. As a lonely kid, he'd loved his foster families with the ease and purity of the innocent child he'd been. But every time his new family would send him back to the orphanage, his young heart had been ripped from his body. It hadn't taken him long to equate love with pain, and he quickly learned to steer clear of it. He'd broken a cardinal rule when he fell for Landis. He'd let her get inside him. Into his mind. Into his heart. In the end he'd paid a very steep price.

So why was he setting himself up for the same thing all over again? Even if he beat the odds and cleared his name, he knew things would never work out between them. Not because she'd walked away from him all those months ago, he realized, but because deep down inside he knew she'd do it again.

Jack contemplated her, liking the way she looked wrapped in that robe. Soft and vulnerable and incredibly sexy. The ends of her hair were damp from her shower. Moistness glistened on her skin. But it was evident the last days had taken a heavy toll on her. Exhaustion darkened the delicate flesh beneath her eyes. Even her mouth was pale, giving her a soft look that made him remember what it was like to wake up with her in his arms.

Maybe that's what this was all about, he thought. Hormones. Chemistry. The fundamental need for sex. Maybe he was tied up in little knots over her because he wanted sex. Maybe it was no more complicated than lust. Jack could handle lust. Lust was simple. Easy to identify; even easier to satisfy—if you had a willing partner.

But if lust were the culprit, why was the sensation centered around his heart and not another part of his anatomy that was a hell of a lot less emotionally involved?

"I did a lot of thinking when I was in prison," he began. "A lot of thinking about us. About what happened."

She looked like she'd rather be facing off with F. Lee Bailey than sitting in this hotel room about to discuss their past. "I'm sorry I hurt you."

Because he could still feel the ache—because that terrible, hollow ache had been a part of him every moment of every day he'd been locked away—he didn't discount the apology. Instead, he tried to absorb it, used it to stanch the flow from a wound that had been bleeding him dry for far too long.

"Walking out...leaving you like that..." She looked

down where her hands twisted in her lap, stilled them. "It was one of the hardest things I've ever had to do."

"It took me a long time to realize why you did it. Once I did, I understood, at least."

Her gaze turned wary. "I don't know what you're talking about."

"I know about your father, Landis."

"My father doesn't have anything to do with what happened."

"Your father has everything to do with the reason why you walked out on me," he said.

He saw the walls go up in her eyes and swore he would break them down. "I walked out on you because I thought you killed my brother," she said.

"That was part of it. But there was an underlying reason why you believed that, when deep down inside you knew I wasn't capable of murdering Evan."

"I'm a lawyer. I listened to the evidence."

"You're a woman and you remember all too well what it's like to be betrayed by someone you love."

Her eyes widened. "I don't blame you for hating me," she whispered.

The words exasperated him. The anguish in her eyes twisted his heart. "I don't hate you," he said. "I was angry and outraged, but I never hated you."

"I saw it in your eyes, Jack. That day I told you I wouldn't be back. You were furious. You hated me."

Frustration swept through him when he realized he wasn't getting through to her. He wanted to go to her, put his arms around her, if only to keep her from shaking. But he knew touching her now would only distract him from what he needed to say.

"In all the months we were together," he began, "you never told me your father was sent to prison for accepting bribes. You told me Reece McAllister was a decorated beat cop who was killed in the line of duty.''

An unsteady hand went to the collar of the robe in a protective, unconscious gesture that told him plenty about her frame of mind. She was shutting herself off from him. Physically. Emotionally. Damn it, he wasn't going to let her do it.

''My father is ancient history,'' she said.

''And we all know history has a way of repeating itself.''

''I don't want to talk about this.''

''It took me a while, but I finally put the pieces of the puzzle together, Landis. I know what kind of man Reece McAllister was.'' Jack couldn't keep the contempt from rolling off his tongue with the words. The thought of what the man had done to her sickened him. ''I found out what he did to you, what he did to Evan. Ian. Your mother.''

''I don't want to discuss my father.''

''The prison has a law library, Landis. And I had a lot of time on my hands. I was working on my defense, but you never left my mind. I was able to get the name of Reece's ex-partner.''

''You were out of line.''

''I made some calls, asked him to visit me.'' Jack had spent the better part of a year researching Reece McAllister, piecing the newspaper stories and court transcripts together until he'd had a picture. A very dark picture that explained a hell of a lot more than he'd ever imagined. ''He agreed to talk to me.''

''He had no right.'' Landis stared at him, her expression stricken. ''And you have no right to dredge that up now.''

Jack stepped toward her. ''He told me about the times your father came home drunk, bragging about the money. He told me about the kind of company he kept when he was off the clock. He told me about the time he put your mother in the hospital. The times he put his hands on you.

About the times he used his fists on you and your brothers.''

"This doesn't have anything to do with what happened between you and me.'' Landis tried to turn away.

Jack snagged her arm and forced her to face him. "You were just a little kid. But you saw the scum that came to the back door in the middle of the night, didn't you, Landis?''

"Stop it.''

"You worshipped the ground your father walked on, didn't you? He was your hero. But he walked that thin line, didn't he? A line you've learned to fear because you know a betrayal is right around the corner, don't you?''

Wrenching free, she backed away, looking like a trapped animal. Jack tracked her, refusing to give her a respite. For the first time his temper stirred. He was furious with Reece McAllister for the terrible scars he'd left on this woman. Scars so terrible and deep, she would rather be alone than risk opening her heart to another human being. To a cop she thought walked the same dark line as her father.

"Reece McAllister was a dirty cop, wasn't he, Landis? A dirty cop with a drinking problem and mean streak. He gave you a taste of that mean streak a time or two didn't he?''

"My father is dead. He doesn't matter anymore.''

"He broke your wrist when you were in third grade,'' Jack said bluntly. "Because you got a bad grade in math. The scar on your knee is from the time he pushed you down the stairs for waking him from a nap. But he was still your hero, wasn't he?''

Her eyes darkened, and Jack knew she was remembering. He saw the agony of it in her eyes. A child's unconditional trust torn from an innocent heart.

"He called it discipline,'' Jack continued, "but Reece

McAllister stepped over a line. He took away your childhood. He took away your trust.''

''I don't want to have this conversation.''

Staring into her shimmering eyes, Jack saw the injured girl she'd been. An innocent child desperately seeking her father's love and approval only to find herself facing the kind of pain no child should ever have to bear. A little girl who'd been betrayed in the worst possible way a child could be betrayed.

''You were nine years old when the cops came for him in the middle of the night. When they handcuffed him and took him away. You were eleven when he hung himself in his prison cell.''

Her face had gone sheet white. She stared at him, her eyes stricken, her expression accusing. ''How dare you dig into my past?''

''I needed to understand you, damn it.''

Tears spilled over her lashes and ran unchecked down her pale cheeks. For a moment, she stood vacillating, staring at him as if he'd just pulled the rug out from under her. ''I'm sorry I hurt you,'' she whispered. ''But none of this changes anything.''

''It changes plenty for me.''

''I'm the same person I was before.''

''But at least now I understand.''

Hugging herself as if from a sudden chill, she turned from him and crossed to the opposite side of the room. ''I couldn't control any of the things that happened to me when I was a little girl. It's like I was riding in a car that was barreling out of control and all I could do was hang on and hope the crash didn't kill me. I couldn't control my father or what he did. What he did to my mother and my brothers.''

She turned to him, her expression fierce. ''I swore that when I grew up, no one was ever going to hurt me like that again. I swore I would be in charge of my own destiny. I didn't even realize it at the time, but it boiled down to control. I controlled every aspect of my life. My education. My career. My relationships. Everything.'' She searched his gaze as if looking for something vital, something that eluded her no matter how badly she wanted to find it. ''I could control everything,'' she said, ''except you.''

She crossed to him, her steps halting, her expression uncertain. ''I couldn't control you, Jack. I couldn't control my feelings for you. When I met you, it was as if you were a drug, and I was a junkie and I couldn't get enough. I found myself willing to risk things that were important to me just to be with you. I lost control of my life.''

A fissure of tension went through him when she lifted her hand and touched his face. He endured the contact silently. But his heart raged in his chest, a beast anxious to be released from its cage. He could feel the sexual pull to her, an uncomfortable heaviness in his groin. The heady pound of blood. The clench of tension in his shoulders and neck. The need winding up inside him.

He looked down at her, keenly aware of her hand trembling against his cheek. He hadn't expected her to touch him, and his resolve to do the right thing faltered. He wanted to say something that would snap both of them back to their senses, but his mouth was so dry he didn't trust his voice.

''On the outside, you might walk a thin line, Jack. But on the inside I know where you stand. I know you're nothing like my father. I just don't know where that leaves us.''

''The same place we were before,'' he said roughly. ''On opposite sides of the fence. It has to stay that way.''

But he didn't move away when she stepped close and put her arms around him. His world rocked when her body came gently against his. The contact shocked his system. Vaguely, he was aware of his arms going around her, the softness of her body against his. Her scent titillated his senses, and he closed his eyes against a rush of longing, a hot burst of lust.

"I'm sorry I hurt you," she whispered.

Jack couldn't remember a time when he'd been so overwhelmed with emotion—or felt so wrenchingly vulnerable. When he was a kid and had been lost in the foster home system, he hadn't had any control. Over what had happened to him. Over what he'd felt deep inside. He felt that same lack of control now, and it was scaring the hell out of him. He knew they were tempting fate by getting this close. He might be a risk taker, but putting his heart on the chopping block for a fate that could be cruel was something he had no desire to partake in. If only she didn't feel so damn good against him...

"No matter what happens, I'm going to keep working on your case," she said. "I'm going to get you out of this. I'm going to help you. I'm going to keep digging until I find the evidence that will exonerate you."

Even though the hotel room was chilly, Jack broke a sweat beneath his flannel shirt. This wasn't working out the way he'd intended. Her closeness was getting to him in a way he didn't want to pursue. In a way that would hurt them both if he didn't stop this right now.

"As much as I want to make love to you," he growled, "I think we both know it would be wrong for us to let this go any further."

"Maybe it would be even worse not to see where it leads us."

"For God's sake, Landis, I'm a convicted murderer. I'm on the run. I can't let you ruin your life."

"I'm not sure which of us you're trying to convince." She shifted against him, ran her fingers over his shoulders. "But it's not working."

The intellectual side of his brain told him to pull away.

Before things went too far. But the side of him that was a man—a man who'd been alone for a very long time—longed to touch her, to hear her sigh, taste her mouth, feel his body encased within her heat.

"Landis, where I'm going I can't take you with me...."

His resolve faltered when her mouth brushed against his. For the first time he sensed real danger. Not from some outside threat. But from within himself because he knew if she touched him now he wouldn't stop.

He hated it that he was the one who was falling apart. He'd wanted it to be her. But, God help him, she was standing so close, he could feel the warmth of her quickened breaths on his face, the softness of her breasts against his chest. He could hear the rush of blood in his veins, a freight train barreling down treacherous tracks toward an inevitable crash.

Heart pounding, he eased her away just enough for him to look into her eyes. But if he thought looking into her emerald depths would help him do the right thing, he was sorely mistaken. Because it was there that he saw his fate. He felt the truth of it stab him like a steely knife.

"I'm not going to do this," he whispered without conviction.

"Neither am I," she said and pressed her mouth to his.

Landis had always thought of herself as a level-headed creature. She'd always prided herself on her capacity for good judgment without emotions or impulses muddying things up. She valued her ability to stay cool under fire. They were the qualities that made a good lawyer. Qualities she'd cultivated and honed since the day she'd decided to go into law.

It was the ultimate irony that those qualities ceased to exist when it came to Jack LaCroix.

She was starkly aware of the wet, satiny texture of his

mouth as he kissed her. Her breasts grew heavy. She could feel the pang of arousal in her womb. The wet heat between her legs. And an ache in her heart that didn't have anything to do with any of those physical sensations.

"You make me lose control." Never taking his eyes from hers, Jack lifted her hand and pressed her palm against his erection. Shocked by his boldness, she tried to tug her hand from his, but he held her palm firmly against his shaft.

Heat flooded her when he drew her hand slowly over the hard ridge of him. He was like heated steel beneath her fingertips. She could feel the pulse of him beneath against her palm. She could feel that same heat pulsing through her body to gather in her breasts and pool in her womb.

"This is your last chance to change your mind," he whispered.

"I'm not going to change my mind," she said.

Cupping her face with his hands, he dipped his head and crushed his mouth to hers. His lips were firm and demanding and infinitely clever as they devoured hers. She marveled at the scratchy feel of his whiskers against her face, the warmth of his breath against her cheek, the restrained urgency she felt in his touch.

She opened to him when he probed her mouth with his tongue. She entwined hers with his, loving the taste of him. His breaths came hard and quick, filling her senses with the sound of male need. Heat built inside her, burning her until she felt feverish. Until she felt herself melting like hot wax beneath a desert sun.

Even as the voice of reason screamed for her to stop and protect herself from the inevitable hurt this man would bring her, Landis tightened her arms around him. Right or wrong, she wanted this time with him. He filled something empty inside her no other human being had managed to touch. And it was a void that had ached every day he'd been out of her life.

Breaking the kiss, Jack pulled away just enough to make eye contact. Landis stared at him, shocked by the power of the emotions inside her, the intensity of the things happening to her body.

"I've dreamed of touching you like this." His fingers combed through her hair, skimmed her face and throat, lingered on her shoulders. "I love the way you smell. I love the way you taste. I love the way your skin feels against my fingertips."

She leaned close, brushed her lips across his mouth. "I've dreamed of kissing you like that. Of hearing your voice in the night. Of feeling you against me and knowing in my heart everything is going to be all right."

He began unbuttoning his shirt. Even though his hands shook, his gaze never faltered. "I can't make any guarantees, Red."

"Maybe not. But of all the crazy things that have happened in the last year, this is the only thing I can make sense of."

She hadn't realized it was possible to feel so many emotions at the same time. She felt besieged by them, pulled in a thousand different directions. The memories of the way things had once been between them raced through her mind. But all of it was tempered by a future that was uncertain at best. Suddenly she wanted to cry out against the injustices that had been cast upon them. By fate that wasn't always fair. By choices that hadn't always been smart. By a system that wasn't always perfect.

Jack removed his shirt, let it fall to the floor at his feet. Landis lowered her eyes, stared at the broad span of his chest where a thatch of black hair tapered to the waistband of his jeans. Her heart pounded against her breast when his fingers went to his belt.

The need to touch him overrode caution. She skimmed her hands over muscles that were as hard as granite. A shudder went through him when her fingertips traced over his nipples. She could feel the tension vibrating in his muscles as she ran her hands over his abdomen, then lower to his belt. "Let me."

She struggled with his belt buckle for several eternal seconds, but her hands were shaking so badly, she couldn't finish. Gazing intently at her, he set her hands aside and unfastened the belt, then his fly. The muscles of his chest rippled as he worked his jeans down over lean hips and stepped out of them.

The sight of him completely naked and fully aroused unnerved her, thrilled her, sent a shiver of anticipation through her. Without speaking, he took her hands in his and backed her toward the bed. Landis started when the backs of her thighs came in contact with the mattress. Eyes burning into hers, Jack reached for the lapels of the robe. "I want to see you. All of you."

Landis began to tremble. Lovemaking had always been difficult for her. The vulnerability involved with the act itself unsettled her. The power of the emotions involved disturbed her. That Jack could so easily steal her control terrified her....

The terry cloth whispered over her nipples as he slipped the robe from her shoulders. A tremor raced the length of her as it puddled on the floor at her feet. Her nerves jumped when Jack's eyes swept over her. She felt his gaze as if it were a physical touch, warm fingers skimming over her flesh....

She didn't miss the darkening of his eyes or the rigid set of his mouth when his eyes latched on to hers. "You're more beautiful than I remember," he said in a thick voice.

Landis had never seen his emotions so visible on his face. She'd always known he was an intense man, but he'd never shown her this gentle, vulnerable side of him and it moved her profoundly that he would share it with her now.

She jolted when he raised his hand and swept a strand of hair away from her face. Embarrassed by her overreaction, she laughed, but the sound was fraught with nerves.

A smile touched the corners of his mouth. "I guess I'm not the only one who's nervous."

"It's been a long time since I've been with anyone," she said. "Since you."

"A year is a long time. Maybe we're both a little out of practice." Gathering her into his arms, he pulled her to him and kissed her. She thought she'd been prepared for the onslaught of pleasure, but nothing could prepare her for the hunger of his kisses. She accepted his tongue, opened to him. Her thoughts tumbled inside her head until she could no longer form a single, rational thought.

A gasp escaped her when he cupped her breasts. She jolted, then arched when he took her nipples between his thumbs and forefingers. Dizzy with sensation, she closed her eyes. Never taking his mouth from hers, Jack swept her into his arms and laid her on the bed. Vaguely, she was aware of him lying down beside her. Of her breaths coming hard and fast. Of her heart beating out of control.

She threw her head back when he kissed the hollow of her throat. His mouth lingered at her collarbone. A shiver swept through her as he trailed wet kisses to her breast. She cried out when he took her nipple into his mouth. Another cry escaped her when he flicked the engorged tip with his tongue and began to suckle.

Landis writhed beneath his ministrations, shocked by the intensity of the sensations streaking through her. Anticipation coiled tightly inside her, a high tension wire stretched to the limit. Dazedly she wondered how she had survived for an entire year without this man. How she had gotten through a single day without his touch.

She wanted badly to touch him, but every time she tried to move, his mouth besieged her with a new sensation that had her muscles tensing and then going slack. A shudder ran the length of her when he traced kisses from her breasts to her navel. She could feel the wetness of his mouth heating her flesh, teasing her with the promise of something forbidden and sweet. A keen sense of vulnerability made her tense when he moved lower, but he didn't stop.

"I want all of you," he whispered. "Let me kiss you there."

Landis had never shared that part of herself before. Had never been able to bear the vulnerability of it. A shiver moved through her when he set his mouth against her mound. He kissed her softly, and sensation vibrated through her. The power of the pleasure stunned her; the intimacy of it shattered her. She cried out when his tongue slid between wet folds. Every nerve ending in her body zinged when he stroked her. Thoughts fragmented and splintered and her control tumbled away.

He kissed her with a ravenousness that took her quickly to the peak. Pleasure washed through her, a wave cresting higher with every stroke of his tongue. Sensation assaulted her senses. The intensity of it wrenched a cry from her. She heard his name on her lips, realized she'd called out his name. Jack answered in kind, kissing her deeply, stroking her, never giving her a respite.

One by one her senses shut down until she was aware of nothing except his mouth against the most private part of her body. She relinquished her control, let him guide her. White light sparked behind her closed lids as he flicked over her with his tongue.

"That's it," he whispered. "Let go…"

The climax struck her with stunning force. Wave after wave of pleasure gripped her. Landis rode each wave, a roller coaster rising and then falling until she felt as if she would shatter.

Jack took her apart piece by piece, atom by atom. In a

small corner of her mind that still clung to rationale, she wondered if she would ever be able to put those pieces back together the way they were before.

"I want to look into your eyes when I make love to you."

She opened her eyes. Her heart stumbled in her chest when he took her face between his hands and smiled down at her. She met his gaze, but she could feel her mouth quivering, the fist of emotion in her throat. She opened her body to him. His eyes darkened, intensified as he moved between her knees. The muscles of his shoulders corded. His breaths came shallow and quick.

He entered her with slow and devastating control. Quicksilver pleasure lashed at her, as sharp and cutting as a bull whip. She whispered his name when he began to move. Her vision blurred as the pleasure rose, a rogue wave crashing over her. He moved within her, stretching her, filling her, moving her as she'd never been moved before.

As her second completion bore down on her, she tried desperately not to acknowledge what she knew to be true in her heart. What she'd known to be true all along. What she'd feared more than anything in the world. She'd never stopped loving Jack LaCroix.

Chapter 12

Jack stood beneath the spray of the shower, trying not to think about what he'd done or how it was going to affect his plans. He'd thought that by sleeping with Landis, by making love to her, he would finally be able to exorcise the demons that had haunted him for the past twelve months. He'd thought a few hours of mind-numbing sex would get her out of his system once and for all. That when the time came, he would be able to walk away and not look back.

What a pathetic fool he was.

All he'd managed to do was get himself more deeply entangled in a web that was threatening to suffocate him. The more he struggled to free himself, the more ensnared he became. How in the name of God could he have been so arrogant as to believe making love to her wouldn't mean something? How could he have ever believed he would be able to walk away? A man didn't walk away from a woman like Landis. Not unscathed, anyway. She was part of him whether he liked it or not. He would carry his feelings for her with him for the rest of his life. He would carry his feelings for her to the grave.

The way Jack saw it, he had three choices. He could turn himself in and fight for his life within the same system that had failed him so terribly once before. Or, he could flee to South America where he would invariably spend the rest of his life wasting away in some muddy grass hut, wondering what might have come of his life if he'd had the courage to fight. Or, he could continue with his original plan of breaking into Duke's mansion on the outside chance that he would find some scrap of information that would clear him and end the nightmare once and for all.

None of the choices were ideal. All held a very high probability of failure. Ironically, the one that held the most reward also carried the most risk.

That brought him to another problem that wasn't quite as cut and dried. If he decided to go into Duke's mansion, he knew Landis wouldn't sit on the sidelines and watch. The dangers involved—whether she recognized those dangers or not—wouldn't matter to her. Like the tough prosecutor she was, she would insist on going with him.

Jack couldn't let that happen.

He knew firsthand how Duke dealt with those who crossed him. The thought of what could happen if Duke's thugs got their hands on Landis made him physically ill.

Cursing the situation, he turned off the water and yanked a towel off the rack. Cold, hard fear churned in his gut. A fear that had nothing to do with his own life and everything to do with the woman he'd just made love with. He was in so far over his head, he hadn't even considered the possibility that what he was about to do could end up getting her killed.

Jack stepped into his jeans, then shrugged into his shirt. He found Landis sitting cross-legged on the bed with an egg roll in one hand and a pencil in the other. Wispy tendrils of flame-colored hair framed her face and fell in tousled disarray around her shoulders. Papers and documents were spread out around her like playing cards. Sitting there in her oversize-robe and disheveled hair, she looked more like a law student than a practicing lawyer.

Jack stared at her, shaken as much by her beauty as he was by his reaction to her. He tried hard to see her as the tough prosecutor she was. Instead, he saw her as the woman with whom he'd just shared one of the most erotic experiences of his life. A woman who meant a hell of a lot more to him than he wanted her to.

God in Heaven, how was he going to handle this?

The need to protect what was *his* jumped through him with surprising force. He knew she wouldn't like it, but he wasn't going to let her go with him into Duke's mansion. Only he had the sinking suspicion she was going to be his toughest opponent.

She shot him a smile that stopped his brain cold. "There have been at least two precedence-setting cases in the state of Utah in which convicted law enforcement officers have been exonerated of charges against them and reinstated."

"First-degree murder cases?" he managed.

"Well, no, but that doesn't—"

"I think we both know formulating a legal strategy at this point is premature."

She cut him a sharp look. "How about if you stick to the cop stuff and leave the legal mumbo jumbo to me?"

"I just don't want you to get ahead of yourself."

Tapping the pencil, she looked down at her notes. "I can file a—"

"Don't waste your time." He knew she was only trying to help, but he'd reached a point where he knew accepting help from her now would only lead to her getting hurt—or worse.

Rising from the bed, she approached him. Her eyes were soft, the color of a forest at dusk. Her mouth was full and wet, making him remember what it had been like to taste her there. He could just make out the swell of her breasts beneath the robe and felt a hard tug of lust.

"What's going on with you?" She reached for his hand.

Suddenly furious with her, with the situation, but most of all with himself, Jack pulled away. "Cut it out."

She stared at him, waiting, her expression perplexed and expectant. "You want to explain the surly mood or are you going to make me guess?"

He stared at her, unreasonably angry, frustrated and more scared than he'd been in a very long time.

Taking his hand, she pressed it gently to her lips. "Don't shut me out," she said.

The sensation of her mouth against his palm stirred him as no simple kiss could have. He tamped down on the slow heat building in his groin. He couldn't let his attraction to her keep him from doing the right thing. Damn it, he would never forgive himself if something happened to her.

Troubled, he eased his hand from hers and lowered it to his side. "I don't need you messing with my head right now, Landis."

"Is that what I'm doing? Messing with your head? I thought I was helping you clear your name."

"You're not. You're not helping anything. In fact, you're making the situation worse."

Her eyes narrowed. "Why don't you tell me what's really going on?"

"I'm going to take you back to Ian's. I want you to—"

"I'm not letting you go to Duke's alone, Jack. You can rant and rave and throw male temper tantrums until you turn blue, but I'm not going to let you do that."

"It's out of your hands," he said nastily.

"You're not the only one with a stake in this. Damn it, I've risked everything helping you."

"I'll send you a medal from prison."

"Don't you dare talk to me that way."

"I'm giving you an out, Landis. If you're half as smart as I think you are, you'll take it."

"Sometimes the smart thing isn't the right thing, Jack."

"That's a bunch of crap and you know it."

"I'm not going to walk away. I'm sure as hell not going to sit this out while you get yourself killed."

Jack crossed to her. She gasped when his fingers closed around her biceps. Without finesse, he drew her to him and kissed her hard on the mouth. The need inside him clenched, a fist squeezing so hard he couldn't breathe. He hated doing that to her, hated showing her such disrespect. But the alternative was infinitely worse, and he couldn't think of another way to save her life.

He pushed her away so she was arm's length, let his gaze skim down the front of her. "You served your purpose, Landis. Now that I've scratched my itch, I don't need you anymore."

Her face paled, but she didn't look away. "I'm not going to let you manipulate me that way."

A sudden, desperate anger crashed through him. "Do you think this is some kind of game? I've seen Duke's handiwork, Landis! I was a cop for twelve years. I've seen the blood and the twisted, butchered heaps he leaves behind. Do you think you're immune to that?"

She tried to pull away, but he held her, forced her to listen. "I've seen what he does to decent people like you! I've had to tell mothers and wives that their sons and husbands were gunned down in the street. I've seen the pain and the ravaged faces he leaves behind."

"Stop it!" she shouted.

He wanted to shake her, wanted to make her bend to his

will. But he knew she wouldn't. That was one of the things he'd always loved about her. When Landis put her mind to something, she was like a terrier with a bone and God help anyone who got in her way.

He could feel her trembling, feel the tremors quivering through his own body. He loosened his grip on her arms, tried not to think about the bruises he'd put on her. "You have no idea what that bastard is capable of," he said.

She stared at him for an interminable moment, the only sound coming from their harsh breathing. "It's insulting for you to stand there and tell me I'm not capable of helping you. I thought you were more enlightened, Jack. I thought you've always known I'm as strong and capable and determined as you are."

"Landis, for God's sake, you've got your entire life ahead of you. Don't throw it away."

"I'm in a position to help you do this. Please, *let me help you.*"

"I won't be able to live with myself if I let you go in with me and something goes wrong. Damn it, Red, for once in your life, let it go."

Her eyes were fierce. "If you shut me out, I swear I'll do it on my own. I'll find a way. You know I will."

Heart pounding, Jack turned away. He didn't want her to see that she'd rattled him. He didn't know what to do, didn't know how to convince her to walk away, how to keep her safe. Another layer of fear enveloped him when he realized that if he were killed tonight, or sent back to prison tomorrow, Cyrus Duke could still target Landis—if only to prove a point.

"You need someone to drive," she said. "You need a lookout. I can help you with the computer system. I'm relatively good with software. I took a networking class last fall."

The need to hold her safe in his arms, to feel her heart

beating against his, overwhelmed him. Abruptly, he went to her, pulled her to him. A hundred conflicting emotions unfurled in his chest. Vaguely he was aware of her arms going around him. Her warmth eased the ice freezing his heart. He closed his eyes, against the ebb and flow of emotions, held her tighter. As if it were the most natural thing in the world, she rested her head against his chest and sighed.

Reaching out, he stroked the back of her head, marveling at the silkiness of her hair beneath his fingers. "I don't know how to keep you safe. That scares the hell out of me."

"Life isn't safe, Jack. We've already been terribly hurt. Both of us. But it's within our power to stop it. Please don't take this chance away from me."

"I could never live with myself if something happened to you because of me. Landis, that would kill me."

"Is that feeling any less for me, Jack? Do my feelings not count? I have enough regrets. I don't want to regret walking away from our only chance. We don't have a choice but to do this."

He dug deep for an argument, but came up short. He wished with all his heart he could dispute her, but couldn't. "You never did know when to walk away from a fight."

She looked up at him, a smile touching her mouth. "That's a hell of a character flaw for a lawyer, huh?"

He only hoped it didn't get them killed.

The alley was as narrow and dark as a cave at three o'clock in the morning. Garbage bags, fifty-gallon drums and broken pallets lay haphazardly along the scarred brick walls. A graffiti-streaked Dumpster hulked like a battered sentry outside the rear door of Café DeVille, the upscale restaurant owned and operated by Cyrus Duke.

Jack stopped the truck and cut the headlights, giving his eyes a moment to adjust to the dim light.

"What if there's someone inside?" Landis's voice cut through the tension creeping over him.

"The restaurant has been closed for a few hours," he said. "The employees should be long gone, but I'll make sure before I set the fire."

"What if the fire spreads to one of the adjacent shops?"

Jack didn't like the variables any more than she did; the last thing he wanted to do was jeopardize the safety of innocent bystanders. But without a diversion, there was no hope of them getting past the security system and into Duke's mansion. The way he looked at it, they didn't have a choice.

"We're talking about a kitchen fire, Red. Just big enough to warrant the fire department and get Duke and his entourage out of the mansion."

"How do you know he'll show? I mean, it's three o'clock in the morning. Doesn't he have underlings who take care of this sort of thing for him?"

"He'll come, believe me. Back when I was a cop, it was common knowledge that Café DeVille is his pride and joy. If there's a fire—particularly if it's of a suspicious nature—you can bet he'll come running like a pig to chow."

He looked at her. Determination shone in her eyes, but its sheen was dulled by a fear she couldn't hide. A fear he wished like hell she never had to feel. "You sure you want to do this?"

"More sure of anything I've ever done in my life."

He resisted the urge to slide across the seat and pull her into her arms. As much as he wanted to hold her, touch her, taste her, he couldn't afford to let himself get distracted. Not when the most dangerous part of the plan lay dead ahead.

Turning away from her, Jack studied the brick exterior,

the scarred wooden door and tried not to think about all the things that could go wrong. "I'll start the fire in the kitchen, then call 9-1-1. To help expedite, I'll contact someone at Duke's estate, tell them I'm with the fire department and that they need to get someone to the site. The fire should give us enough time to drive to the mansion, get inside, into his network, then get out. We're talking fifteen minutes inside max."

Knowing he didn't have any more time to spare, he reached into the back seat for the backpack filled with tools he'd picked up at an all-night convenience store. "Slide over to the driver's seat," he said.

Her hand was already on the door latch. "I'm coming in with you—"

He swore softly. "I need you in the truck. If something goes wrong, I want your hands on the wheel so we'll be able to get out of here quickly."

Myriad emotions scrolled across her face. He saw fear tempered with courage, a thin bravado and a determination he admired despite the fact that he didn't want her here.

"Okay," she said. "I'm just…afraid for you."

"Yeah, well, I'm afraid for both of us."

Without warning, she slid across the seat, leaned close and kissed him full on the mouth. Shock and pleasure punched through the adrenaline and nerves. He forgot about the job ahead of him and kissed her back. Her lips were wet and demanding as they devoured his. Need struck him squarely in the gut.

Before he could wrap his arms around her, she pulled away. "Be careful."

Shaken by the depth of his feelings for her, Jack reached for the door latch. "If I'm not out in ten minutes, I want you to drive around the block. If I'm not standing here waiting for you after that, I want you to drive back to the motel and wait for me there."

Objection entered her eyes, but she didn't voice it. He knew if worse came to worse, she wouldn't leave him behind. He supposed he'd just have to make sure he didn't screw up.

"I'll be here," she said. "Be careful, okay?"

Jack opened the door and stepped into the cold night. What he was about to do went against everything he believed in, against everything Mike Morgan had instilled. Jack might have walked a thin line during his career as a cop, but it was always for a greater good and he'd never once crossed over. Tonight, he was crossing that line, willingly breaking the very laws he'd been sworn to uphold. He knew it was foolish at this point, but it made him feel dirty. Like maybe he was no better than the scum he'd spent twelve years trying to get off the street.

Shoving the thoughts aside, he crossed to the rear entrance of Café DeVille, checking both alley entrances as he went. He'd been inside the upscale restaurant several times—mostly to let Duke know vice was keeping an eye on him. While Duke had spent tens of thousands of dollars renovating the interior, the alley exterior looked as if it hadn't been updated since the Great Depression. The red bricks and mortar had been worn by decades of the harsh Utah elements. The wooden door was weathered and slashed with graffiti. Above the tarnished brass knob, a shiny new bolt lock mocked him.

He studied the small window set into the door. Through the grime, he spotted the alarm wire that ran the length of the glass. Stupidly, he'd underestimated Duke's security measures, and knew getting inside wasn't going to be as easy as he'd hoped.

For a full minute, he studied the scene, tried to establish the best way to gain entry. To the left of the door, a good eight feet off the ground, a small window with etched glass and two steel security bars snagged his attention. Bathroom,

he thought. Or perhaps a bathroom that had been trans
formed into a storage room. Jack studied the tiny window
wondering if it was wired, wondering how solidly the bar
were imbedded into the mortar.

Spotting a metal garbage can a few feet away, he strod
to it, dragged it to the window and set it upside down. Hi
injured shoulder twitched uncomfortably as he hauled him
self onto the can. Removing the flashlight from his back
pack, Jack shone it on to the glass, searched quickly fc
alarm wires. Relief skittered through him when he foun
none.

He drew back the hammer, averted his face and shattere
the glass in a single stroke.

An alarm shrilled.

Shock jumped through him, followed by a jolt of fea
For an instant, he considered aborting the mission, bu
knew he wouldn't get another chance. Blood pounding, h
used the hammer to dig away the mortar from the lowe
security bar. To his relief, the mortar gave way easily an
within a few seconds he pried out the bar and dropped
to the concrete below.

He figured he had less than a minute to get inside, sta
the fire and get out before the cops showed up. Not givin
himself time to debate the insanity of what he was abor
to do, he cleared away the remaining glass with the han
mer, then thrust himself through the window.

Once inside, he jumped to the floor. "Police!" h
shouted. "Fire! Get out of the building!"

The ear-splitting alarm continued its deafening cry. Fee
ing the press of time, Jack sprinted to the main dining roon
found it deserted. "Police! Get out of the building!" Turn
ing, he ran through the dining room and into the kitche
barely noticing the aromas of basil, old grease and th
yeasty smell of bread.

In the kitchen he withdrew the lighter fluid from th

backpack. Flipping it open he sprayed the stove, the fire-wall, the commercial-size ovens, the refrigerators, then tossed the open can on the floor. He turned to the nearest cooktop and twisted the burner, jumping back as the blue flame engulfed the stovetop. He backed up a step, watched the flame creep down the side of the stove and rush toward the far wall. Satisfied the room would burn, he sprinted back to the dining room. Spotting a phone behind the bar, he picked it up and dialed 9-1-1. He barely heard the dispatcher's voice over the pounding of his heart.

"There's a fire at Café DeVille. I suggest you get the fire department here pronto." Setting the phone on the bar, he sprinted through the dining room and headed for the window.

Chapter 13

Landis's nerves snapped like hot wires as she watched Jack writhe through the window and drop to the ground. He'd been inside a little over two minutes, but with the alarm screaming and her heart raging like a panicked beast, it felt like an eternity.

Her hand was poised on the shifter when he yanked open the door and slid onto the seat beside her. "Drive!" he shouted.

She hit the gas. The truck jumped forward and streaked down the alley toward the street. "Are you all right?" she asked.

"I'm fine. Make a left."

Barely avoiding a police car with emergency lights flashing, Landis spun the wheel to the left. The truck fishtailed but she turned into the skid and regained control quickly.

"Nice and easy, Red. Slow down. We're okay."

Adrenaline burned like acid in her stomach, and she had to take several deep breaths before she could speak. "Why did the alarm go off? I thought—"

''So did I.'' Jack turned in his seat to look out the back window. ''Just one of those nasty little surprises that happen when felons act like felons.''

''I think I'm getting carsick.''

Jack looked over at her, grinned. ''That's the adrenaline. Just settle down. You're doing fine. Take a right here.''

Slowing the truck, she turned the wheel. ''Did you get the fire started?'' She couldn't seem to keep her eyes off the rearview mirror. In a small corner of her mind, she wondered if she would stop or run if she saw flashing lights behind them.

''Yeah, but I didn't have time to call Duke,'' Jack said. ''I suspect he'll be getting a call in the next half hour or so. We'll find a safe place to watch the mansion and go in the moment he leaves.''

She hated it, but her courage faltered. Oh, good Lord, how did she ever think she could go through with this? ''What if he leaves someone behind? I mean, isn't that a possibility?''

''We'll cross that bridge when we come to it.''

Landis glanced over at him. He looked calm, controlled and incredibly handsome as he watched the street, his eyes taking in every dark alley and car they passed. Even through the fear and nerves that had her stomach in knots, she felt the now familiar draw to him. She thought of everything that had transpired between them in the last hours. They'd covered a lot of ground in a very short span of time. Emotional ground that had left her raw and shaken inside— and dangerously close to a man who meant a hell of a lot more to her than she'd ever realized.

''Jack, no matter what happens, I want you to know…this time we've had together. It means something to me. More than I ever thought possible.''

Jack shot her a questioning look. ''Landis, this probably isn't the time or the place to talk about this.''

She wasn't sure why her emotions chose that moment to betray her. Not when she should be thinking about the very dangerous task ahead and all the things that could go wrong. But she was suddenly afraid that this would be their last chance to talk. "I've been blind, Jack. And I'm sorry for that. You came back into my life and forced me to see things clearly. About you. About my father." She looked down, vaguely aware her knuckles were white on the wheel. "About us."

He looked away, into the night spinning by. The muscles in his jaw worked, and Landis wished she knew what he was thinking. How many times had she wished that in the past two days? How many times had he refused to tell her?

His eyes were dark and somber when they met hers. "Landis, at this point, all I can tell you is that there are some things that are best left unsaid."

"We may not get another chance to talk," she said.

He grimaced. "The odds of our pulling this off are pretty slim, but we knew that before we'd decided. You know I won't go back to prison. If things don't work out tonight— if I don't get shot—I'm going to run." He looked out the window, his jaw clamped tightly. "You know I won't take you with me."

The thought of never seeing him again made her feel gut punched. Sick to her soul. Hollowed out. The thought of him spending the rest of his life in prison broke her heart. She knew if she had to choose, she would prefer that he run. Even if she had to live the rest of her life without him, at least he would be free.

"We've got to be prepared for the worst," he said. "If things don't work out, I want you to get on with your life."

"But I can help with your case—"

"If I get sent back to prison, I'll refuse to see you. I won't put either of us through that."

She hated the distance in his eyes. She felt as if he were

slipping away, even though he was close enough for her to reach out and touch.

"If I get caught, I'm going to tell the cops I forced you to help me. If you're smart, you'll corroborate that. Hopefully, it will keep you from being disbarred."

"I won't go along with it."

"If we get busted tonight all I want from you is for you to forget we were ever lovers. If you want to help, send a good criminal lawyer my way."

"You're innocent—"

"I'm in deep trouble! I'm piling up new charges with everything I do. And if you don't start using your head, I'm going to drag you down with me. Are you getting that?"

The road in front of her blurred. Hot tears burned behind her eyes. She tried to blink them away but her emotions were boiling. The truth of what she felt in her heart stunned her, shook her from the inside out.

"Pull over," he said.

She barely heard him over the drum of her pulse. She felt a sob building in her throat. The tears blinded her, scalded her cheeks, reminding her that she was not in control. Not of the situation. Not of the man sitting next to her. Not of the emotions shredding her heart. "I won't let you go to prison for something you didn't do. I won't let—"

"Pull the damn truck over."

Blinking furiously, Landis turned on to a quiet side street. It was stupid, but she felt like a failure. She was such an emotional wreck, she couldn't even drive. "I suppose you want to drive," she said.

Jack leaned over and turned off the ignition. Wordlessly, he reached around her and punched off the headlights. She reached for the latch to get out of the truck. He grasped her upper arm and pulled her to him. "Shut up, Red," he murmured.

His strong arms wrapped around her. Then Landis felt his hands in her hair. His breath against her ear as he whispered her name. The warmth of his body as he held her tightly against him. "I just want to hold you a moment," he whispered.

Her mouth sought his. Desperation tangled with something deeper and burned through her with an urgency that made her feel wild and out of control. "I love you," she whispered.

"Shhh," he said. "Don't say it."

"I have to. I need to say this. Because it's there. In my heart. I love you. Oh, God, Jack, I've always loved you. All those months we were apart…" Only then did she realize that she was crying. She kissed him openmouthed, tasting tears and anguish and a mutual hunger that would never be sated. Heat engulfed her as his hands found her breasts. She moaned when he molded her flesh, brushed his fingertips over the sensitized tips.

Forgetting the dangers they faced in the coming hours, shutting out everything except the moment between them, Landis traced her fingers over his face, his neck, the corded muscles of his shoulders. Her hands shook as she fought with the buttons of his shirt. A tremor rippled through him as her hands drifted over his chest. She marveled at the feel of his flesh, the male hair, the hard-as-rock muscle.

He moaned and whispered something wicked in her ear. Words that thrilled her, filled her with anticipation, expectation. And hope.

Tilting her head, he kissed her long and hard, without the finesse he'd shown her when they'd made love. It was a reckless kiss, laced with urgency and hunger. And she wondered if he were somehow branding her, marking her as his.

As quickly as his mouth had assailed hers, he released her. Growling low in his throat, he moved away, his eyes on the darkness beyond the windshield. "That wasn't a very good idea."

"No, but I...needed to get that off my chest."

He cut her a hard look.

Even with her senses vibrating with the remnants of his kiss, it hurt that he hadn't told her he loved her. She knew he wouldn't now, and her heart broke with the knowledge. As impossible as it was for her not to hurt, she knew it would only make things more difficult if he had. Still, she hated it.

"Drive," he said.

Refusing to let herself consider all the variables of what they were about to do, she put the truck in gear and pulled onto the street.

The Duke estate was nestled behind a high stone wall and an ornate wrought-iron gate in one of Salt Lake City's most prestigious neighborhoods. Parked on a quiet side street one block away, Jack and Landis watched two gleaming white limousines glide through the gate and head toward the downtown area.

"He got the call."

Landis jumped at the sound of Jack's voice. She was so scared she could taste fear at the back of her throat, all coppery and thick. "Looks like he has quite an entourage."

"We have to assume there are people inside."

"Sleeping people hopefully."

His eyes met hers for an instant, then without speaking he reached for the door latch and got out of the truck. She did the same, and stepped into the cold night air, refusing to acknowledge that her knees were shaking.

"Follow me." Sticking to the shadows cast by the trees along the street, Jack took the sidewalk to the front gate of the mansion.

"How do we get inside?" she asked, breaths puffing out in front of her.

"We go over the gate."

Trepidation shot through her as she took in the evil-looking spears twelve feet up. "Piece of cake if you don't mind getting skewered."

Jack glanced toward the rear of the estate. "Let's see if the rear gate is any less deadly."

Landis wasn't sure whether she was relieved that she hadn't had to clamber over the gate or annoyed that he didn't think she was capable. "No argument here."

"There's a first."

Pleasure rippled through her when he took her hand. Even through her gloves, she could feel his warmth and it was incredibly reassuring.

They jogged to the rear of the estate where the servants' entrance was located. The gate was smaller and not nearly as ornate. No spears, Landis noted with a vast sense of relief.

"Not many lights on in the house," Jack said. "Even so, getting inside is going to be tricky."

Landis's nerves jumped at the statement, but instead of letting the fear get the best of her, she stepped up to the gate. "Give me a leg up, will you?"

Interlocking his fingers, he formed a stirrup of sorts with his hands. "Put your foot in my hands. I'll lift you. All you have to do is pull yourself up, then swing your leg over the top. Do it quickly. Don't make any noise. Starting now, we move quickly. Okay?"

Pulse racing, she put her foot in his clasped hands. He lifted her with amazing ease. Once she was chest level with the top of the gate, she swung her leg over the bar until she was sitting precariously on the rail.

"Jump," he said. "I'm right behind you."

Landis closed her eyes and slid off the fence. She landed

hard enough to jar her teeth, but managed to stay on her feet. She looked up to see Jack come over the gate with the agility of a panther. He landed with a quiet thud a few feet away, his knees bending to absorb the impact.

"Not bad for a lawyer," he said.

"My ankles aren't broken. I think that's a good sign at this point." She glanced toward the house thirty yards away. It looked ominous cloaked by cold and shadowed by the night. "You're good at this."

"I'm just getting warmed up." He took her hand and hauled her into an easy jog toward the house. "Follow me. Stay close. Don't say anything. Don't make any noise. Got it?"

Landis nodded and tried not to think about what would happen if someone inside saw them crossing the lawn.

The Tudor-style mansion was constructed of stone and stucco. A sweeping circular drive led to a four-car garage on her right. To her left, an Olympic-size swimming pool replete with a cabana and stone diving platform monopolized the backyard. They followed a narrow flagstone path to the patio. Using the shadows for cover, Jack led her along a manicured hedge, between two wrought-iron tables to a set of French doors at the back of the house. Yellow light flickered from an overhead gas lamp. It didn't give off much light, but Landis felt exposed nonetheless. If someone were to look out the window…

"Stay here." Jack strode to the dual French doors, knelt, ran his hand along the seam.

Landis watched, fascinated by his surety and physical grace. He moved to the second door. Cupping his hands, he peered inside. "There's an alarm," he whispered.

"Can you disarm it?"

"I don't know." He rose, followed the trail of the wire with his hand. "I'm going to cut the phone lines."

"You mean if the alarm dials out automatically to the police?"

"Or to Duke."

She swallowed, not wanting to imagine such a scenario. "What if it's wireless, or something?"

"I don't know. I'm going to do this the best way I know how."

"Why can't anything be easy?"

"I'm sure that's a questions all felons ask themselves."

"We're not felons, Jack. Not really. We're the good guys."

For the first time, he paused, turned to look at her over his shoulder. A smile tugged at his mouth. "Thanks for reminding me."

Landis watched him jog to the end of the house, then around to the side. She wasn't cold but at some point she'd begun to shake. Her hands. Her knees. Her legs. One minute dragged into two. Two into five. By the time he returned, her teeth were chattering.

He gave her a thumbs-up. "I took out the phone line."

"I got gray hair while I was waiting. How do we get in?"

Without speaking, he strode to the French door. Landis trailed him and watched, fascinated, as he pulled duct tape from his backpack. He quickly tore off three long strips and placed them vertically over the pane nearest the lock.

A renewed wave of uneasiness washed over her when he reached for the hammer. "When I open the door," he began, "I want you to go inside and look for the alarm system panel. It'll probably be set into the wall, or hidden in a utility or laundry area nearby. Since we're at the rear of the house where the servants work, it shouldn't be too hard to find. I'll go left—you go right. We've got about forty-five seconds to find it or all hell's going to break loose. Are you ready?"

A lump of fear rose in her chest. "We don't know the code."

"Pete Boyle told me."

A laugh escaped her, but the sound was fraught with tension. "What if it's been changed since then?"

"We improvise." His jaw flexed. "Come here."

When she didn't move, he grasped her hand and pulled her to him. Landis wasn't expecting him to kiss her. Not at a time like this. But he did. It was a hard, sexless kiss that touched her more deeply than it should have. When he pulled back, she saw the reckless light in his eyes, felt something quiver in her chest. "What was that for?"

"Luck." He started for the door.

She was still thinking about the kiss when the sound of breaking glass splintered the air. Jack reached through the broken window, unlocked the door, shoved it open. "We've got forty-five seconds to find the alarm panel. Go."

She barely heard him over the drum of her pulse. On unsteady legs, she followed him inside. The door opened to a tiled hall with high ceilings and muted yellow light. Landis barely noticed the exquisite architecture or the lavish furnishings. With their very lives at stake, her mind was on finding the alarm panel.

Vaguely aware of Jack disappearing to her left. Landis started down the narrow hall to her right. Beyond, she saw a refrigerator and stove, beyond a washing machine and clothes dryer. A closed door to her right beckoned. Mentally counting the seconds, she opened the door, flipped on the light. An intricate-looking panel set into the wall blinked at her with a glaring red eye.

"I found it!" she whispered. If her mental clock was correct, they had about twenty seconds before the alarm sounded.

Jack appeared a moment later. Without speaking or looking at her, he punched in four numbers. The red light continued to blink. "Look for a code written down somewhere nearby," he snapped and started punching buttons. *"Damn it."*

Landis searched the room frantically, looking for sticky notes or a calendar on the wall, but found nothing. The tiny red light blinked at quick intervals. "What do we do now?"

Jack studied the panel, his brows knit in concentration. He reached up and flipped a switch, but his hand was shaking. The light continued to blink.

He pulled the hammer from the waistband of his jeans. "We turn it off the old-fashioned way."

On an oath, he drew back the hammer and smashed the panel. Shards of plastic flew. A thin veil of smoke rose into the air along with the pungent smell of burning plastic. Landis watched, feeling helpless and frightened as he hammered at the panel until there was little more than a few colorful, frayed wires sticking out of the wall.

"If the alarm is wireless, we're cooked," he said.

She stared at the caved-in Sheetrock, the burn marks on the wall and the shards of plastic on the floor with a combination of horror and disbelief. "You've got a real knack for the electrical stuff."

"I guess now would be a good time to start praying there's no one else in the house."

Breathing hard, Jack turned to her. Landis saw something in his eyes, then his face went ashen. "Jack?"

"Don't look now," he said quietly, "but we've got company."

Chapter 14

The Rottweiler was the size of a Brahman bull. It stood just outside the utility room, intelligent eyes sliding from Landis to Jack as if trying to decide which of them to maul first. Having spent two years working with a K-9 unit, Jack could tell by the excited light in the animal's eyes that it wasn't the least bit intimidated. Knowing Duke, it was probably a trained attack dog. So much for getting out of this mess unscathed.

"At least he doesn't have a gun." Landis's voice was high and tight with fear.

"Just really big teeth."

"I'm sure you have an alternate plan."

"Fresh out, honey."

The dog crept toward them, its hackles rising.

"Get behind me," Jack said softly. "No quick moves. No loud noises."

Without making direct eye contact, he watched the animal's every move. When the dog's jowls drew back in a snarl, Jack knew it was no longer a question of if the animal would attack, but when—and which of them it would tear into first.

Once Landis was behind him, Jack positioned himself between her and the dog. He knew what kind of damage a dog could do to a person. He had no intention of either of them becoming mincemeat. "Good dog," Jack whispered. "Good boy."

The dog snarled. The muscles in its hind legs bunching and quivering with tension.

"Back away," Jack told Landis. "Toward the kitchen behind you. Don't turn your back. Don't look him in the eye. Do it now. Nice and easy."

The dog jumped forward, barking and baring its fangs. Behind him, Jack heard Landis moving away. He turned his head to see her slip into the kitchen. Relief skittered through him. An instant later the animal lunged.

Jack raised his arms to protect his face and throat. He knew that to survive, he must stay on his feet. But the dog was huge, and its weight sent him reeling backwards. Pain seared through his forearm when the dog's jaws clamped down. Cursing, he shoved at the dog, heard the fabric of his coat tear. Fear seized him when he lost his balance. He stumbled, crashed into the wall, managed to stay on his feet.

In his peripheral vision, he saw movement from the kitchen. Something large and dark sailed through the air, missing the dog by inches. The dog's attention split, followed the object. The death grip on Jack's arm loosened. He stared in amazement as a large ham splattered on the tile floor, and slid into the utility room.

He shoved hard at the dog. The animal fell to all fours, then vacillated as if trying to decide whether to finish off the intruder or feast on the ham. Never taking his eyes from the animal, Jack backed toward the kitchen. The dog looked at the ham, then turned and trotted toward it. The instant the animal was inside the utility room, Jack rushed forward and shut the door.

"Jesus." He leaned against the wall and looked down at his forearm. His coat was ripped clear through. A crimson stain blossomed on the fabric, but he could tell by the pain he was more bruised than cut.

"My God, you're bleeding."

He glanced to see Landis rushing toward him. The concern in her eyes moved him more than it should have, and for the first time since they'd gotten inside he was glad he wasn't alone. Unable to keep himself from it, he reached out and pulled her against him. "You okay?"

"Yeah, but I'm not the one who's bleeding."

Holding her tightly, he closed his eyes against the emotions churning inside him. God, how he wished things had turned out differently. He wanted to spend the rest of his life with this woman. Holding her just like this. Loving her. Healing her. Healing himself.

He'd thought he'd known hell in prison. Being locked away, deprived of decency and freedom and dignity. But having spent the past two days with Landis, having fallen in love with her all over again, he knew the torture he'd suffered behind bars would be nothing compared to the pain he faced when he walked away from her for the last time.

"That was a smart move with the ham, Red." He stroked her hair, marveling at the silkiness of it against his fingers.

"Good thing I came along, huh, LaCroix?"

"You saved my butt," he grumbled.

"It's such a nice butt."

"That's my line."

"Don't be a chauvinist."

He knew this wasn't the time or place for a silly conversation, but it took his stress down to a manageable level.

A moment later, he pushed her to arm's length. "If there's someone in the house, we're probably toast."

She nodded. "In that case, we'd better hurry."

He tried to ignore the uneasiness pulsing through him as they did a cursory search of the lower level. But Jack knew if Duke or one of his thugs caught them, they wouldn't bother calling the police. Cyrus Duke had his own brand of justice, and it was as swift and violent as a bullet.

They took the curved staircase to the second floor. Halfway down the wide hall a set of double doors opened to a study. It was a dramatic room with a leather sofa and glossy rosewood desk. Twin recliners huddled beneath a mullioned window that looked out over the pool. Books of every shape and size lined an entire wall from floor to ceiling. The smell of expensive tobacco mingled with the more subtle aromas of lemon oil and leather. A dark hardwood floor gleamed beneath a multitiered brass chandelier. The room was cold in a way that had nothing to do with the temperature. And Jack knew they had finally found Cyrus Duke's inner sanctum.

"This is it," he said.

Landis started toward the desk where a sleek computer and flat screen monitor beckoned. Without speaking she pressed the power button, then pulled out the leather chair and slid into it. "What's the login and password?" she asked.

Jack met her at the desk and pulled the information from his memory. "The login is DUKECYRUS. Upper case."

Her fingers flew over the keyboard.

"The password is maryelaine. Lower case."

She craned her head around to look at him. "Maryelaine?"

Jack shrugged. "I hear Duke's a real mama's boy."

"Sort of makes you wonder about his mother." She typed in the name. "It accepted it."

The drive whirred softly. The monitor began to roll. He looked down at her small, slender hands as they rested on the keyboard and saw that they were shaking. "You doing okay, Red?"

"I'll be a lot better once we get what we need and get out of here."

"Another five minutes or so, and we'll be home free." But he hated it that she was afraid. Hated it even more that it was his fault. He shouldn't have brought her here. Shouldn't have put her in danger. If something happened to her he would never forgive himself.

Somewhere in the house, a clock chimed. Jack started at the sound, a sense of foreboding pressing into him. He glanced at the clock on the desk and cursed. "We've been inside for almost ten minutes."

"Just give me a few more minutes here, okay?"

He looked at the screen, tried to ignore the zing of nerves running through him. "Try his contact information."

"Good idea." She clicked the mouse. "Damn. It's asking for an authorization."

He searched his memory. "Type deville. Lower case."

"Not very creative, is he?" Her fingers played over the keys. "No go."

"Damn it." He thought about it a moment. "Try upper case."

She clicked more keys. "We're in."

Leaning forward in anticipation, he watched the contact software scroll. "Pull up the contact lists."

"There are several."

"Open that one." Jack pointed to the largest of the files. "Got it."

A page containing names, addresses and other contact information materialized. Most of the names were unfamiliar. Several contained dollar amounts and various notes. Birthdates. Children's names. Professional titles.

"Scroll down," he said.

"Oh, my God."

The hairs at the back of his neck rose. Her slender finger went to a name at the bottom of the screen.

Aaron Chandler.

The name hit him like a set of brass knuckles. Next to the name, the figure of one hundred fifty thousand dollars stared back at him. "What the hell?"

"Jack, you don't think…"

He didn't hear the last part of the sentence as the significance of his finding the name on Cyrus Duke's computer hit home. Fury rumbled through him, an approaching storm promising a violent end. The sense of betrayal nearly choked him. "That son of a bitch railroaded me."

"That's why they killed him."

Jack reached forward and pressed the page down key. More names. People who'd sold their souls for the likes of money, illicit favors or power.

Resisting the urge to use his fist, he hit the key again and again. "Copy it to a disk. We've got to get the hell out of here." He jerked open a drawer, found nothing, jerked open another. He spotted the compact disk case, opened it and pulled out a blank disk. "Use this." He shoved the disk into the drive. Suddenly furious, he flung the remaining disks across the room. "That son of a bitch."

"Jack, calm down."

"I am calm, damn it."

Landis rubbed her temples while the disk copied. "A couple of those names looked familiar. I'm not sure when or where, but I've seen them before. Maybe the courthouse County inspectors, maybe. Tax collectors. God, Jack maybe judges."

Leaning back in the chair, she looked expectantly a Jack. Her eyes were a kaleidoscope of emotions. Jack sav all of them. Fear. Outrage. Pain.

"I'm sorry about Chandler," she said.

"I trusted the bastard." Bitterness rose inside him like vomit. He knew it was an impotent reaction, but he felt incredibly betrayed. Worse, he felt like a fool. "I should have seen it coming. I'm a cop for chrissake."

"There's enough information here to warrant an investigation. Who knows, maybe there's enough here to exonerate you."

His brain absorbed the words, but he didn't let himself feel their impact. He didn't let himself hope. He knew all too well what it was like to have that hope yanked from his grasp.

"I want my life back." He wanted more than that—a hell of a lot more—but didn't think now was the time to voice it.

His heart stuttered when she smiled at him. In the depths of her eyes he saw hope and faith and the utter certainty that good would prevail over evil. Something he hadn't believed in since the day they put him in a cage.

"It's going to be okay," she whispered. "This is exactly the kind of information we were looking for."

Shaken by the emotions roiling inside him, he looked down at the computer, realized the disk had finished copying. "Let's get out of here."

Landis stopped him when he reached for the disk. "I want more."

"We don't have time," he snapped. "I'm getting you out of here."

Anger darkened her features. "Don't blow this chance to save yourself."

Ignoring her, he removed the disk from the drive and shoved it into his pocket. "We're leaving."

"I'm not leaving until I see what else is in that computer." Surprising him, she reached for another disk, shoved it into the slot. "I'm doing this as much for myself as I am you. Don't try to stop me. I know what I'm doing."

He hadn't wanted to use force, but his instincts were screaming for him to get her out of the house. It had been foolhardy for them to come here tonight. It had been downright insane for him to have brought Landis along. If Duke caught them, he'd kill them both.

Grasping her beneath her shoulders, he lifted her from the chair. "I know you don't believe in gut instinct, but mine is working just fine and right now it's telling me to get the hell out of here."

She tried to twist away, but he muscled her toward the door with relative ease. "It's crazy to leave without seeing what else is on that computer!" she hissed.

"Yeah, well, it's even crazier to get ourselves killed over it."

She spun away from him, glared at him with large, angry eyes. She raised her hand as if to stave him off, but it was shaking violently. "Give me five minutes, Jack. Please. Don't take this away from me."

The fierceness of her expression took him aback. That she was willing to risk everything for him—her career, her freedom, her very life—shocked him all over again. Knowing he was going to regret it, Jack shook himself, stepped back. He knew it was a mistake that would probably cost him. He only hoped it didn't cost Landis her life. "You've got two minutes."

She stalked back to the computer. Jack watched her for a moment, shaken by the power of what he felt for her. "I'm going to make sure there's no one else in the house."

"Two minutes," she said without looking up.

He started for the door. A couple of minutes should give him time to check on Fido and make sure there weren't any cars in the driveway. If she wasn't ready to leave when he returned, he'd haul her out by the scruff of her neck.

As he stepped into the hall a noise behind the door jolted him. *The dog,* he thought, and started to turn toward it. The blow came out of nowhere. The force of it snapped his head back. Pain billowed at his right temple. A starburst of color exploded in his brain. The floor bucked beneath his feet. His only thought as he went to his knees was that Landis was in danger. That it was his fault. And if he didn't do something to rectify the situation, they were both going to die.

Chapter 15

The sickening thud of steel against flesh spun Landis away from the computer. Terror punched through her when she saw Jack sprawled on the floor in the hall. Cyrus Duke stood over him with a shiny semiautomatic pistol in his hand.

"Jack! Oh my God." She bolted from the chair. Vaguely, she was aware of Duke shifting the weapon from Jack to her.

"Stop right there," he said.

But Landis didn't stop until she reached Jack. She dropped to her knees, tried to keep him from rising, but he shook off her hands. The blow had been vicious. She could see a thin line of blood trickling from a cut at his temple. It didn't look deep, but a knot was already forming beneath it.

Cursing, he struggled to a sitting position. His eyes met hers, and even though he was disoriented from the blow, she saw the fear, felt that same fear grip her like a spindly claw.

"Easy," she said. "You're bleeding."

"We've got worse problems than that." Before she could stop him, Jack lurched unsteadily to his feet. His eyes landed on Duke and suddenly it was as if he and Duke were the only two people in the room.

Landis had never met the drug kingpin, but the local media loved him so she recognized him immediately. Thick brows rode low over cruel, intelligent gray eyes. The double-breasted Armani he wore matched the steel-gray of his hair. He was taller than she'd imagined. A few inches taller than Jack, in fact. His muscular shoulders contrasted sharply with a waistline that told her he was accustomed to fine dining.

"Ah, Detective LaCroix. We finally meet." Duke held the gun steadily on Jack's chest, his eyes sliding from Landis to Jack. "Only you're not a cop anymore, are you?"

Jack contemplated him, his expression dark. "You set me up, you son of a bitch."

"An unpleasant necessity that worked out quite nicely, don't you think?" A coldly amused smile touched the other man's face. "I'm sure you realize it was nothing personal. I needed a fall guy. You were looking to...how do you cops say it? Bring me down? So I simply killed two birds with one stone."

His gaze never faltering, Jack reached up and touched the cut on his temple, grimacing when his fingers came away red.

"I must say, I'm very impressed by your...resourcefulness. You've eluded the police. You've outsmarted two of my finest men." He considered Jack, rubbing his chin. "If the circumstances were different, I could use a man of your talents."

"Where you're going all you're going to need is a cell mate with a decent disposition," Jack said.

"I'm afraid you're getting a little ahead of yourself, Mr. LaCroix."

"I don't think so."

"Ah, but I've got the gun. That puts me in charge." Machiavellian eyes flicked to Landis. "You wouldn't want to see anything happen to the lovely Ms. McAllister, would you?"

Jack went perfectly still, so still Landis could see the rise and fall of his chest as he breathed. Though he seemed outwardly calm, the tension rolling off him was tangible. She'd always known he had a dark side. A side that was as dangerous and unpredictable as the storms that rolled down off the mountains. She knew that side of him had been wakened, that it was dangerous as hell, and she knew that somehow he was going to get his chance with Cyrus Duke.

Duke's eyes lingered on Landis. "I must say, Ms. McAllister, I'm touched by the…rapport you've developed with your brother's killer. It's amazing how flexible our loyalties become when our hormones are involved, isn't it?"

She knew he was baiting her, that a reaction would only feed the cruelty she saw in his eyes, but the anger snapped through her like the flick of a bull whip. "What's really amazing is how the truth always manages to find its way to the surface no matter how thick the scum."

Duke arched a brow as if she'd amused him, then his gaze flicked to Jack. "She handles herself well, doesn't she? Keeps her cool. How well did she keep her cool when she found out you put a bullet in her brother?"

Enraged, Landis started toward Duke. "You murdered Evan, you bas—"

"Landis," Jack said firmly. When she didn't stop, he stepped forward and set his hands on her shoulders. She tried to shake off his grip, but his fingers dug into her skin, warning her to keep a handle on her temper.

His gaze went to Duke. "This is between you and me. Don't bring her into this."

"Ah, but she's already in this up to that very pretty neck of hers."

"She doesn't know anything. Let her go now and you and I will deal."

"Deal?" Duke threw his head back and laughed. "This is all quite amusing. I wish I had more time to indulge, but I don't. You are no longer useful to me. Unfortunately, you've caused me some problems. I'll need to spend the day making reparations." A cruel smile whispered across his features. "I'm going to make you pay for the damage you did to my restaurant."

Landis felt Jack nudging her aside, realized he was slowly positioning himself between her and Duke. "I'll do whatever you want," he said. "Just let her go."

Without warning, Duke swung the pistol, leveled it at her face. A shiver moved through her when she found herself looking down the barrel. "Come here," he said to her. *"Now!"*

Pulse hammering, she started toward Duke, but Jack stopped her. Duke shifted the pistol, fired a shot that missed her by inches and slammed into the wall. Jack froze, raised his hands to shoulder level. "Leave her alone," he said. "I'm the one you want."

Duke glared at Landis. "I said come here!"

She could feel her entire body shaking as she moved toward Duke. She felt Jack's eyes on her, saw the fear in his expression. Felt that same fear rushing through her in a torrent. "It's okay," she said, but her voice was taut.

When she only had a foot to go, Duke lunged at her. Landis tried to scramble back, but his perfectly manicured fingers wrapped around her bicep, jerked her to him with such force that she stumbled. In her peripheral vision she saw Jack move toward her, teeth clenched, lips drawn back in a snarl. But before he could get close, Duke put the pistol to her temple.

"Stop right there, LaCroix," Duke said. "Or I swear to God I'll ruin this pretty face."

Jack stopped, his hands still raised, his gaze never leaving Duke. "She doesn't have a part in this. Let her go."

"Get the hell back," Duke snarled. *"Do as I say!"*

Landis could feel the muzzle shaking against her cheekbone. She could see his finger curved around the trigger and tried hard not to imagine the horror of what a bullet would do to her face.

Jack retreated slowly. "You can be out of the country in less than an hour. You've got your own jet. Money."

Duke looked around the expensively furnished room. "And leave all this behind? For the likes of some two-bit cop? I don't think so." He jabbed the pistol against her temple hard enough to cause pain. "Not when it would be so much easier to do away with the both of you."

Landis wanted to believe Jack would get them out of this, but didn't see how. Duke had a weapon and any number of thugs at his beck and call. He was ruthless, and she knew he wouldn't hesitate to murder them. For the first time she considered the very real possibility that they wouldn't survive. That they would die on this terrible night and no one would ever know the truth. The injustice of it made her shake with outrage.

"You won't get away with murdering us," she said. "I'm an assistant prosecutor with the D.A.'s office. My brother's a cop. He knows I was working on Jack's case."

Tilting his head, Duke glanced down at her. She glared back, trying not to shake, thinking she'd never seen such cold, empty eyes. "Jack LaCroix is a cop killer. He escaped from prison. Murdered his lawyer. You're his accomplice.

His lover. Driven by lust to aid and abet a convicted killer. The two of you showed up at my home to rob me of cash and guns.'' He shrugged. ''I had no choice but to protect myself, my family, my property. As a prosecutor you know I'm within my rights.''

Cold, hard fear seized her when she realized everything he'd said was feasible. He was going to kill them. The realization that he would probably get away with it made her feel sick.

As if sensing her terror, Jack looked at her, held her gaze. She sensed a message in the depths of his eyes, but didn't know what he might be trying to convey. Perhaps he was trying to calm her. More than anything, she wanted to go to him. She wanted to step into his embrace, feel his arms around her, his heart beating against hers. In the back of her mind, she wondered if she would ever feel his arms around her again....

Holding the gun to a spot just above her right ear, Duke glanced over his shoulder toward the door. ''Ryan, would you come in here, please?''

A stocky man dressed in an ill-fitting suit stepped into the room. Flat, brown eyes took in the scene, moving from Landis to Jack, then to Duke. ''Yes, sir?''

''Bring the SUV around to the back. We'll need tire chains for a ride into the mountains.'' He looked at Landis, his eyes rich with amusement. ''And a couple syringes of Demerol to keep our passengers in line.''

A silent understanding passed between the two men. With a nod, the big man in the suit left the room.

Demerol, she thought. Oh, God, he was going to drug them, and then murder them. Landis closed her eyes against the horror of the thought. Dread curled inside her like palsied fingers. She couldn't believe their lives were going to end this way. With so much unfinished between them. So much life left to live.

She looked at Jack, felt her heart shatter. He stared back at her, his face like stone, the muscles in his jaw clamped tightly. She thought of everything that had led up to this moment, and the unjustness of it destroyed her. She loved him. She'd always loved him. Would forever love him.

Even in death.

Duke turned his attention to Jack. "I won't have a problem framing you for her death, Mr. LaCroix. After all, you're a cold-blooded killer. A cop killer. Do you think anyone will be surprised to learn you killed Ms. McAllister when you were finished using her?"

"You won't get away with it," Jack said. "I left word with the police."

"You'll forgive me if I'm not terribly concerned by that. We both know your credibility is at an all-time low." Duke smirked. "When the police find Ms. McAllister's body— and not yours—they will draw the logical conclusion that you fled the country. That tidies things up nicely, doesn't it?"

Outrage had her trying to twist away, but Duke held her firmly. "I told my brother everything," she blurted. "He's a cop. Even if you kill us here today, he'll spend the rest of his life making sure you get what you deserve."

"It's truly refreshing that you still have so much faith in people, Ms. McAllister. Even after everything that's happened. Faith is an admirable trait."

Another layer of fear settled over her when Duke removed a pair of chrome handcuffs from his jacket and handed them to her. "Put the cuffs on your lover, or I'll kill him."

She stared at the cuffs, aware that her breaths were rushing in and out, too fast, too shallow. She felt panic encroaching. When she didn't move, he shifted the gun to Jack. "It doesn't matter if I kill him now or later. I suggest you do as you're told."

She glanced at Jack, looking for direction. His nod was almost imperceptible, but she discerned it. She didn't know what he was thinking. Once he was cuffed there would be nothing he could do to get them out of this. Unless, perhaps, he was simply trying to buy them some time.

Her hands shook uncontrollably as she reached for the cuffs.

Duke brushed his hand across hers with a touch so gentle gooseflesh raced up her arms. "Don't try anything stupid," he whispered. "You know I'll put a bullet in his brain."

"Ian will make sure you get what's coming to you." Choking back hatred and fear, she looked at the cuffs in her hands. She could feel the tremors moving through her body. Hear the roar of blood in her veins, the quick rush of her breaths. Panic edged through her. She could feel its spindly fingers stealing her control, letting her emotions out of the gate. She looked at Jack, wondering how he could be so calm when the fear was tearing her apart. Oh, dear God, she couldn't do this. She couldn't bring herself to cuff him. She knew that to incapacitate him now would be a death sentence for both of them.

The sound of footsteps from the hall drew her attention. The bodyguard, she thought, and fresh panic gouged her, a sharp spur tearing into flesh.

"What is it, Ryan?" Duke snapped over his shoulder.

But it wasn't Ryan standing at the door. Disbelief shocked her system when Ian walked in. Relief swept through her with such force that her legs went weak.

"Duke's armed!" she cried. "My God... Ian, he was going to kill us both." In her peripheral vision, she saw Jack move toward Duke.

"Stay where you are, LaCroix." Ian pulled his service revolver from the waistband of his jeans, leveled it at Jack. "Get your hands where I can see them."

Jack raised his hands to shoulder level, his eyes narrow and hard. "Get Landis out of here," he said.

"Shut up." Ian started toward Duke, but his revolver remained on Jack.

The hairs at the back of Landis's neck prickled. Of the two men, Duke was infinitely more dangerous. He was armed with a pistol. He'd threatened her life. So why in the name of God hadn't Ian disarmed him?

Duke threw his head back and laughed. "Very timely entrance, Officer McAllister. For your information, I was accosted by these two...burglars upon my return from the restaurant. I think the fire marshal will find the fire was intentionally set." His gaze met Jack's. "Won't they, Mr. LaCroix?"

Landis watched her brother, uneasiness stealing through her. She took a step toward him. "Duke set up Jack," she said. "The money. The gun. All of it. Ian, my God, he killed Evan. He was going kill both of us in cold blood if you hadn't—"

"Stay where you are, Landy."

She stopped, a chill rippling up her spine. "Ian, for God's sake, this isn't about Jack."

He looked at her, shook his head. "You have no idea what this is about."

A terrible realization dawned on her. Everything inside her went still and cold, a knot of dread unraveling in her stomach. She stopped breathing, vaguely aware that her heart pounded wildly. She looked at Jack, but his eyes were already on her. In their depths, she saw the answer she hadn't wanted to see. A truth that hurt her more than any bullet.

"No." She looked at Ian. "Not you."

Jack scowled at Ian, his expression incredulous. "You sold your soul for the likes of this scum?"

Ian's face darkened. "I should put a bullet in you right

now for dragging her into this! I didn't want her hurt, damn it! Why couldn't you just leave her out of it?''

Shock vibrated through her as the meaning of the words hit home. It hadn't been Evan who'd been working for Cyrus Duke, but her younger brother. The younger brother she'd been so proud of. The idealistic young police officer who'd dishonored himself, his family.

Just like their father...

Disbelief and fury and a damnable amount of hurt stabbed through her, a knife going deep and hitting bone. It was a cruel twist that she and Evan and Jack were the ones whose reputations had been sullied.

The urge to launch herself at him was powerful. She wanted to hurt him. The same way he'd hurt Evan. The way he'd hurt Jack. The way he'd hurt her. But Landis hung on to her control, if only by a thread.

"How could you?" she heard herself say. "How could you betray your own brother?"

He lifted his lip in a poor imitation of a smile, but his eyes were incredibly sad. "I didn't kill him, if that's what you're asking."

"That's exactly what I'm asking." She didn't even realize she was moving toward him. She wasn't sure what she would do when she reached him. Strike him. Throw her arms around him and beg him to stop the insanity and make things right. But she knew the law well enough to know things would never again be right with her brother.

Jack stopped her. "Easy, honey."

Landis tried to shake off his hands, but he held on to her, pulled her back. She felt numb on the outside, as if she'd been given a too-strong dose of pain medication. But she was coming apart inside. Jack tried to pull her against him, but she shook off his hands. As badly as she wanted to be held, the need to know the truth was stronger. "You let Jack go to prison. You knew he was innocent all along."

Emotions she couldn't readily identify clouded Ian's eyes. Remorse. Shame. A measure of fear. "I did what I had to do to protect myself. I'm a cop. I couldn't go to prison."

Jack shot Ian a killing look. "You let his killer go free. You let me take the fall for you, didn't you, you cowardly little bastard?"

Ian's gaze swept from Landis to Jack. That he didn't dispute Jack's words confirmed them. Landis felt them like a knife sinking slowly into her back.

"Evan covered for you, didn't he?" Jack said. "He found out you'd hooked up with Duke and covered your sorry ass."

Landis jolted as the words registered in her brain. Backing away from Jack, she looked from man to man, her mouth dry. A few feet away, Duke leaned against the desk, taking in the entire scene with an expression of supreme amusement.

"I loved him, Landy," Ian said. "I swear it. I didn't kill him. I wouldn't. It just…happened. That night, in the warehouse. Evan shouldn't have been there, damn it. One of Duke's thugs shot him." He ran his hand over his mouth. "There was nothing I could do. He was dying. I didn't want to go to prison. I panicked."

Pain lashed her like a whip. Fury followed, pumping through her with the same force as her life blood. She couldn't believe her younger brother would betray his own brother and then lie about it to save himself. She couldn't believe he would betray the man she loved, that he would let her believe the lies. The unjustness of it sent a wave of raw outrage slicing through her.

Blinded by grief and rage and she launched herself at him. "You *bastard!*"

"Landy…for God's sake." Ian raised his hands to protect himself.

Landis barely heard the words as she lashed out at him with her fists. In a small corner of her mind, she was aware that she was sobbing. That they were deep, wrenching sobs that came from somewhere deep inside her. She felt Jack's hands on her shoulders, digging into her flesh, pulling her back.

"Get her off me!" Ian stepped back, his hair falling into his face, the gun on Jack. "Keep her the hell away from me."

Aware that Jack was holding her tightly, that she was suddenly too tired to fight him, Landis glared at Ian, sick to her soul by what he'd done. "I'll never forgive you," she said.

"Bravo!" Duke brought his hands together in applause. "Bravo! Such drama! Touching performances by all. I couldn't have written a better script myself."

Lowering the gun to his side, Ian looked over at Jack. "I didn't want her involved! Damn it, now what the hell do you expect me to do?"

"Be a man for once in your life and stop this here and now," Jack said. "Do the right thing and turn yourself over to the police." He looked over at Landis. "That's the only way your sister is going to get out of this alive."

Lips drawn back in a snarl, Ian raised the gun, pointed it at Jack. Tears streamed down his face. His barrel shook uncontrollably, but he didn't take his finger from the trigger. "I'm not going to prison!"

"I don't want bloodshed here!" Duke said. "Evidence is getting extremely difficult to hide in this age of forensic science." Never taking his eyes from Jack, he tugged a cell phone from his pocket, pressed a button. "Ryan, is the UV ready? I need someone up here to take out the trash."

"What are you going to do with them?" Ian asked.

"I'm going to dispose of them the way I've disposed of every other piece of trash that got in the way."

Ian paled, raked a hand through his hair. "I don't want to be part of it. Damn it, this wasn't part of the deal. My own sister…"

"If you don't have the stomach for it, Officer McAllister, I suggest you leave."

Jack watched the two men closely, interested in the dynamics of their relationship. He knew Ian was the weak link. Just as he knew Landis was the key to breaking that link. The only questions that remained was whether or not he was willing to take the risk.

She stood a few feet away, staring out the window, her eyes unseeing, her face as pale as death. He hated seeing her like that. Hurt and betrayed and facing a violent death at the hands of a ruthless scumbag like Duke. Jack couldn't bear the thought of her life ending this way. With so many things left unfinished. He hadn't even told her he loved her. But he did. He loved her more than life itself, would gladly give up his own life to save hers.

They only had a few minutes before Duke's thug returned to drug them and haul them away. While Jack had watched Duke and Ian, a plan had formed. It was dangerous as hell with an outcome that was unpredictable at best. Worse, in order for it to work, he would have to use Landis.

Cyrus Duke sat at his desk, the gun in his hand. Ian stood at the door, looking shaken and angry. Never taking his eyes from Duke, Jack eased closer to Landis and whispered, "cry."

"Shut up." Duke pointed the gun at Jack, motioned him back. "Get away from her."

Lowering her face into her hands, Landis made a keening sound. Her shoulders began to shake. "Jack…" Never raising her head, she walked over to him.

Duke stood, his gun shifting to Landis. "Tell her to shut up."

She went into Jack's arms. He could feel her heart pounding in time with his own, the fear pumping through him with every beat. He put his arms around her, turned so that his back was to Duke in case the drug kingpin decided to pull the trigger...

"I'm going to get us out of this," he whispered to her. "I want you to talk to Ian. Talk him down. He's our only hope."

She jerked her head in agreement.

Praying he wasn't making a mistake, Jack let go of her, pushed her toward the window. "Stay away from him," he said loud enough for Duke to hear.

She glared at him. "He's my brother."

Jack glared back, praying Duke bought it. "I don't care."

Eyes ravaged, she turned to Ian. "It's not too late for me to fix this for you. There's still time. I could help you with a plea bargain."

Cursing, Duke snatched the cuffs from the desk and approached Jack. A few feet away, he stopped, trained the pistol at his chest. "Turn around and give me your wrists."

Heart racing with pure adrenaline, Jack turned and offered his wrists. A few feet away, he could hear Landis speaking to her brother. Behind him he heard Duke open the cuffs.

"Don't try anything stupid," he said.

"Wouldn't dream of it."

"You've got a smart mouth. I'm going to enjoy making you hurt. Or maybe I'll kill her while you watch. How would you like that?"

Jack shifted his weight from one foot to the other. Duke grasped his right wrist, snapped the cold steel in place tightly enough to cut off his circulation. "What are you going to do with us?" he asked.

"Shut up and give me your other—"

Jack spun, slammed the dangling handcuff against Duke's forehead. The other man grunted, raised the gun, fired once. Jack went in low and rammed his shoulder into his solar plexus. Duke reeled backward. Using his body weight, Jack shoved him against the desk. He heard Landis scream, prayed he was right, that Ian wouldn't shoot his own sister in cold blood.

Grasping Duke's wrist, he squeezed hard, but the other man didn't relinquish the weapon. Jack muscled him across the room to the window, slammed him against it. Glass shattered. Duke cursed, tried to twist away. Jack smashed his wrist against the wall. Once. Twice. Bone cracked and the gun flew from his hand, clattered to the floor. Duke raised his knee, tried to ram it into his groin, but Jack was prepared and danced sideways.

"Shoot him!" Duke bellowed to Ian. "Kill the woman!"

Terrified Ian would do it, Jack glanced over his shoulder to make sure Landis was safe. In the instant he was distracted, Duke grabbed Jack by his collar and forced him toward the window. Displaying incredible strength, Duke shoved him hard. "I'll see you in hell!" he snarled.

"Jack!"

Landis's voice penetrated the haze of rage and fear, gave Jack the focus he needed to save himself. Using every bit of strength he possessed, he lunged back, freeing himself from Duke's grip.

Screaming profanities, face contorted in fury, Duke charged. Jack stepped aside. The momentum took Duke out the window. He twisted, made a wild grab for the sill, made contact with one hand.

"No!" Jack lunged toward him, reached for his hand, but wasn't fast enough. The other man's eyes met Jack's an instant before he fell backward and plummeted to the paving stones twenty-five feet below.

Jack turned to see Ian run out the door. A few feet away,

Landis had picked up Duke's pistol, had it aimed at her brother. She stood in the center of the room, vacillating, blinking back tears. She looked at Jack when he approached. "I couldn't shoot him."

He crossed to her. "Nobody expected you to."

He tried to take the gun from her, but she held it so tightly he had to peel her fingers from the grip. "Easy, honey. It's over."

"I can't believe Ian was involved."

Setting the gun on the desk, he ran his hands over her, checked her for blood. "Are you all right?"

"I'm okay. Just shaken and...shocked." Her gaze met his. In her eyes, he saw the depth of her pain, the betrayal, felt the familiar slash of it in his own soul. "You knew he wouldn't hurt me."

Jack nodded. "I knew."

"I begged him to turn himself in, but...he wouldn't listen."

"The police will get him." The need to hold her was alive and eating at him, as urgent as the need to take his next breath. "I'm going to call the police."

She jerked her head.

Only when he'd reached the desk did Jack realize his entire body was shaking. He picked up the phone and punched in 9-1-1. "This is Jack LaCroix," he said. "I want to speak with Lieutenant Fulton."

Holding the phone in the crook of his neck, he walked over to the broken window. Duke's body lay sprawled on the paving stones below, motionless.

Only then did it hit him that the nightmare was over. Duke was dead. Ian's illicit dealings would soon be uncovered. Jack would be exonerated. If all went well, he would be a free man in a matter of days.

He kept his emotions in check as he explained to his former lieutenant everything that had happened. He knew he would still be arrested, that he would spend the next few days in lockdown while the case was being investigated. But at least now he knew he had a future. The only question that remained was whether or not he would be spending that future with Landis.

He was still pondering the question when he hung up the phone and turned to Landis. Her eyes were already on him, shimmering with unshed tears and all the same emotions boiling inside him.

"Come here," he said.

She crossed to him. He didn't remember reaching for her, pulling her to him. He wrapped his arms around her, and the emotions he'd been holding at bay fractured. Closing his eyes, he buried his face in her hair and simply held her.

"It's over," he said. "I can't believe it."

She trembled against him. "Everything's going to be all right."

He hadn't shed a tear for more than thirty years. After spending the past year in hell, he hadn't believed he was capable of showing such a basic human emotion. But holding the woman he loved, seeing that love returned to him in her eyes, undid him as nothing else could have.

Pulling away slightly, he brushed the hair from her face. "When the police arrive, they're going to take me into custody."

"I'm sorry you have to go through that."

"Knowing it's temporary makes a hell of a difference."

"I'll make some calls. I'll be with you when I can."

"I know." He set his hand against her face, marveling at the softness of her skin. She covered his hand with hers. A tear slipped down her cheek, but he stopped it with his thumb.

"I got my life back," he whispered.

"And your future."

More than anything he wanted to know if that future

included her, but he was so shaken by the emotions churning inside him, he didn't trust his voice.

She started to speak, but he quieted her with a kiss. "There will be time for talk later," he said.

"Plenty of time," she echoed.

"All the time in the world," he said as he covered her mouth with his.

Chapter 16

Landis parked her Jeep in the driveway and hefted the grocery bag in one arm, her briefcase in the other and started for the cabin. Around her, snow whispered down from a starless sky to catch in the pine boughs and twinkle against the frozen ground. As she stepped on to the porch, she wondered fleetingly if the sight of snowfall would always remind her of Jack....

Shoving the thoughts of him aside, she unlocked the cabin door and stepped inside. The familiar smells of home embraced her like an old friend. Vanilla from the candles she'd burned the night before. Old pine from the rustic paneling that would one day need replacing. Hazelnut from the coffee she'd brewed just that morning. BJ, her cat, sat regally on the sofa back, licking his paws and eyeing her with the cool indifference of royalty. Landis took it all in with a sort of heightened appreciation, knowing she would never take anything for granted ever again.

It had been two weeks since the terrible ordeal at Cyrus

Duke's mansion. After the police had arrived, Jack had been arrested and processed in to the Salt Lake City jail pending a full investigation by myriad law enforcement agencies ranging from the Department of Corrections to the Provo County Sheriff's Department. Duke was pronounced dead at the scene by the county coroner. An autopsy later revealed the drug kingpin had broken his neck in the fall from the second-story window.

Ian had gone on the run. After taking Landis's statement, the police had launched a massive manhunt. Two days later, he'd called Landis from Denver. Convincing him to turn himself in to the police had been difficult, but in the end he'd acquiesced. She'd helped him make arrangements with the Salt Lake City police. He was arrested upon his arrival at the department and charged with racketeering, accepting bribes, perjury and interfering with an official investigation. The trial wasn't scheduled until spring, but she knew he would do prison time for his crimes. Landis only hoped the time behind bars would rehabilitate him. Call her a hopeless idealist, but she knew that deep down inside her brother was a decent man.

All in all, life was good, she thought. Just because she cried a lot didn't mean she was unhappy. It didn't mean her heart was broken. Or that she was so lonely she'd taken to sleeping with her cat. Just because she hadn't seen Jack in over a week didn't mean she was coming apart at the seams.

Setting her briefcase next to the coffee table, she scooped BJ into her arms and hugged him against her. "How about a fire and a tall glass of merlot, big guy?" she asked.

She set the cat on the sofa and started toward the French door to gather some wood from the woodpile in the backyard. She would build a fire. Pour herself a glass of wine. Heat the casserole she'd made over the weekend. And spend the rest of the evening working on her opening argument for a trial that was scheduled to begin next week. It was the way she'd spent every evening for the past two weeks. She worked until she was too tired to think. A good theory in concept, but no matter how exhausted she was, her mind invariably found its way to Jack.

She was nearly to the kitchen when the doorbell rang. Puzzled that someone would be visiting so late, she changed directions and started toward the foyer. At the door, she stood on her tiptoes and peeked through the peephole. Her heart spun into a wild freefall when she saw Jack LaCroix standing on her porch, looking calm and in control and so handsome that for several seconds she couldn't catch her breath. He wore a blue parka over snug jeans, a faded flannel shirt, and lace-up hiking boots. He'd gotten a haircut at some point, though she could see the shadow of a goatee. The sight of him standing on her front porch with snow in his hair and a small wrapped gift in his hand unnerved her as much as it thrilled.

Stepping away from the door, Landis put her hand to her wildly pounding heart and tried hard to calm down. He could be here for any number of reasons, she reminded herself. But she could feel herself shaking inside as her nerves began to sizzle and snap.

Refusing to let herself read too much into the visit—or the present in his hands—she tugged open the door. She barely felt the cold air that wrapped around her legs. Barely noticed that the snow was coming down hard. All she was aware of was the man standing on her porch, holding a gift wrapped in red foil, contemplating her with dark, enigmatic eyes she couldn't begin to read.

''Hi,'' he said quietly.

A hundred things needed to be said, but she couldn't think of a single one. The words tumbled around in her brain, but she was so taken aback by the sight of him, the fact that he'd come to see her, that she couldn't come up with a coherent sentence. She settled for, "Hi back."

He looked good, she thought. His color was back. The cut on his temple had healed to nothing more than a small pink line. He even looked as if he'd gained a couple of pounds since she'd last seen him. His cheeks no longer had that hollowed quality that had made him look so harsh and dangerous. She didn't let her eyes drop to his mouth. She didn't want to know if it was exactly as she pictured it in her dreams.

"You look really good," he said after an awkward silence. "A little thin."

"So do you. Good, I mean." She couldn't stop looking at him, couldn't slow the pace of her heart or catch her breath. "I like the goatee."

Smiling, he scrubbed his hand over his chin. "I thought maybe while I'm between jobs..."

"When were you released?"

"Last week."

Why didn't you come to see me? The words were on the tip of her tongue, but she couldn't bring herself to speak them. He didn't owe her an explanation. If he'd wanted to see her upon his release, he would have. "How are you feeling?"

He shrugged. "I feel good. I went to see my foster mom. Played a little hockey. Did some skiing. Got back in touch with some of my cop friends at the department." His gaze turned heady. "Most of all, I did a lot of thinking, Landis."

A twinge of alarm rippled through her. Suddenly, she felt incredibly vulnerable and utterly certain that he'd come here to say goodbye. To tell her that too many things had happened. Things that could never be fixed and it would be better for both of them if they moved on...

"Yeah, me too," she said. "Thinking, I mean."

He grimaced. "Did I catch you at a bad time?"

"Oh. Well, no." Because she was flustered and didn't know what to do next, she stepped back. "Would you like to come in?"

Jack stepped into the foyer. He passed so close to her she smelled the mix of soap and a piney aftershave that titillated her senses.

Trying to get a handle on nerves that were close to skittering out of control, Landis started for the living room. "I can make some coff—"

Every nerve in her body jumped when he gently grasped her arm. "I don't want coffee."

Landis stared at him, but his gaze was so intense, she had to look away. She could feel her pulse pounding off the scale. Reaching out, he put his fingers beneath her chin and forced her gaze to his. "I've missed you, Red."

The words rang in her ears like the final chords of a sad, sweet love song. Her heart tumbled end over end in her chest. It was as if all her hopes and fears and the tumultuous feelings inside her had been tossed into a furiously spinning vortex, and she couldn't get a handle on any of them.

"God knows I tried, but I couldn't stay away from you," he growled. "I didn't know if you wanted me to stay away."

She hated it that he was so damn calm while she was about to go to pieces. "You've been a free man for a week, Jack. You didn't come to see me."

"I had some things to take care of. I had some thinking to do. Some decisions to make."

"I don't know why you're here," she blurted.

"I'm not sure, either." A smile touched the corners of his mouth. "I thought maybe we could figure it out together."

Landis closed her eyes, struggling for composure, hating it that she was on the verge of tears. "I know you've had a lot to deal with in the last twelve months. It's not unreasonable for you to want to get on with your life. I mean, I walked out on you a year ago. I didn't believe in you when I should have.'' She knew she was blubbering, and it appalled her because she never blubbered. But the words kept tangling on her tongue and pouring out and she was getting every one of them wrong. ''What I'm trying to say is that I'll respect your decision, Jack. It doesn't matter that I'm—''

He went still, his eyes narrowing. ''You're what, Landis?''

In love with you. The words were on the tip of her tongue, but she couldn't say them. She couldn't bring herself to tell the truth because she was afraid that truth would hurt her more than any lie.

Never taking his eyes from hers, he reached out and put his fingers beneath her chin, forcing her gaze to his. ''How can you possibly not know that I'm crazy about you?'' he asked.

The words reverberated in her brain, the repercussions zinging like a ricochet. She stared at him, torn between pouring out what was in her heart and preserving what little dignity she had left.

She searched his face, searched the depths of her own soul, and found the words she needed to say. ''You never told me you loved me,'' she whispered.

Jack couldn't take his eyes from hers, couldn't stop looking at her lovely face because within her gaze he saw everything he'd ever loved about her. Everything he'd longed for in the terrible months he'd been locked away. Everything he'd ever wanted in a life partner. Strength. Courage. The kind of rare and precious love that came once in a lifetime—and only to a lucky, chosen few.

And suddenly, after all the agony and uncertainty of the past year, he knew coming here tonight was the only thing he could have done. He felt the rightness of it all the way to his soul.

He didn't remember moving, didn't see her move. But in the next instant her arms were around him, and his mouth was wrestling with hers. She tasted exactly the way he wanted her to taste—like heaven—and the sweetness of the kiss intoxicated him. He held her tighter, remembering all the nights he'd spent alone, all the nights he'd spent wanting her and fearing he would never hold her again.

"I love you, Landis. I've always loved you, and I always will. Nothing will ever change that."

"You taught me to trust my heart," she said. "And now I know that when it comes to you, my heart will never steer me wrong."

"Hearts never lie." Pulling back slightly, he reached into the pocket of his parka and pulled out the wrapped present. "I thought we might celebrate Christmas a couple of days early."

She reached for the box, shook it. "I don't have to wait until Christmas morning?"

"Not on your life."

Smiling, she tugged at the delicate gold bow. The paper fell away to reveal a tiny velvet box. Her fingers trembled when she opened it. And her heart simply burst. She stared at the small, but exquisitely cut diamond ring. "Oh, Jack…it's stunning." She laughed. "I'm stunned."

"I think there's something to be said for keeping a woman on her toes."

Tears shimmered in her eyes when she looked up at him. "You're proposing?"

"That's generally the idea when a man gives a diamond ring to the woman he loves."

She punched him good-naturedly on the shoulder, but the breath she let out shuddered.

"Now might be a good time to say yes." Tilting his

head, he kissed her mouth, her temple, the tip of her nose. "That is, if you're interested."

"I'm interested. But only if it's forever."

"Love is forever, Landis."

Lifting her hand, he slipped the ring on to her finger. Her hand trembled when she held it out. The diamond glinted like a star between them. "It's beautiful and perfect."

"I take it that's a yes?"

"An unequivocal yes." Standing on her tiptoes, she kissed him on the mouth.

Jack returned the kiss, loving the feel of her in his arms, the taste of her on his tongue. He closed his eyes against the hot burst of emotion that moved through him when she put her arms around his neck.

He didn't know if the tears he tasted on her lips were his or hers. But he drank them in, knowing they didn't matter because they were tears of joy. He could feel that joy welling inside him, like a fountain overflowing, and he reveled in the sensation.

Lifting her off her feet, he held her tightly and spun her in a tight circle. When she laughed, he joined her. The sound of their laughter mingled to form a single note that spoke of simple human joy. And the sound of their happiness echoed through the cabin, the peaceful place they would soon call home.

* * * * *

Your opinion is important to us! Please take a few moments to share your thoughts with us about your experiences with Harlequin and Silhouette books. Your comments will be very useful in ensuring that we deliver books you love to read.
Please take a few minutes to complete the questionnaire, then send it to us at the address below.

Send your completed questionnaires to:
Harlequin/Silhouette Reader Survey, P.O. Box 9046, Buffalo, NY 14269-9046

1. As you may know, there are many different lines under the Harlequin and Silhouette brands. Each of the lines is listed below. Please check the box that most represents your reading habit for each line.

Line	Currently read this line	Do not read this line	Not sure if I read this line
Harlequin American Romance	❑	❑	❑
Harlequin Duets	❑	❑	❑
Harlequin Romance	❑	❑	❑
Harlequin Historicals	❑	❑	❑
Harlequin Superromance	❑	❑	❑
Harlequin Intrigue	❑	❑	❑
Harlequin Presents	❑	❑	❑
Harlequin Temptation	❑	❑	❑
Harlequin Blaze	❑	❑	❑
Silhouette Special Edition	❑	❑	❑
Silhouette Romance	❑	❑	❑
Silhouette Intimate Moments	❑	❑	❑
Silhouette Desire	❑	❑	❑

2. Which of the following best describes why you bought *this book?* One answer only, please.

the picture on the cover	❑	the title	❑
the author	❑	the line is one I read often	❑
part of a miniseries	❑	saw an ad in another book	❑
saw an ad in a magazine/newsletter	❑	a friend told me about it	❑
I borrowed/was given this book	❑	other: _____	❑

3. Where did you buy *this book?* One answer only, please.

at Barnes & Noble	❑	at a grocery store	❑
at Waldenbooks	❑	at a drugstore	❑
at Borders	❑	on eHarlequin.com Web site	❑
at another bookstore	❑	from another Web site	❑
at Wal-Mart	❑	Harlequin/Silhouette Reader	❑
at Target	❑	Service/through the mail	
at Kmart	❑	used books from anywhere	❑
at another department store or mass merchandiser	❑	I borrowed/was given this book	❑

4. On average, how many Harlequin and Silhouette books do you buy at one time?

I buy _____ books at one time	❑
I rarely buy a book	❑

MRQ403SIM-1A

5. How many times per month do you shop for any *Harlequin and/or Silhouette* books? One answer only, please.

1 or more times a week	❑	a few times per year	❑
1 to 3 times per month	❑	less often than once a year	❑
1 to 2 times every 3 months	❑	never	❑

6. When you think of your ideal heroine, which *one* statement describes her the best? One answer only, please.

She's a woman who is strong-willed	❑	She's a desirable woman	❑
She's a woman who is needed by others	❑	She's a powerful woman	❑
She's a woman who is taken care of	❑	She's a passionate woman	❑
She's an adventurous woman		She's a sensitive woman	❑

7. The following statements describe types or genres of books that you may be interested in reading. Pick *up to 2 types* of books that you are most interested in.

I like to read about truly romantic relationships	❑
I like to read stories that are sexy romances	❑
I like to read romantic comedies	❑
I like to read a romantic mystery/suspense	❑
I like to read about romantic adventures	❑
I like to read romance stories that involve family	❑
I like to read about a romance in times or places that I have never seen	❑
Other: _____	

The following questions help us to group your answers with those readers who are similar to you. Your answers will remain confidential.

8. Please record your year of birth below.

19 _____

9. What is your marital status?

single ❑   married ❑   common-law ❑   widowed ❑
divorced/separated ❑

10. Do you have children 18 years of age or younger currently living at home?

yes ❑   no ❑

11. Which of the following best describes your employment status?

employed full-time or part-time ❑   homemaker ❑   student ❑
retired ❑   unemployed ❑

12. Do you have access to the Internet from either home or work?

yes ❑   no ❑

13. Have you ever visited eHarlequin.com?

yes ❑   no ❑

14. What state do you live in?

_____

15. Are you a member of Harlequin/Silhouette Reader Service?

yes ❑   Account # _____   no ❑   MRQ403SIM-1B

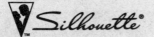

COMING NEXT MONTH

I N T I M A T E   M O M E N T S

#1261 TRACE EVIDENCE—Carla Cassidy
Cherokee Corners

Someone had vandalized teacher Tamara Greystone's classroom, and it was up to crime scene investigator Clay James to find out who was behind it—and whether they'd be back. Mesmerized by Tamara's ethereal Cherokee beauty and desperate to keep her from harm, would the man of ice finally melt from the heat of their passion, or crack under the pressure of guarding his own heart?

#1262 THE TOP GUN'S RETURN—Kathleen Creighton
Starrs of the West

The government had told Jessie Starr Bauer that her husband was dead. And in many ways, the time spent as a POW *had* killed the Tristan Bauer Jessie had known. Eight years later, Jessie and Tristan reunited as strangers with only one common ground: the memory of a love worth fighting for.

#1263 SURE BET—Maggie Price
Line of Duty

In order to solve a series of murders, rookie officer Morgan McCall and police sergeant Alex Blade had to pose as newlyweds. Though they were reluctant to act on the obvious attraction flaring between them, danger led to desire, and soon their sham marriage felt all too real....

#1264 NOWHERE TO HIDE—RaeAnne Thayne
The Searchers

FBI agent Gage McKinnon's many years on the job had taught him to recognize a woman with secrets—and his new neighbor, Lisa Connors, was certainly that. Lisa couldn't help the attraction she felt for Gage but vowed to keep her distance. It was the only way to protect the ones she loved most....

#1265 DANGEROUS WATERS—Laurey Bright

When professional diver Rogan Broderick and beautiful history professor Camille Hartley each inherited half of a boat that held clues to a sunken treasure, they learned that Rogan's father had been murdered for his discovery. But could they find the treasure before the murderer did—and survive the passion that threatened to consume them?

#1266 SECRETS OF AN OLD FLAME—Jill Limber

A year ago, police officer Joe Galtero's felony investigation had led to a steamy affair with the chief suspect's daughter, Nikki Walker. But when she discovered he was using her to get to her father, she left him. Now she had returned to San Diego with a secret of her own—his child!